RUN
Away
HOME

RUN *Away* HOME

a novel

Jennie L. Hansen

Covenant Communications, Inc.

Covenant

Published by Covenant Communications, Inc.
American Fork, Utah

Printed in the United States of America
First Printing: September 1993

04 03 02 01 00 99 98 97   8 7 6 5 4 3 2

Library of Congress Cataloging-in-Publication Data

Hansen, Jennie L., 1943-
    Run away home, / Jennie L. Hansen.
        p.   cm.
    ISBN 1-55503-567-1
    Fiction. I. Title
    PS3558.A51293R86 1993
    813'.54--dc20   93-36277
                                              CIP

For the two Marys in my life:

Mary Smith, my mother,
who always believed in my talent

and

Mary Jo Rich, my daughter,
who kept me working at it

One

"HE BLAMES YOU, YOU KNOW."

"I don't care. He deserves everything he got and then some." Megan crossed her legs and leaned back in her chair. She was glad the trial was over. In her work as a television investigative reporter, Megan found that every abuse story she covered stirred painful memories.

"Well, it was a great story, but I wouldn't want to be in your shoes when that guy finally gets out!" said her boss, Prescot.

"I'm not scared. Jasper talks a tougher game than he plays. He's really a sniveling coward." It wasn't the first time she'd met a man like Jasper. In her work Megan had met a lot of Jaspers, men who fed off the vulnerability of those smaller and weaker than themselves.

"Maybe. I'll admit it doesn't take much courage to cripple and starve children, then make them the focus of a solicitation scheme. After all, most people are only too willing to give to hungry, homeless children. But he won't forget he might have gotten away with it if you hadn't poked your pretty little nose into his scam and made it the highlight of the six o'clock news."

"What are you complaining about? I thought that's what you paid me for. I thought I was supposed to make certain your news team has—and I quote—'relevant, local, hard news' for your six and ten o'clock shows."

"Right—that's what I pay you for. What I don't pay you for is to do the prosecuting attorney's job for him. You could have gotten several exclusives out of the material you gift wrapped and handed to the prosecutor."

"But he wasn't even looking for a previous pattern of abuse. He might not have gotten a conviction without the testimony of Jasper's ex-girlfriend." Leave it to Prescot to be more concerned about the station's ratings than whether or not justice was served.

"I know. I know. You consider him an incompetent boob, and it isn't just him, is it? You don't have a very high opinion of men in general. Come to think of it, I don't think you like women much either, judging by the way you exposed that Bradshaw woman and her Women's Clinic last fall."

"Battered and neglected women and children have enough strikes against them without allowing scavengers to manipulate them and siphon off the already insufficient funds available to the few protective service programs out there," Megan said.

"Try to remember you work for Channel Two, not the social services department!" Prescot leaned across his wide desk, a stubby highlighting pen gripped in his thick fist. His round face was serious as he shook the pen at her for emphasis. "Maybe I've assigned you too many family problem stories. You take them too personally. That kind of emotional involvement can affect your work."

"Am I being complimented or reprimanded?"

"Complimented, I guess," Prescot chuckled. "You're tough and bright, the best reporter to come this way in a long time. I'll admit you're as good in the field as you are on that computer in there. I like you, but I don't understand you. A woman who looks like you should be in front of the camera, breaking your own stories on the air."

Bristling at his personal tone, Megan said dryly, "As you've mentioned before. But I don't want to read the news. I want to investigate and write it. Yes, you said I could do both, but really Prescot, I don't want to." She was sick of men who thought she should use her appearance to further her career. Sometimes she considered dyeing her pale blond hair brown and buying thick glasses to avoid the attention her silvery blue eyes seemed to draw.

"All right, I won't push you, not today anyway. Only tell me why a little thing like you can stare down the toughest crooks and politicians in town, but will turn tail and run the moment someone points a camera your way!"

"I just don't like cameras." She stood up. "See you Monday, Prescot." She waggled two fingers at him and started toward the door.

"Not so fast. I called you in here for more than to compliment you on a story. It's come to my attention that you haven't taken any vacation time for more than two years. Personnel frowns on that. You do recall paid vacation is one of the benefits listed in your contract, don't you? I'll see you the first of September, not Monday." Holding up one hand to prevent being interrupted, he added, "That's an order."

Megan left Prescot's office with mixed feelings. What was she going to do with six weeks free of pressure and deadlines? She couldn't remember a time when she hadn't had to work. From the corner of her eye, she noticed the speculative glances of her co-workers as she made her way to her desk and began gathering up some of her personal items from its drawers. Their stares made her uncomfortable, and she stiffened. She had no intention of satisfying their curiosity.

Just as she reached for a tray of computer disks, two strong, male arms wrapped firmly around her. Megan instantly went rigid although not a flicker of emotion crossed her perfectly made-up features.

"Megan, I'm sorry. I should have known better." The arms holding her relaxed their grip and slowly turned her about. Warm brown eyes met hers in a questioning look before A.J., the cameraman, stepped back. Glancing at the items in her hands, he raised one eyebrow quizzically. "Surely the old ogre didn't fire you? After the journalistic coup you just pulled off, he's probably promoting you to the upper echelons and moving you into your own swank office!"

"Don't be silly, A.J. He just ordered me to use up my vacation time—beginning right now."

"Now that sounds like a cause to celebrate. Come, your chariot awaits. Let me just carry these things for you. Wave good-bye to the nice people." Taking her arm, he hustled her swiftly toward the door.

"A.J."

"Uh-uh. Don't stop to think. Don't pause to give Mr. P. time to reconsider. Just vamoose!"

"Really," she tried to protest as the laughing man ushered her through the door and into the elevator. "I can find my own way to my car." She put up with more nonsense from A.J. than she ever had from anyone else. Unlike most men who tried to get close to her, he didn't really frighten her. Sometimes he made her uneasy, but down deep she sensed a kindred vulnerability she couldn't brush off.

"Great! You can drop me off at my apartment on your way. I could even invite you up to see my etchings," he added with an exaggerated leer.

"In your dreams!" Megan's laughter floated across the parking garage as she unlocked the doors of her practical, navy blue Ford Escort. A.J.'s laughter followed hers as he slid into the passenger seat even though he knew there was more truth than laughter to the joke. He had been blatantly chasing Megan for three years, ever since he arrived at Channel Two, just six months after Megan had signed on. Megan would be shocked if she knew he'd seen her in San Antonio when she'd gone there to bury her grandfather. When she left San Antonio for Missoula, A.J. decided to move north. With some luck and perseverance he had managed to get hired at Channel Two as well. She didn't know that he had known her briefly in her earlier life.

"How about dinner tonight?"

"You never give up, do you? You know I don't date." The little car accelerated sharply away from a traffic light.

"Why not?"

"You're about the only friend I've got; I can't risk losing a friend by dating him."

"Why can't friends have dinner together?"

"Too dangerous. I don't want any entanglements. Entanglements have a bad way of starting over dinner for two."

"Where did you pick up that brilliant bit of philosophy? It sure wasn't from experience. I'll bet you could count on one hand the number of guys who have taken you to dinner."

Megan's face took on a shrouded look. A little white line formed at the corner of her mouth.

He knew she was hurt. "Oh, Megan. I'm sorry. Look, I know perfectly well you could have all the dates you wanted, but you just don't want to let any man in your life. That's the whole problem. Somebody hurt you so badly there's no way you'll even give the rest of us poor slobs a chance!"

The car lurched to an abrupt stop as Megan narrowly missed running a red light.

"Oh, great! Me and my big mouth! This is neither the time nor the place. You concentrate on driving, and I'll concentrate on keeping my mouth shut. Deal?"

"Deal."

He wasn't getting anywhere. What was he going to have to do to get Megan to confide in him? He'd like to build a more personal relationship, but there didn't seem to be any way past the barrier Megan erected every time he tried.

Silence filled the car. She didn't have to close her eyes to see the face of the one man who had made it impossible for her to accept the relationship A.J. offered her. No matter how many times she banished that face, it still intruded when she least expected it. In order to escape her own thoughts, she turned on the radio. As Randy Travis's voice filled the air, A.J. raised one eyebrow.

"Jason's station," Megan explained apologetically, but despite her tone, A.J. knew she was enormously proud of her young son.

"I might have known. You two have big plans for your vacation?"

"Hardly! Jason doesn't know there's going to be a vacation. Remember, I just found out myself."

"Oh yeah, that's right. Bet he'll see this as the answer to his prayers. I recall very clearly his efforts to convince you he's much too old for day care."

"I know. Nine really is too old to need a baby-sitter, but it's too young to be on his own. He has another week of Little League games, then I was thinking of sending him to summer camp for a couple of weeks. I'll have to think of something. This might be a good time to fly to New York; there are several shows I'd like to see."

"New York in August with a kid! You're either awfully brave or not as smart as I thought you were! Besides, I'll bet Jason would rather go camping or to someplace where he can ride a horse."

"You're probably right. Oh well, I'll think of something," she said as she pulled to the curb.

"Thanks for the lift."

"See you around!"

"Sooner than you think!" A.J. winked.

Megan shook her head as A.J. walked away, then pulled out during a break in traffic. She continued on toward the outskirts of town. Her mind continued to dwell on the jaunty figure she'd left entering the condo where she knew he owned an apartment, though she'd never been inside it. A.J. frequently left his bright red Ferrari behind as an excuse to con her into giving him a lift home. He also showed up uninvited at her house on the outskirts of Missoula at frequent intervals with his rhythmic tune on her doorbell.

Shaking her head, she wished she could be head over heels in love with the guy. He was fun, intelligent, and talented, and most importantly, Jason liked him.

His looks weren't the macho, broad-shouldered cowboy image women in Montana seemed to go for, but he possessed a kind of grace she always appreciated in professional skaters and dancers. Megan knew from his occasional attempts at closeness that although his 5' 9" frame might not look big, it was solid. She had noticed that other women practically swooned when they met him. "He is really good looking," she admitted to herself—and he was one of the few people, especially men, she really felt comfortable around. She liked to think if she ever found Buddy, her brother, he would be a lot like A.J.

Megan entered the curving driveway of the Kids Korral Day Care Center. Ten minutes later a glowering Jason was fastening his seat belt.

"I'm not going there anymore," he threatened.

"Okay."

"You can't make me. I'm not a baby anymore. I hate being the biggest kid there."

"Honey, you're the biggest kid almost everywhere you go." Her heart swelled with pride as she glanced quickly at her son. She could scarcely believe that this handsome, bright boy was her own child.

"I know, but at school even if I'm bigger, the kids are still my same age, so it's different. I mean it, Mom. I'm not going back."

"I said okay." She controlled an urge to laugh.

"You did? Really, Mom? You're not going to make me go back?"

"Really, really. At least this year." She smiled when she saw the look of delight on his face.

"Can I stay by myself? Probably not," he added suspiciously. "Who's going to take care of me?"

"How about me?"

"You, Mom? Really? Wow! Aren't you going to work at the TV station anymore?"

"I'm on vacation starting right now. I don't have to go back until September first when school starts. That okay with you?"

Megan laughed as a wild war whoop filled the car.

"Mom, you left my uniform in the dryer too long again. It's all wrinkly."

"Just put it back in with a damp towel for ten minutes. It'll be okay."

"Are we going to stop at McDonald's on the way to my game?"

"No, you know your coach said to eat after, not before games. Get a glass of orange juice. That should hold you."

"Aw, Mom!"

In less than a minute Megan heard the refrigerator door slam and the unmistakable sound of a chair being dragged across the kitchen floor. Smiling, she stepped out of her skirt. After snapping it in place on the hanger that already held its matching jacket, she hung it in its place in the large walk-in closet covering one end of her bedroom. Moments later the sharp sting of warm water struck her bare skin. Not lingering in the shower, she quickly lathered with a fragrant rose-scented soap, hurriedly rinsed off, then reached for a thick clean towel. Ten minutes later, she was dressed in pale green linen pants and a neat, white pullover. With her beige-pink polished toes peeping through white sandals, she sat before her make-up mirror to urge her short, sleek curls into their usual flawless, sunny cap.

"Mom, aren't you ready yet?" Jason tapped on his mother's bedroom door before strolling in. Megan eyed her son through the mirror, checking that he was properly clean and dressed. Absently she noticed that his tight, stretchy blue and white uniform highlighted his gangling arms and legs. *He's getting so tall. When he's grown he'll be as tall as* . . . Sharply clamping down on her thoughts, she reached for her makeup brush.

"I'll just be a moment. Do you have your glove?"

"A.J. has it. Come on. We get to ride in A.J.'s car with the top down."

"A.J.?"

"He came to see me pitch. Hurry, Mom. I can't be late. Coach Jensen said if anybody is late they have to sit out the first inning. If I'm not there, he'll let Monica pitch. Then we'll lose."

Taking one more glance in the mirror, Megan stood up. "All right. I'm ready, but we're not riding with A.J. We'll take our own car."

"But Mom, I never get to ride in A.J.'s car. Please . . ." The argument continued as Megan locked the door and approached the startlingly red Ferrari blocking her driveway.

"Please," A.J.'s voice joined her son's. "Besides, if we sit here arguing Jason will be late, and you know what that means!"

"Oh, all right!" Megan agreed reluctantly and pulled a green silk scarf from her handbag. "But you guys know I hate convertibles!" Trying not to show how much she detested riding in the windy car, she huddled in the passenger seat while Jason settled onto the short back seat. A.J. and Jason discussed the upcoming game and worked out a strategy for dealing with the undefeated Lobos all the way to the park.

When they reached the park, Jason scampered out of the car and raced to the home dugout, yelling over his shoulder, "Thanks, A.J. That was cool!"

Megan followed Jason with her eyes until he joined the group of blue and white clad ball players surrounding a skinny young man with dusty blond hair standing on end. For a couple of quiet minutes she watched the obviously harassed coach attempt to calm his excited team and send them onto the field to warm up.

"Whew! Guess we'd better find seats." A.J. lightly brushed his knuckles across Megan's cheek before opening his door. The unexpected touch sent a shiver down her spine. She jumped out of the car before he could reach her side.

"You find seats. I'll be back in a minute." Needing an excuse to escape his presence for a moment, she hurried to the ladies' room to straighten her hair. "Why can't he leave me alone?" she muttered crossly to herself as she tucked a curl behind her ear and lifted the crown, which had been flattened by her scarf. "I can't give him what he wants." Giving herself one final glimpse in the mirror, she left to rejoin A.J.

"Batter up!"

"Perfect timing, they're just starting." A.J. patted the space beside him. She knew he noticed the careful space she left between them on the bleacher bench. To her relief he didn't comment.

"Your right fielder is too deep!" A.J. yelled at the coach a few minutes later. "Bring her in! Jason, watch the way that batter is choking up on the bat! Keep an eye on first base!" Megan smiled in amusement. Their position behind the backstop didn't deter A.J. When Jason hit a line drive and managed to make it all the way to second base, she found herself standing and clapping too. "He's safe!" A.J. roared.

Sometimes Megan wasn't really certain how she felt about Jason's consuming interest in sports. So far she had refused to let him join a football or soccer league, considering them too rough, but she had subscribed to a cable television sports channel so Jason could follow the NBA and NFL games he talked about constantly. Sports heroes occupied positions of honor on his bedroom wall. Actually it had been A.J. who had persuaded her to let Jason play Little League ball this summer, and she had to admit it had worked out well for the boy. Sitting on a hard wooden bench in the sun or rain while every breeze whipped dust in her face was not Megan's idea of a good time, but as long as it mattered to Jason she would be there.

"Safe!" bellowed the umpire as Jason's teammate Monica slid into home. Dusting off the seat of her pants she swaggered, red pigtails dancing, toward the Blue Jays' dugout while the Lobos' coach screamed insults at the catcher for letting a girl get past him. Megan smiled at Monica, who waved at her. It irritated Megan the way the Lobos' coach ordered his team around as though he were a Marine drill sergeant. His team might win games, but the kids weren't having any fun. The big man with his belly hanging over his belt and his bald head glaring in the sun was the direct opposite of the Blue Jay's coach. Billy Jensen appeared to be just an overgrown kid having a great time.

"If Jason ever had a coach like that oaf, I'd pull him out of Little League," Megan whispered to A.J.

"Aw come on, Megan," A.J. argued. "Sure, he's a pompous jerk. He probably doesn't even like kids or baseball, but that's not the issue. Volunteers are hard to come by. Besides, every kid comes up against a few big-mouthed, armchair jocks in his life. You won't punish Jason because he draws a bad coach once in a while, will you?"

Megan shaded her eyes with one hand against the glare of the late afternoon sun before she answered with fierce intensity. "He's my son. I won't let anyone treat him that way."

"You can't always fight his battles for him, Megan. Too much protection hurts more than it helps."

"I won't let him be abused!" No way would Megan sit by and see Jason burdened with physical or emotional scars.

"Okay, don't get upset. Let's just watch the game."

"Pass the chicken, champ!"

"Sure, A.J." Jason wiped his fingers on the grass before handing the paper bucket to A.J. The three sat on A.J.'s car blanket in a shady spot in the park.

"See, this isn't so bad, is it, Megan? We're having dinner together, and it doesn't hurt a bit." His brown eyes laughed into her blue ones.

"You've got to be kidding! I'm sitting on the ground like some kind of contortionist, trying to keep grass and dirt out of my plate, getting grease all over my fingers, and you think we're having fun?"

"At least you can't call this getting involved."

"Mom, we can go now if you want to."

A.J.'s mouth tightened as he caught the look of concern in the boy's eyes. He'd noticed the uncanny way Jason immediately zeroed in on any hint of physical discomfort from Megan. Mother and son were close, but Jason assumed an adult responsibility at times that left A.J. uncomfortable.

"No, I'm all right," Megan reassured Jason. "Eat your chicken. We're celebrating, remember? It's not every day the Blue Jays beat the Lobos!"

"How about those Blue Jays!" A.J. pretended to slug Jason's shoulder. After a brief tussle, Jason sat quietly staring into the distance. Turning thoughtfully to the man beside him he asked, "Are you my dad, A.J.?"

"What—?" A.J. coughed as the soft drink he was attempting to swallow seemed to get caught in his throat.

"Jason! You know he isn't your father!" Megan turned embarrassed eyes briefly to A.J. before giving her attention back to her son. "Whatever made you ask that?"

"Well then, are you my uncle, A.J.?" the boy persisted.

"Jason!"

Jason hung his head sheepishly. "Monica said when dads don't live with moms, then uncles come to visit, and A.J. is the only man who ever comes to visit us." He looked challengingly at his mother.

"Oh, Jason!" Megan's cheeks flared red.

"I don't believe it. The unflappable Megan Nordfelt is embarrassed!" A.J.'s laughter rumbled from deep within him, making her even more mortified, and A.J. found his laughter met with a stony glare.

Jason looked contrite. "I'm sorry, Mom. I didn't really think A.J. was my dad. I just thought he might be an uncle, and if he were, he could tell me about my dad."

A.J.'s laughter disappeared. He sat very still.

"Jason, I've always answered your questions about your father." She avoided thinking about the past as much as possible, but long ago she had determined to be honest with Jason about his father. She'd always known a time would come when her child would want to know his father's name and possibly contact him. She hoped that time hadn't come. She wasn't ready. Why was Jason asking these questions now? Puzzled, she faced her son. "What do you want to know that I haven't told you already?"

"Oh, just stuff." The boy paused, digging one sneakered heel back and forth in the grass.

Megan put her arms around the troubled boy. "He's just like a bigger you." She tried to smile.

"Mom, you told me he looks like me, only bigger, and I know he had to go away to a far-off country, and you were too young, so he doesn't know about me. But you said you didn't know if he likes sports or what position he played when he played Little League. Maybe he didn't even play Little League."

"You're right," Megan whispered. She felt a haunting sadness. "I don't know about things like that. I just know he's big and strong and very kind . . . and he likes to climb mountains. That's a sport, isn't it?"

"Really, Mom? He climbs mountains?"

"Oh, yes. He's a very good mountain climber."

"Gosh, Mom. You never told me that before."

"I guess I didn't."

"I wish I could meet him."

"Someday, son." Her arm went around his shoulders to pull him closer for a quick hug.

"It's not really fair, Mom. Other guys live in the same house as their dads. Even Monica's uncle lives at her house, and he's cool and really funny."

The word "uncle" reminded Megan of A.J.'s presence. Abruptly she lifted her chin to find herself staring directly into A.J.'s face. For long seconds their eyes held. A.J. was the first to look away.

"Perhaps we should get this young man home." A.J. rose to his feet and began gathering up the remains of their impromptu picnic. Megan helped him. Her movements felt jerky and uncoordinated. She wished A.J. hadn't been a witness to the things she'd told Jason.

The pinks and golds of sunset had faded away, and the first early stars of evening were coming out when Megan found herself alone with A.J. on her small patio. They watched silently as gray shadows turned inky black.

"Are the things you told Jason about his father true?" A.J. put the question to Megan abruptly. After taking Megan and Jason home, he had stayed until Jason was in bed, blandly ignoring Megan's hints that he should leave. Shadows lengthened as day turned to night. She welcomed the protection of shadows.

"I've never lied to Jason," Megan bristled, "about his father or anything else."

Staring at the deepening night sky, she observed how the stars looked remotely like chips of ice on warm, black velvet spread across the vast sky.

"Was he really kind to you? Jason's father?"

"He saved my life." She wished A.J. would go away. She didn't want to remember.

"I thought he hurt you badly."

"Why would you think that?" Pain was creeping in, but not the kind of pain A.J. referred to.

"I don't know. Some man hurt you. I assumed it was Jason's father."

"You assume a lot." The pain was there, deep and dark.

"Do you still love him?" The words were barely a whisper.

"It's really none of your business, but no, I don't. I never did." In the back of her mind a nagging doubt questioned whether she was really telling the truth. "As I'm sure you've guessed, we hardly knew each other.

He rescued me when I was hurt and frightened, then he married me."

"Does he know about Jason?"

Megan couldn't answer. He was twisting her soul.

"Why didn't you tell him?"

"How do you know I didn't?"

"I just know."

"It didn't seem right."

"I don't understand."

"You don't need to understand." She fought to maintain her smooth, cool facade. She could feel great cracks spreading across her protective shell. "Please go, A.J. I'm really tired, and it's all really none of your concern."

"It's more my concern than you realize. But okay, I'll go. Just answer one more question. Are you still married?"

Megan didn't bother to respond.

Without a word A.J. understood that she had no intention of discussing her private life with him or anyone else. He stood, his fists clenched then unclenching, his mind six hundred miles and ten years away. For a long time he watched the silent woman cloaked in a distant sadness. She was the most self-contained, closed person he had ever met. Only where her son and her work were concerned did she ever exhibit passion and vitality. Even there, something was missing. Grimly his lips tightened and his knuckles whitened. It was time to wake the sleeping princess.

Turning on his heel he abruptly walked away.

Megan listened to the red sports car roar to life. Leaning back in her chair, she surveyed the brilliant stars glittering in their rich heavenly setting above her, but in her mind's eye she saw only the intense shine of two eyes that had once gazed down into hers, full of promises. She remembered reaching for those stars, only to find her hands were left holding ashes. Shivering in spite of the warm summer evening, Megan rose to her feet and hurried inside, locking the patio door behind her.

Two

OVER JASON'S HEAD MEGAN COULD SEE THE SPIRES OF the Mormon temple and the precise north-south wide streets of Salt Lake City, a city she had never intended to see again, let alone visit on her vacation. She gripped the armrests as she stared out the aircraft's window while her son leaned forward, pressing his nose against the glass. Megan told herself that she was being silly—that even if she walked right past someone who knew her then, no one would recognize or remember her now. It was too long ago and she had changed too much.

Gone was the shabby little girl who had run from here nearly ten years ago, clutching her guilt and fear along with a plastic bag containing all her worldly possessions . . . and a few that weren't hers. For a moment Megan grieved for the girl she had been, a child who hadn't been able to grow up as a child should. She was proud of her accomplishments since that time because she was now a confident, poised woman in a "power suit," a woman who earned a good income and supported herself and her son fully, not only with the necessities of life but with a good number of luxuries as well. She was respected by her colleagues and loved by her son. For the first time in her life she also had a friend.

No, she reminded herself sadly. Once before she had had a friend. Even after so many years, tears stung the back of her eyes as her thoughts returned to the man who had held her in his powerful arms so briefly, wiping away her pain and fear. Close on its heels came that other memory of terror and betrayal, which had sent her fleeing from this city as well as the one man she had wanted to love.

In the aisle seat beside her, A.J. appeared to be sleeping. How had she let A.J. talk her into this? Easily. He'd let Jason do it. When A.J. suggested she and Jason stay in his cabin near Park City, Utah, until Labor Day, she had declined. But Jason pleaded—as A.J. had no doubt intended—until Megan finally gave in. She had stalled as long as possible, reminding Jason of his commitment to finish the Little League season, then spent several days shopping for jeans and hiking boots and all the other odds and ends she thought they might need.

Five weeks in a mountain cabin certainly wasn't her idea of the ideal vacation. The thought of being isolated in a primitive cabin so far from a city merged with memories she had struggled to put behind her. A.J. might mean well, but he was interfering in her life. On the other hand, she and Jason had never taken a vacation together before. There had been an occasional long weekend, but not a real vacation. She found she liked the idea of a family vacation, an experience as new to her as to Jason.

Jason had been so excited when they reached the airport in Missoula that he'd run in every direction chattering nonstop. She admitted reluctantly she was glad to have A.J.'s assistance in answering his questions and keeping Jason entertained. A.J. bought him the latest edition of *Sports Illustrated* before boarding and kept Jason busy by pointing out the Bitteroot Range and the sites of famous Indian battles the plane flew over during the early part of the flight. She was glad when Jason turned to his magazine and A.J. fell asleep.

A network of freeways spread below as the ground rushed by ever faster. Megan swallowed convulsively, and her muscles tensed as her mind wandered back fifteen years when she had first arrived in Salt Lake City. The heater had been broken in Lee's old Chevy and it had been well past midnight. It had been alternating between snow and rain ever since the family had left Denver early the previous morning. Without warm clothing, the long hours in the unheated car had left its three occupants tired and chilled. Mama and Lee were arguing, but Megan knew enough to keep quiet. Her life in Texas had not prepared her for this cold. Her inadequate wardrobe had consisted of shorts, a couple of faded T-shirts, and the crumpled pink sundress she wore as she huddled in the back seat trying to get warm enough to sleep.

She had wished Buddy were snuggled up close to her, and tears seeped from her eyes as she thought of her brother. During the trip she'd lost track of time so that she didn't know if days or weeks had passed since Lee had taken her brother away.

The sequence of events of that awful night ran together in her mind as she recalled the car breaking down, Lee shouting at her mother, police officers with flashlights, and a big room with wall-to-wall beds of sleeping women and children. She remembered a woman with an ugly black and yellow bruise spreading from one eye almost to her chin, but strangely, she couldn't remember if the woman was her mother. Blocking out thoughts was something Megan learned to do at an early age.

A slight bump told her the plane had landed and was taxiing toward the terminal. A slight pressure brought her attention to her lap. She hadn't even realized that A.J. and Jason were each holding one of her hands.

"You were really scared, weren't you, Mom? I thought you liked flying. When we went to Seattle last year you weren't scared." A shadow crossed the boy's face. Turning away he muttered, "'Course I was pretty little then. Maybe I just didn't notice."

"No, I wasn't scared. I just have a lot on my mind today. Thanks for taking care of me." She brushed the persistent dark curl that fell across her son's eyes back into place. Casually she straightened her own jacket, allowing a look of calm assurance to close across her face like a shutter.

"You okay?" A.J. whispered as he reached for their carry-on luggage.

"Yes, thank you." She concentrated on keeping her hands from shaking. Everything would be fine if she stayed calm and poised. She could do it. She knew half the people at the TV station saw her as an iron maiden, the other half dismissed her as a stuck-up snob. She didn't mind so long as it kept people from getting too close.

With relief, Megan watched Salt Lake City disappear behind them as the car A.J. had rented at the airport began the climb up Parley's Canyon to the east.

Jason wondered aloud about the soaring mountains and the chair lift he glimpsed through the trees. He asked why all the trucks were moving so slowly. Megan had opted to sit in the back seat, allowing the two males to sit together in the front. She listened as A.J. described the deep powder skiing for which Utah was famous, and then he launched into the hazards of trucking over the steep mountain pass. After that, he pointed out a sharp dirt road cutting away from the westbound lane. It angled steeply upward and was used, he explained, by trucks when their brakes failed going down the sharp mountain road. By changing to an upward grade a good driver could bring a runaway truck, careening dangerously down the canyon, under control. She heard the words, but her mind kept drifting to another time.

Rolling down his window, Jason breathed in the tangy mountain air. "It smells like going to the lake."

"Lake! It doesn't smell anything like the Lake," A.J. protested.

"Flathead Lake, not Great Salt Lake." Megan differentiated between the beautiful freshwater mountain lake north of Missoula, Montana, and the huge inland, salty sea west of Salt Lake City. She had taken Jason to Flathead Lake in the spring to celebrate his birthday.

"You've been to Utah before?" A.J caught her eyes in the rearview mirror.

"Yes." Megan didn't elaborate.

In a very short time they pulled off the freeway to follow a winding dirt road that climbed higher and deeper into the pine forest that covered the craggy mountains. Occasionally they glimpsed the steep roof of a summer cabin, though human habitations seemed to be fewer and further apart the higher they climbed. Several times they caught quick glimpses of deer. Long after Megan felt they had left civilization completely behind, the car slowed, then turned onto a narrow track that seemed to lead into raw wilderness.

"This car wasn't designed for this," A.J. groaned as rocks and brush scraped its sides. "I should have rented something with four-wheel drive at least." A particularly loud thump brought a grim expression to his usually cheerful face. "Just another mile."

Megan wasn't certain whether he was reassuring his passengers or the car.

Ten minutes later the car came to a shuddering halt before a small log house with a sharply pitched roof, tucked against a steep granite cliff. Pine trees formed a sheltering semicircle around the small clearing. A wide porch stretched across the front of the cabin, and a faint trail disappeared into the trees from the south end. As the car's engine stopped, a deep stillness filled the air.

"Gosh! Is this it? Wow!" Throwing open his door, Jason scrambled out to run laughing onto the porch. "Hurry, Mom!"

"I told you he would love it." A.J. pulled the seat forward so she could climb out.

They walked together to the door of the cabin. A.J. fit a key into the lock and swung the heavy, wood door open. "After you," he bowed dramatically to Megan.

Stepping inside, Megan immediately noticed how clean and airy the cozy room appeared. A huge stone fireplace occupied one wall while two large windows let in light from the east. Grouped in front of the fireplace was a long sofa and two love seats. A large braided rug protected the gleaming pine plank floor. To her right was a comfortable kitchen area featuring a gas stove and a refrigerator, along with a huge, round pine table and a dozen matching wooden chairs. A carefully crafted, wooden high chair sat beneath another window.

"A high chair?" Megan looked askance at A.J.

With a burst of laughter A.J. reminded Megan the cabin wasn't his alone, that he shared ownership with a couple of friends. The cabin had been a joint graduation present given to them by the father of one of his friends in hopes that it would be a link keeping them as close to one another in the future as they had been as boys.

"One of the guys is married," he added. "At last count, he's a papa five times over, which explains the high chair. In the bedroom you'll notice a matching cradle."

Ushering her toward an open doorway on the right, he indicated she should lead the way. A tiny hallway barely separated the living area from a snug bedroom occupied by a wide, rustic log bed against one wall. A prickle of alarm sent Megan across the room when her eyes settled on the inviting bed. Her mind noted that there was only one bedroom.

Attempting to appear casual, she stretched out one hand to touch the cradle that stood at the foot of the bed. Slowly it rocked to and fro. A pine desk and matching chair were beneath the small window, and a wooden rocking chair occupied a corner of the room. One wall was composed entirely of closet space and built-in drawers. Her eyes returned uneasily to the bed covered with a predominantly red and black star quilt. A matching cushion on the rocking chair gave a homey touch to the room.

"You can have the bedroom. I'll bunk with Jason upstairs." A.J. hadn't followed her into the room. He still stood in the doorway. She wasn't sure she liked the way A.J. seemed to almost read her mind at times; nonetheless, she felt tension seep out of her muscles.

Moments later she was delighted to discover a small bathroom complete with flush toilet and a shower stall. With a sheepish grin, she admitted she had anticipated something decidedly more primitive. It was nice to learn the small cabin boasted hot and cold running water, electric lights, a gas stove, and even gas heat to supplement the fireplace.

A loud thump sounded overhead. A.J. ran toward the living room with Megan on his heels. She followed him to a spiral staircase leading upward to a roomy sleeping loft. Jason sat on the floor near a sturdy bunk bed made from debarked and polished logs. As he rose to his feet rubbing his behind gingerly, he admitted he had tried to jump from the top bunk to the double bed nearby that was made from the same beautiful timber. However, he had landed off balance, sliding backward onto the floor.

After Megan had reassured herself that he really wasn't hurt, she looked around. She noticed the heavy railing separating the sleeping loft from the room below. Beside her were another set of bunk beds and two narrow dormer windows. Across the back of the loft ran a long, smooth countertop with shelves and knee hole openings at regular intervals, providing ample storage for clothes, treasures, and rainy day projects.

Before it grew dark the three explored the area immediately around the cabin. A.J. proudly showed them that the cabin had its own septic tank, a large propane tank, and a generator housed in a shed tucked in the trees nearby. A.J. led the way to a small, swift stream a short distance from the cabin and assured Jason there would be plenty of time and opportunity to fish there and in ponds further downstream.

For dinner, they had chili, hot dogs, and chunks of melon. Jason was so tired he argued only halfheartedly when Megan insisted he sleep in the bottom bunk rather than the top one he had jumped from earlier. His happiness and delight made Megan glad she had agreed to bring him.

With Jason asleep in the loft, Megan felt a slight tremor of nerves as she joined A.J. before the fireplace. He had started a small blaze there earlier for Jason's sake, and the coals still gleamed red. A.J. leaned back against the sofa with his eyes closed and his hands clasped behind his neck. Megan settled quietly in one of the love seats. She stared blindly at the red coals before her. Gradually she relaxed, deciding the man across from her must have fallen asleep. In moments her eyes began to drift closed too.

"Megan."

At the sound she opened her eyes warily, only to observe A.J. hadn't moved, hadn't even opened his eyes.

"Tomorrow I have to take the rental car back. I'll spend the night with my friends, then come back up with a four-wheel drive vehicle. If I'm late, don't worry. I'll be back." After a long silence he went on. "Megan, if things don't work out here . . . if you really can't stay, I'll understand. But please try—not just for Jason's sake—but for your own, too."

They were both quiet for a long time listening to the occasional popping of the fire. The curtains were drawn, creating an island in the dark of the cabin.

"There's hot water if you want to shower before you go to bed. I'm just going to check the generator before I turn in. Don't worry about Jason; if he wakes up, I'll be right there. If either of you are nervous here alone tomorrow night, move Jason down here to one of these couches and bar the door, though there's really nothing to worry about."

She felt a rush of relief, followed by a stab of guilt for doubting him. A.J. was as good as his word; he had promised he wouldn't try anything or expect any romantic involvement from her. She rose to her feet and made her way sleepily to the bathroom where in seconds the hot needles of spray soothed her into the exhausted slumber that held her tight in its grip until the sun's rays streamed through her window the next morning.

By the time Megan was dressed, with her gleaming silver blond curls sleekly in place, A.J. and Jason were finished with their breakfast. She savored golden pancakes swimming in strawberry syrup, while from the window she watched A.J. lift the hood of the rental car and lean over the engine.

A short distance away she could see Jason strewing a trail of tiny bits of pancake from a nearby tree stump to the porch. It wasn't long before two quarreling ground squirrels accepted the invitation. Sitting quietly on the porch step, Jason grinned his delight as the furry little gluttons worked their way toward his outstretched hand. They stopped only a foot away to chatter a warning before scampering back to their hole beneath the stump.

Megan washed the few dishes and tidied the room before stepping outside to join Jason. Redwood furniture now adorned the wide porch. A.J. must have carried the pieces from the shed earlier that morning while she still slept. Making her way to an inviting porch swing, she curled up in one corner.

Jason ran to her side, laughing as he tried to tell her about the little squirrels.

The car hood slammed into place, and A.J. strolled back into the cabin, emerging shortly after with a small travel bag in one hand.

Leaning casually against the door frame, A.J. silently watched Megan bend her pale blond head toward the deep chestnut brown waves of her son's head. He knew she wasn't as fragile as she appeared—slender and almost childlike with huge blue eyes surrounded by thick golden lashes. The first hint of sun had brought out a flush of faint freckles on her nose, but he knew those eyes could turn to ice. She had a will of steel that could buckle anyone she caught attempting to abuse power or trample on those she considered smaller and weaker. More than once he'd also watched her topple the ego of some man who looked at her well-rounded figure and thought it was his for the grabbing.

"This better work out," he muttered softly under his breath. The more he'd seen the boy, the more he knew Jason could only be one man's son. A.J. had followed Megan to Missoula and had grown to know her and to love the child who constantly reminded him of the childhood friend who had always been there for him. He'd known for a long time that under Megan's smooth, polished veneer hid a fright-ened little girl who had been badly hurt. At first he saw Megan as the woman who had torn his friend's life apart and shattered a friendship built on time and trust. But the more he came to know her, the more he'd begun to question the friend who had been his hero. Megan had indeed been hurt. Had it been Doug? A.J. could hardly believe it. But Megan's revelation of his friend's innocence of any crime showed him that these three people he loved deserved a second chance.

Megan and Jason walked with A.J. to the car. He placed his hands on the boy's shoulders. Giving them a squeeze, he instructed Jason to look after his mother. Being careful not to touch Megan—who he knew still didn't fully trust him—he asked if there were any other supplies she would like brought back. "I asked a friend's wife a week ago to stock the cupboards and refrigerator for us. Cathy is a health food nut—and a Mormon—so you won't find any coffee, let alone anything stronger to drink. She probably filled the whole place with fruit and granola."

Megan laughingly told him she had wondered about the four gallons of milk, eight cantaloupes, basket of peaches, and three quarts of strawberries, but since she and Jason both loved fruit she looked forward to eating their fill. She had also discovered six loaves of homemade bread in the ice box and a gallon size mayonnaise jar full of oatmeal cookies. Every shelf in the kitchen was loaded with cans, boxes, and bottles of food she looked forward to sampling.

"Mom, I found a whole shelf full of all kinds of soda pop and sixteen packages of Fig Newtons upstairs," Jason volunteered. "There's a great big can of hot chocolate mix and tons of marshmallows, too."

"I'll bet Cathy doesn't know they're there!" A.J.'s snort of laughter ended the discussion. "Seriously, is there anything special you would like, anything to eat or drink, books, magazines?"

"No, we've got everything we need. We'll be fine."

A.J. let his eyes drift over her face. Then he swallowed and turned his eyes toward the small clearing. Suddenly making up his mind he met Megan's eyes once more. "Megan, it sounds like you know the area. Is there anyone you would like to send a message to?"

He saw a flash of fear flicker through her eyes before her mask of serenity slid into place.

"No, of course not." She looked into his eyes without flinching. "I don't know anyone in Utah."

His serious mood continued. "Remember, I'm your friend. I really do want you to be happy, and I will never knowingly hurt you. Trust me please, Megan."

"I wouldn't have come if I didn't trust you." But her eyes told him a different tale as they hinted at secrets not to be shared.

After the rental car disappeared from sight, Megan let Jason coax her to accompany him to the little stream they had visited the previous evening. Settling on a blanket with the newest Tom Clancy thriller in her hands, she read and dozed intermittently, encouraging Jason as he tried unsuccessfully to catch a fish with the rod A.J. had prepared for him. Then he tried catching the minnows darting about in the clear water with his hands. When that proved unsuccessful too, he sifted sand and pebbles through his hands, pretending he was panning for gold. Eventually he succumbed to the warm sun and the aftermath of the long trip, the early start to the day, and the hours of running and exploring. He snuggled down on the blanket beside her and was soon asleep.

It was peaceful in the little clearing and for more than an hour Megan relaxed with only an occasional insect to disturb the slumbering quiet. She was deeply engrossed in her book when a slight noise broke her concentration. Her startled eyes hastily scanned the surrounding area. She caught her breath, then reached to shake her sleeping son's shoulder. She placed her finger across his lips signaling him to be silent as he opened his eyes.

Lifting his head, he turned puzzled eyes to follow his mother's pointing finger. He almost forgot to be quiet as his eyes focused on two lovely deer drinking the cold water with only the width of the tiny stream separating them from their entranced audience. The two deer stretched their slender necks toward the cool water as they delicately tasted its icy sweetness, the sun glinting on their sleek hides. One doe's ear flapped brusquely at an annoying insect, before she resumed drinking. Several minutes passed before the deer became aware they were being watched, then they turned, unconcerned, and drifted back into the forest.

Megan placed one hand on Jason's shoulder, enjoying the peace and closeness she shared with her son. Life hadn't afforded them many such moments. Survival had kept her scrambling for an education, then job security. Perhaps the time had finally arrived when they could be together more.

Picking up the blanket, Jason helped Megan shake free the grass and needles that clung to it, then carried it back to the cabin for her. At first he talked softly as though under the spell of the wild creatures or perhaps hugging to himself the lingering enchantment of the beautiful animals, but by the time they reached the cabin his chattering exuberance had returned.

"Wait till I tell Monica. She's not going to believe it!"

"You and Monica!" Megan tousled his hair. She loved the happy grin on his face.

Having missed lunch they set about preparing an early dinner of fruit salad with warm, crusty bread topped with melted cheese, along with tall glasses of milk.

Darkness came early, even for the mountains. Still they both jumped when the first loud growl of thunder rumbled through the air. Quickly they secured the windows and door, then mixed mugs of hot chocolate topped with melting marshmallows. They settled down before the fireplace with their comforting drinks and a plate of oatmeal cookies. Megan felt snug and secure from the wind and rain raging beyond the sturdy log walls. She was glad she'd been given this time to spend with Jason.

When she suggested it was time for bed, Jason appeared reluctant to go upstairs alone, so she suggested it might be fun for her to sleep upstairs, too. Together they climbed the stairs to retrieve the boy's pajamas. Megan insisted Jason shower, then quickly did the same. When both were ready for bed, she made certain the fireplace screen was in place before the dying coals, then she began turning off the lights.

As the cabin lights went out, the storm appeared to grow louder. Lying in bed directly under the steep pitched roof, she listened to the screaming wind and the rapid beat of the rain. A loneliness filled her like that she had known as a child in her grandfather's wooden shack. She listened to Jason's steady breathing and was glad he was there sleeping beside her. Nervousness gave way to fatigue, and before the storm beat out its fury she too gave in to sleep.

Gradually Megan became aware of a rhythmic pounding at the door below followed by the deep tones of a man shouting. Frightened, she reached across the narrow space between her bed and Jason's bunk to assure herself he was safe and still asleep. Her hand met only an empty, mussed bed. Shivering now, she jumped out of bed.

"Jason," she called softly for her son. There was no answer. Hastily she turned on a low bedside lamp. She couldn't see him anywhere. She rushed to the rail overlooking the living area.

Jason stood at the door lifting the bar that reinforced the lock on the heavy wooden door.

"No!" she screamed.

Too late, she saw the door swing open. A huge, heavily-bearded man stepped into the room toward her defenseless son. In the dim light of the glowing coals and the weak rays of the one tiny lamp she could see his shaggy hair and rough beard. His hair appeared as dark and as wet as the camouflage khaki pants and jacket that clung to immensely wide shoulders and long, long legs. Slowly he lifted his chin until his eyes caught hers.

"Megan?" She heard his hoarse whisper.

"No! Oh, no!" Slowly she sank to the floor. It couldn't be! How did he find her? From farther and farther away she heard Jason screaming for her. She heard the man shout, followed by his heavy boots pounding up the stairs. Frantically she reached for her son, but blackness claimed her first.

Three

CONSCIOUSNESS RETURNED SLOWLY. SOMETHING WAS wrong! Why was she lying on a hard wooden floor? Instinctively Megan lay still, feigning sleep, until she was certain of her whereabouts. Memory came rushing back . . . the cabin . . . the intruder!

"Jason!" Her mind recoiled when she realized she had passed out, leaving her son unprotected. As every muscle tensed, preparing to leap into action, she became aware of small arms clutching tightly about her neck.

"Mom! Mom!" There was a definite quaver in her son's voice. "Wake up, Mom."

Relief brought tears shimmering to her eyes as she willed her arms to gather him into a comforting embrace.

"Get back," came a deep-voiced order. "She can't breathe with you practically strangling her." Large hands reached to draw the boy back.

"Don't you touch my mom," Jason screamed, turning on the man who was attempting to draw him away from her. The panic-stricken child kicked frantically at the shins of the man holding him, bruising his own bare toes. Then like a cornered animal, he sank his teeth into the restraining hand.

"Stop that!" The man easily shook the child off. Once more he reached for the boy. This time his eyes met Megan's. Within her she felt the icy steel of a mother lion protecting her cub as she sat up and pulled Jason to her side. Her eyes never wavered as they met the intense blue eyes of the man standing over her. Fury and fear blinded her to everything but protecting her child.

"Megan." His voice was low and sounded harsh to her ears.

"Get out!" she screamed.

Silence met her cold demand. For long seconds she thought he would not respond. Something lonely and sad flickered in his eyes. A muscle twitched beside his mouth. "Not, 'Hello, Doug? It's been a long time. How are you?' Just, 'Get out'?"

"That's right. Leave."

"Megan, you're in shock," he began with weary patience. "I know you didn't expect to see me. Please, just relax. Go back to bed. We can talk in the morning."

"No! I want you out of here."

"You're not being reasonable. It's two o'clock in the morning; it's raining outside, and this is my cabin. Besides you know we have to talk."

"This is not your cabin. It belongs to a friend of mine. He loaned it to us for the rest of the summer."

"Megan," the big man's voice rumbled gently in the tones reserved for speaking to a frightened child. "Your friend, A.J., is my friend, Allen James. Didn't he tell you he shares this cabin with two friends, Brad Williams and me? Brad's father, Judge Williams—you remember the judge—gave this cabin to the three of us as equal partners."

Shaking her head in disbelief she stared numbly at the man towering over her. Nothing made sense. It wasn't like her to faint like some Victorian maiden in a too-tight corset. *Why is Doug here? Did he tell Lee that she was here, too? No! Lee is dead! And A.J. But I thought he was my friend.*

Her eyes widened further, radiating a glaze Doug recognized as shock. Fearing she might collapse again, he reached a hand forward to support her.

"No!" Jason, in a sobbing whirlwind, attacked him once more.

Ignoring the small furious fists pounding his chest and arms, Doug gathered Megan into his arms and placed her resisting body on the bed she had just left.

"We're leaving!" She glared at him while struggling futilely to get to her feet.

"Not tonight. I'll be sleeping on the sofa right at the bottom of the stairs, so don't even think of doing anything stupid. In the morning we'll talk."

"I don't want to talk to you."

"I don't imagine you do, but you're going to." He locked his arms around the still struggling boy, swung him onto the bed beside his mother, and pulled the quilt over them both. "Stay put until morning."

Turning to walk away, he never looked back until his feet touched the bottom step. They never saw his shoulders slump, nor the way his large body sank wearily into the sofa cushion where he sat for most of the remainder of the night with his elbows braced on his knees and his bowed head resting in his cupped palms.

The woman upstairs really was Megan. He could hardly take it in. He hadn't quite let himself believe Allen's words. He'd searched so long. Now she was here. But nothing was the way he'd dreamed all those years. In his dreams she always welcomed him with open arms. He sighed. There certainly hadn't been anything welcoming about the reception he'd received tonight. He knew he'd frightened her, but her fear went deeper than tonight. He knew that. He felt a clenching pain deep inside. What happened to his Megan during those awful years they'd been apart?

Horror held Megan paralyzed for long minutes until gradually the mother in her recognized her son's need for comfort and reassurance. "Shh," she whispered hugging him close. "He's not really a bad man. He won't hurt you."

"Why are you so scared of him if he isn't bad? I thought he was going to hit you."

"I'm not really afraid of him." Her voice shook, belying her words. "I was just surprised to see him, and at first I didn't recognize him. I must have jumped out of bed too quickly when I couldn't find you, then when I saw you opening the door to someone I thought was a stranger, I got scared."

"Why does he know your name?"

"He's not a stranger," she admitted reluctantly. "But I haven't seen him for a long, long time and didn't think I would ever see him again. I guess the surprise made me faint. It was really kind of silly. When I started to wake up I was confused, and for a minute I thought he was trying to hurt you." Megan sensed she was babbling, but couldn't help herself. She was determined to be as honest as possible, but what could she tell Jason?

"But, Mom, who is he?"

Megan was unsure how to answer. She didn't want to tell him the truth, but she wouldn't lie either.

"He's someone I knew a long time ago," she began softly. "You remember I told you when I was a little girl I lived with my grandpa and that one day my mother got married to a man who didn't take care of us. He took us away from Grandpa's house, and I didn't have a home anymore. Sometimes we lived in motels or apartments, but most of the time we just lived in his car."

"Is he the man who took you away?"

"No, Jason. That man's name was Lee. He brought my mother and me to Salt Lake after a while. We lived in an old house in the middle of the city, but I wasn't happy there. Sometimes the man hit me." Her voice took on the pain of a hurt and confused child.

"I wish I'd been there," Jason declared. "I wouldn't let anybody hit you."

Megan hugged him closer.

"One day something bad happened to me. That man downstairs— he found me when I was hurt and scared. At first he was very kind to me, but later something happened, so I knew we could never be friends anymore."

"What happened, Mom?"

Megan's voice continued softly without directly answering, "He made a bargain with Lee." Feeling the tension leaving the child's shoulders, she continued her whispered monologue, though she suspected Jason was too nearly asleep to really hear her words.

"So I ran away from him—the man downstairs. Oh, I don't think he minded that I ran away, but I did something very bad too. I took some money that didn't belong to me. I didn't really steal it; I only borrowed it, but it took a long time to pay him back. I think that made him angry. Now I'm afraid he wants to take something of mine, something he won't ever give back."

As Jason slept he made a little whimpering noise, making Megan aware that she was clutching him much too tightly. Easing away from him a bit, she stared sightlessly into the blackness surrounding her, knowing she wouldn't be going back to sleep.

Memories she had buried in the deep recesses of her mind refused to stay where she had struggled so long to keep them. Once set free, she knew they would torment her again for a long, long time. Returning to Utah had opened a crack in the door to the past, and the man downstairs threatened to blow apart her whole life. She couldn't stay here. In the morning she would find a way to get Jason safely away. Shortly before dawn she finally drifted into a restless sleep.

Doug awoke as light began to fill the cabin. He hadn't slept much, and a slight sound from above drew his eyes to the overhead rail. Clasping the rails tightly, the boy peered between the smooth pine spindles. Doug wondered how long the child had watched him sleep, sprawled across the large sofa before the cold fireplace.

Allen had warned him Megan had a child, but he'd chosen not to think about it. Pain tore at his heart. He didn't want to think of Megan with some other man, nurturing someone else's child. Was the boy's father still in her life? He felt certain the child was going to be an obstacle to convincing Megan she still belonged with him.

He ran the palm of his hand across his mouth, down across his thick, full beard. Suddenly he had a picture of himself as the boy— and Megan—must have seen him the night before. His beard was nearly black although it had strong hints of red. It was rough and untrimmed. He hadn't had a haircut for several months. His knit shirt was matted and wet from the rain, and his khaki pants were crumpled and baggy. He was a big man, and he knew from experience that his sheer size often intimidated grown men. He must have appeared a monster to Megan and her child.

His eyes returned to the watching boy. He met deep blue eyes staring back at him. The boy sucked in his breath but did not retreat. Sitting up carefully, Doug motioned silently for him to come downstairs. Glancing hesitantly at his mother, Megan's son made his way carefully to the stairs. Keeping his back to the wall, he cautiously edged his way to the lower level. A scowl served to warn Doug to keep his distance. The boy disappeared into the little hall leading to the bathroom, and Doug realized it was nature, not an overture of friendliness, that had drawn the boy down from the loft where Megan still slept.

Doug reached for his boots. If the child's reaction to him was any indication of what Megan's would be when she awoke, he'd better do something about it. He shrugged into his jacket, hesitated a moment, then took the door bar with him as he walked outside.

When Megan joined Jason minutes later, it was to find the large room empty, with the front door standing slightly ajar. A quick glance through the window explained Doug's disappearance. As they watched, the man reached into his pocket then proceeded to unlock the back of a mud-spattered Ford Bronco. Soon a battered duffel bag rested beside his feet and he bent forward, digging farther into the Bronco.

Jason turned when his mother touched him lightly on his shoulder.

"Go into the bedroom and lock the door," she said quietly. "You can dress there, but don't come out until you hear me leave the bathroom." She had no intention of allowing Doug to catch Jason alone. In her work she had covered too many stories where the father had snatched a child away from the mother.

When Doug returned to the cabin the boy was nowhere in sight, but hearing the shower running, he quietly removed a clean shirt, a pair of jeans, and a few toiletries from his bag, then slipped back outside. He carefully trimmed his beard, the cold of the mountain stream bracing him to face the hostile occupants of his cabin.

Reaching the open doorway, he knew Megan hadn't heard his approach. She wore spotless white slacks, and she bent over the stove to stir something in a black skillet. He felt a moment's regret as he lifted his eyes to her short, silvery hair. He remembered a flowing mane of angel hair.

The boy sat at the table noisily draining a tall glass of orange juice. Doug frowned. Seeing the boy stirred feelings of hurt and anger he didn't wish to analyze too closely. Later he would have to come to terms with the boy's existence. Right now it was enough to know Megan was here, here in his cabin.

When Megan turned to lift steaming scrambled eggs onto two plates, he caught his breath. Her eyes were as he remembered, a pale silvery blue, but he had never before seen her face in full light without shadowy bruises and raw scratches. Gone was the lovely, vulnerable girl, and in her place was a beautiful, mature woman. He experienced the same compelling certainty that had jolted him ten years ago when she'd first opened her eyes and gazed at him. It went beyond recognition to a bond older than time.

Unsure how to approach her, he was startled when she took the initiative. "There are more eggs on the stove, Doug. Help yourself," she invited coolly before seating herself at the table. Three places were set with fresh fruit and toast.

As the three shared a silent meal, Megan seemed completely calm. Long ago she'd schooled herself to hide her emotions. She knew Doug was watching her from beneath his long lashes as she forked eggs into her mouth. Taking a cue from her, Jason also ate steadily and quietly, only his eyes gave away his anger and frustration. Doug's attempts to start a conversation were ignored.

When they finished eating, Megan began clearing the table.

"Megan, come sit down."

She turned on the hot water and began scraping at the egg drying on the plates as though she hadn't heard his request. Doug silently reached for a dish towel.

When the last dish was back in its place in the gleaming pine cabinets, Doug placed his hand firmly on her shoulder to steer her toward the couch. She caught her breath. Fear and nausea fought for dominance. Steeling herself to ignore the shock that raced through her at his touch, she shook off his hand before she strolled unhurriedly toward one of the wide love seats. Settling herself in the center, she took a deep breath, and turned to her son who was preparing to sit beside her.

"Jason," she spoke calmly. "I want you to take your fishing pole and go to the clearing where the deer were yesterday. They might be back, you know." She sought to assure her son with a tremulous smile that all was well.

Looking belligerently at the man now seated across from her, Jason announced, "I'm not leaving you by yourself with him!"

"I'm sorry," Megan continued smoothly. "I should have introduced you. "Douglas, this is my son, Jason Nordfelt. Jason, this man is Douglas Beckwith. And, Jason, I really will be all right. You go catch a fish and look for the deer, but don't wander off. I'll be there in just a little while."

After the child reluctantly stepped out and closed the door Megan silently braced herself for the attack she expected. Doug didn't move or speak. His eyes traveled from her hair to her toes. She resisted the urge to squirm. Not by a blink of an eye did she allow him to see just how deeply disturbed she was by his appraisal.

"You're very beautiful."

It wasn't what she expected and only added to her nervousness. She didn't bother to respond.

"I've rehearsed for years what I would say to you if I ever found you. Now I don't even know where to begin."

Still she made no response.

"Megan, talk to me. Tell me why you ran away. Do you have any idea what kind of torment you put me through? My mother lost ten pounds worrying about how a sixteen-year-old girl with one arm in a cast was going to be able to survive alone."

"Well, obviously I survived." It was a low blow to mention his mother. It had comforted her for a time to pretend that Elizabeth Beckwith was *her* mother. Causing Mrs. Beckwith pain was one of the deepest regrets of Megan's life.

"Yes, I see that, but at what price?"

A thread of bitterness crept into Megan's cool facade. "As if you didn't know. That's the whole point of this little talk isn't it? Money and pride!"

"I suppose pride does play a part, but what does money have to do with you and me?" He sounded genuinely puzzled by her attack.

"You think you bought me and now you want me to pay you back. Well, I have news for you. I'm not going to pay anymore and neither is Jason. You don't own us."

"Own you? Of course, I don't own you." Her anger left him reeling. She must be confusing him with someone else. Quickly he latched onto one word, her reference to her son. "Speaking of Jason, Mrs. Nordfelt, where is his father? Did you run out on him, too?"

Startled, Megan stared blankly at Doug. Before she could regain her equilibrium, the color began to drain from Doug's face. Hoarsely he whispered. "There isn't a Mr. Nordfelt, is there? Jason is mine!" Leaping from his chair, he gripped her shoulders roaring angrily, "How could you? I have a son, and you never even told me!"

"He's not your son, he's mine," Megan hurled back. Her heart was pounding and her hands felt damp.

"Oh, he's mine all right. All nice and legal, or have you conveniently forgotten I married you?"

"Take your hands off me! I haven't forgotten anything. You'll never know how much I wish I could forget everything that ever happened in my life up until the day Jason was born."

Doug watched her eyes change from pale blue to steel gray as they filled with bitterness and hate. What had happened to her? Why did she hate him? Was it because of the boy?

"Get out of my life. Leave me alone! Leave my son alone!"

"No, Megan." He spoke slowly as the ramifications of the boy's existence ricocheted through his mind. "I've never been served with any divorce papers, and I certainly never did anything to end our marriage. I'm still your husband, and I'm Jason's father. I won't leave either one of you alone."

"Then we'll leave. You can't force us to stay here."

"No, I can't force you to stay," he responded grimly, "but think twice before you take Jason. If you try to leave this state with him, I'll file kidnapping charges against you, and you know the law will back me up. One word from me, and Judge Williams will see that you never see your son again."

Huge tortured eyes met the ultimatum squarely. Pain twisted her ashen face as Megan recoiled from his threat. She knew he couldn't legally charge her with kidnapping, but she'd seen too much abuse of power to naively trust in justice.

"You hate me so much you would destroy a child to get your revenge? Don't you care what it would do to Jason to learn the man he hates and fears, the man determined to send his mother to prison, is his father?"

Doug closed his eyes. He'd never before experienced such agony. He rocked back on his heels for several long minutes before he spoke. Burying his anger, he spoke softly, coaxing.

"Megan, it doesn't have to be like this. Let me get to know him. Give me a chance to be your friend."

"Never!"

"Please stay."

"Do I have a choice?"

"No, I guess you don't." Suddenly tired, Doug sighed. Running his fingers through his hair he tried to control his temper. "I'm not an ogre. Megan, you have to know I never meant to hurt or frighten you. I don't want anyone to be hurt, but I won't give up my son. Surely you can understand that?"

"Oh, I understand all right. I know all about people like you. You're big and rich and a man so you think you can buy anything you want, and what you can't buy you take or destroy. Women and children, people smaller than you, aren't supposed to have feelings. They can't say no. And if we get in your way we deserve to be kicked until we learn our place. Well, let me tell you something, I'll stay because I have no choice, but if you tell Jason you're his father before I think he's ready to be told, I'll make certain he hates you forever."

She jumped to her feet. Before reaching the door she whirled about, "And don't threaten me. I'm neither stupid nor a child. I have rights, too." Lifting her chin defiantly she turned and walked from the cabin.

Doug watched her go. That wasn't the rational conversation he'd anticipated. He wished he hadn't lost his temper. But it had left him totally vulnerable to learn that Jason was his son. His own son.

When Megan reached the stream Jason dropped his pole to run to her. "Are you okay, Mom?"

"Sure, tiger." She smiled wryly. She loved him so much. She couldn't even contemplate how unbearable life would be if Doug made good on his threat. Seating herself on a large boulder, she pulled both feet onto its flat surface. With her arms wrapped around her legs, she dropped her chin to rest against her knees. Staring pensively into the rushing water she wondered what she should tell her son.

"Is Mr. Beckwith staying here? Do we have to leave?"

"Yes, he's staying."

"But, Mom, I haven't caught a fish yet. A.J. said we could stay until school starts. I don't want to go home yet."

"We're not leaving. It seems we'll have to share the cabin with Doug for a while. He won't go away, and we don't have any way to leave."

"Don't worry, Mom. I won't let him hurt you. Remember, I promised A.J. I would take care of you." Suddenly brightening he added, "When A.J. gets back, I bet he'll make that man go away."

"Don't count on A.J. He isn't the good friend we thought he was. He tricked me into bringing you here and made certain we didn't have any way to leave by ourselves. Then he told Doug where to find us." Seeing her son's hurt expression, Megan regretted sharing her suspicions with Jason. It really wasn't right to burden him with adult worries.

"Jason, we're going to have to make the best of it. He isn't going to hurt you, but I don't want you to be alone with him. You must be polite to him, but stay away from him as much as possible. I don't want you to talk about where we live now or where we used to live, and especially don't mention the places we've visited in the past. Do you understand?" Already her mind was searching for a place where neither Doug nor A.J. could find them.

"I guess so."

"Jason, it won't be too bad. You can still fish, and we'll take long walks down to the beaver ponds. I noticed there's an old basketball rim on the side of the shed. You brought your ball so you can practice. A.J. left a camera and film for you in case you wanted to take pictures of the squirrels and deer."

"Can we still drink hot chocolate with marshmallows and have a fire in the fireplace before going to bed tonight?"

"Yes, we'll just pretend Mr. Beckwith isn't even here. We'll just keep right on doing all the things we planned."

"That's okay then, but when A.J. comes I'm going to tell him I'm glad he's not my uncle. A real uncle wouldn't play dirty tricks on us." Silently they sat side by side until Jason decided he ought to check his fishing line to see if he might have caught something.

Megan continued to sit on the rock. Over and over she devised one plan after another to escape and take Jason with her, only to discard each one as impractical. She knew she would only get one chance; she couldn't waste it on anything foolish. Inwardly she raged. Ten years ago she'd left Doug, determined that no man would ever own her again. She was going to control her own life. Most importantly, she had determined never to be scared again. She had learned the hard way not to depend on men. Grandfather, Lee, and Doug had all hurt her. The men she wrote about for Channel Two had reinforced her low opinion of men. If she kept men out of her life, she wouldn't be hurt. Unlike her mother, she didn't need a man.

She remembered the lonely years she'd played in the dirt beside her grandfather's unpainted shack, always being careful not to make too much noise and hiding under her bed when Grandpa drank too much and roared and shook his cane. She remembered going with her mother to San Antonio where they lived in a little house with an angry man who hit her until a lady took her away to a big house where there were so many rules she got confused. They said she was naughty and made her sit on a chair and go to bed without supper. She was happy when Grandpa came to get her. He took her back to his tired little farm where she tried especially hard to be good so he would keep her.

"Look, Mom!"

Megan looked up to see that Jason had found a heavy rope with a thick knot at one end. The other end was tied to a tree limb that extended over the small pool. Grasping the rope he ran forward, then let it carry him in a swinging arc over the water and safely back to shore. Megan applauded to show her appreciation of his new sport, before letting her mind drift back to another little boy.

Megan had been nine, the same age as Jason was now, when her mother came back. This time her mother had brought Lee and Buddy with her. Lee smiled and talked a lot, and he said he was going to be her daddy because he was married to her mama. He liked to touch her silver-white hair, and sometimes he brushed it until she was so tired she fell asleep in her chair.

On the day Lee got his paycheck, he and Grandpa would sit at the table and drink beer until Grandpa starting yelling and waving his cane. Lee didn't yell, he just got quiet and mean. When he got really quiet, he would always hit someone. Most of the time it was Mama he hit, but sometimes he would knock Grandpa down or slap Megan. One time he punched Buddy, then everyone was really scared because Buddy was just a little baby, and he didn't wake up for a really long time. After that Megan kept Buddy under her bed with her when Grandpa and Lee started drinking.

Grandpa had made a wagon for Megan to carry vegetables from the garden to the stand where he sold them. She always found room for Buddy with her load of vegetables. Buddy had soft, brown hair and big round eyes. His fat little arms and legs waved, and he blew bubbles when she kissed his tummy. When Buddy got too big for his basket, he slept in her bed with her.

After Lee lost his job, she and Buddy slept under the bed most nights. Buddy would hug her neck and blow bubbles on her face while he slept. One night when they fell asleep with his blanket under her bed, she woke up because Mama was yelling at Lee. She was crying and saying, "No, you can't do that. No matter how bad we need the money, we mustn't do that."

Megan's eyes stared unseeing around the small clearing. Instead of noticing sunlight dancing on water and hearing the gurgle of the swiftly moving stream, she saw a dark, cluttered room reeking of stale beer and wet diapers.

"I didn't know what she meant then," Megan murmured to herself. Mama had pulled Megan and Buddy from under the bed telling her to take Buddy and get in Lee's car. Grandpa was lying on the couch snoring; beer cans were all over the table and the floor, and the box Grandpa kept his vegetable stand money in was smashed to pieces on the table. Megan didn't see his money anywhere.

Lee had driven all night. Megan held Buddy while he slept. His wet diaper soaked through her nightgown making it stick to her legs. When morning came Buddy cried for his bottle, but Lee wouldn't stop anywhere to buy milk for him. It was hot and Buddy was getting cranky when Lee finally stopped to buy gas for the car. Lee got a can of pop for Megan to put in Buddy's bottle. After that Buddy went back to sleep.

When they got to Houston, Lee stopped in front of a big house with a long porch and took Buddy into the house. Mama started to cry. When Lee came back Buddy wasn't with him. When he started the car, Megan screamed, "Don't leave Buddy. Go get him!" She pounded on Lee's shoulders, but he just kept driving. Mama told her to shut up, that maybe Buddy was the lucky one.

* * *

Suddenly, Megan became aware of Jason watching her, his eyes round and fearful. She called to him, though she knew her words could not be heard over the sound of the rushing water. Perhaps seeing tears coursing down her cheeks had made him let the rope go to hurry to her side. Megan welcomed his arms around her, and she leaned her head against his cheek. Awkwardly he tried to pat her back.

Doug found them embracing. Standing at the top of the path before it dipped to the stream, he watched silently, hidden by a clump of quaking aspen and wild currant bushes. Clenching his fists helplessly, he longed to go to them, to comfort them, to demand some answers, to make them understand. But sensing that his presence would only precipitate another stormy confrontation, he carefully withdrew.

He made his way back to the cabin knowing they would have to return. His thoughts were in a turmoil. He could scarcely believe he had finally found Megan, and the discovery of a half-grown son left him stunned. Regret and guilt twisted painfully through his insides as he acknowledged that his memories of his and Megan's brief time together were far more pleasant than her memories of those weeks must be. Had he turned her into this bitter, angry woman? Reluctantly, he recognized that Megan needed some time to adjust to the situation.

"Adjust she will," he vowed. "I won't let her disappear again."

With clenched fists he bowed his head and found himself for the first time in his adult life praying to the God his friend Brad had urged him to trust since they were children.

Four

DOUG WAS AWARE OF THEIR UNCERTAINTY AS MEGAN and Jason stepped inside the cabin. He had set the table for three, and steaks were sizzling on the broiler. He whistled tunelessly, pretending this was a normal meal and nothing was unusual about the three of them sitting down to dinner together.

"Dinner will be ready as soon as you two wash up," he informed them cheerfully. Without speaking they turned toward the bathroom.

Megan and Jason returned to the kitchen. They sat down. Wordlessly they picked up their forks.

"Would you like some salad?" Doug passed the bowl to Jason. Without answering, the boy accepted it, helped himself, and passed it on to his mother.

"What grade of school are you in?" Doug tried to start a conversation.

"Fourth." Jason shoved a forkful of baked potato into his mouth.

Now what? Doug wondered how he was going to establish any kind of relationship, let alone be a father to this child who obviously resented his presence. He'd been so close to his own father and had assumed that's how it would be with his son, if he were fortunate enough to have one. Of course, he hadn't expected to miss out on the first nine years of his son's life.

"What kind of work do you do?" He turned to Megan. "Allen said you work at the same place he does."

"I do." She ignored the first part of the question.

"What do you do?"

"A little of everything."

Doug wanted to shake her. She sat there nibbling at her steak and eating precise lady-like bites of her potato and salad as coolly as if he didn't exist. She wouldn't talk to him, and he knew practically nothing about her. He ought to give it up, just say, *Okay, Megan, just forget we ever knew each other. You go your way, and I'll go mine.* He looked at her bowed head, glanced at Jason wolfing down whatever was placed before him, and something twisted in his heart. He couldn't give up. He couldn't ever give up on them. Doug ate and continued to ask questions as though he didn't notice their reluctance to converse with him.

When the uncomfortable meal ended and Megan began washing dishes, he picked up a dishtowel. After the dishes were finished, Megan and Jason spent the evening playing checkers. They quietly refused Doug's offer to play the winner, so he settled in a corner of one of the deeply cushioned love seats with a magazine. Not by the slightest lift of an eyelash did he let them know he noticed Jason's swaggering boasts or Megan's quiet ripples of laughter as they challenged and bluffed each other.

The only indication that they were even aware of his presence came when Megan heated milk for hot chocolate. Jason carefully carried a mug, complete with a fat marshmallow, to the low table beside Doug, who picked up the cup and invited himself to join them on the colorful rag rug before the fire.

An outsider would have thought they were an ideal family sharing the lingering end of the day. Doug reclined on one elbow with his long body and longer legs forming a protective semicircle around Megan and Jason. She, with her slender, womanly form, elfin face, and luminous eyes reflecting the firelight, rested one hand on their child's shoulder. The boy, with hair and eyes like Doug's and a proud tilt to his chin like that of his mother, sat cross-legged in front of her. Doug felt comfortable and relaxed. He discovered a new envy for his friend Brad's warm family circle. He liked the cozy picture of the three of them forming a family.

Idly he lifted his hand to finger a silvery curl. Abruptly Megan jerked away. Her back stiffened and a wary expression filled her eyes.

Shifting away from the large man beside her, Megan found herself resenting his broad shoulders and long, lean body. They made her feel trapped. She didn't like him to touch her hair. Lee had always been touching her hair. She bit down viciously on her marshmallow. She remembered that once she had found Doug kind, and she'd felt safe with him. Abruptly she rose to her feet.

"Jason and I will sleep upstairs. You can have the bedroom."

"No, you keep the bedroom. I'll bunk with Jason."

She cast a look of near panic toward Jason. "Jason stays with me." She began to walk away but stopped abruptly as a strong hand closed around her ankle. Hot flames of shock tore through her. She stood rigid. Her mind willed her to fight, but she couldn't move. Conflicting waves of awareness surged through her body, beginning with the spot where warm fingers touched her skin. The dark torture of knowing a man was holding her, forcing his physical will over hers, swamped her emotions. Pine and dirt filled her senses. She smelled blood. She had to escape! She had to get away from Lee!

"Don't touch her! Let my mom go." Jason threw himself at Doug, kicking at the arm restraining his mother.

Doug released Megan and lunged to his feet. He grasped Jason's shoulders and pushed him onto the sofa. Turning he clasped Megan, who still stood as though frozen, and abruptly seated her beside her son. He took a deep breath, ran his fingers through his hair, and glared at the two of them.

"All right, I've had enough. I've tried being friendly. I've tried to reason with you. I wanted to give you time to adjust to me, but since you're not willing to meet me half way, I'm laying down some rules. First of all, Megan, I'm willing to admit I was at fault in making you my wife while you were still in shock and too young to know what was happening to you. My only defense is I wanted the right to protect you, and I only went to your room that last night because I heard you crying and I wanted to comfort you. What happened wasn't planned, and I deeply regret the pain it caused you. I can even understand, in a way, why you ran away. What I cannot understand or forgive is why . . ." His voice trailed off as his glance turned to Jason.

"Okay, rule one. Megan, you will use the bedroom and Jason will sleep upstairs in the loft with me. Two, Jason, you will not throw temper tantrums or attack me. Three, we share the cooking and cleaning up. Four, no more sulking. We will all talk to each other in a civilized way and make every effort to get to know each other better. Is that understood?"

"How come you get to make all the rules?"

Another time Megan might have laughed to see the smaller version of the same face glare right back at the older version, if she weren't so frightened by the prospect of being separated from Jason. She couldn't trust Doug not to simply take the boy while she slept.

"All right. Fair is fair. What rules do you want to make?"

"Don't touch my mom. She doesn't like anybody but me to touch her."

Startled, Doug looked from Jason's serious face to Megan's pale features. Nodding slowly he agreed. "I won't touch your mom unless she wants me to."

An hour later, Doug lay in bed staring at the stars glittering through the dormer windows. He suspected Jason wasn't really asleep, though he lay still with his back to Doug. From below came the sound of the shower still running, telling him that Megan hadn't settled down for the night yet either.

He tried not to torture himself with imagining her slim form standing beneath the steaming spray, her face tilted upward. He closed his eyes. His arms ached, recalling how her body had felt as he lifted her unconscious form to place her on the bed. Sternly, he ordered himself to take control of his thoughts.

Jason's words, "Don't touch my mom. She doesn't like anybody to touch her." Megan's hostility, the running shower. Everything blended together to leave Doug with a sense of frustration that kept him tossing and restless until he finally yielded to badly needed sleep.

Megan shut off the water and reached for a towel. She wrapped its length around herself, using a trailing end to pat her face dry. She didn't bother to blow dry her hair, but picked up another towel to pat and fluff her hair out before she stepped into the adjoining bedroom. After pulling a long T-shirt over her head she sank down on the low rocking chair.

The first thing I've got to do, she told herself, *is get myself together. I'm not a child this time, and I've got to stop reacting hysterically. Doug is not Lee; he won't physically attack either of us. I don't really think he will take Jason and leave me stranded here, though I can't be sure of that.*

Slowly she began to rock. *He hasn't mentioned the money yet. And even though I paid it back, maybe he could still charge me with theft. He has to know I took the money. I paid him back double what I took, but I'm afraid it won't ever be enough. If it were only the money, he might have forgotten about it years ago; but the ugliness, his mother's heart attack, and now Jason. . . . I have to get away from here.*

Rocking back and forth, she relived the nightmare that began the morning of her sixteenth birthday. She had been excited and happy because being sixteen meant she could finally apply for a real job. With money of her own she could save enough so that some day she could go back to Houston and get Buddy. She would buy nice clothing for both of them and surprise him with all the ice cream he could eat, then they would go live with Grandpa again. Lee came into the kitchen where she sat nibbling on a stale doughnut. He stretched and scratched his belly where it protruded above his unsnapped jeans.

He'd reached out to stroke her hair, just the way Doug had earlier tonight. She bit her lip, wishing she hadn't reacted so strongly. She'd overreacted that day to Lee's gesture too. Jerking her head back to avoid his hand, she'd bumped her head painfully against the corner of the cupboard. Lee had laughed and gripped her hair hard enough to bring tears to her eyes.

"Happy birthday, baby," he whispered into her face, his foul breath making her want to retch. "I've got a surprise for my little girl. We're going on a picnic, just you and me." Gradually his fingers combed through her long hair, lingering where the pale strands lay across her breast.

The fear had started a few minutes later when she saw her mother standing in her bathrobe at the door of the bedroom she shared with Lee. One eye was closed in a narrow red slit and her face looked dark and puffy. As Lee was in the bathroom, Megan's mother looked tiredly at her and nodded her head, confirming Lee's picnic plans with Megan.

"Come with us, please," Megan begged.

"I can't go with you. I've got to work today." She'd turned her back, gone back into the bedroom, closing the door behind her.

She knows and doesn't care! Megan was hurt and frightened but not surprised. Mama had never once stood up for her.

The ride up American Fork Canyon was a horrifying ordeal, with Lee taking the hairpin curves too fast and laughing at her terror. Several miles beyond the summit, he parked his old pickup truck in a meadow where several small streams converged. He pulled her out after him, but didn't release her as her feet met the ground. Instead he pulled her tightly against the length of his body. When he attempted to kiss her mouth, she tried to break free. Laughing at her struggles, he taunted her with all the things he planned to do to her, telling her how good it would feel and how much fun they would have. Megan shuddered as she relived the horror of his mouth and hands, his filthy words.

At last, her attempts to escape angered Lee. His powerful fist slammed into the side of her head knocking her to the soft, spongy ground. When she tried frantically to roll away, Lee lunged toward her. He cursed as his feet slid in the mud and crashed to his knees. This was her chance! She scrambled to her feet, only to feel Lee's hand grasping at her legs. Even now she shuddered remembering the feel of fingers closing around her ankle.

Panic lent strength as she kicked out with her other foot, striking Lee full in the face. Startled, he involuntarily released his grip to clasp his bleeding nose. Megan didn't even hesitate; she ran. She ran until a red mist was swirling in front of her eyes, then she hid until crashing sounds in the shrubbery sent her fleeing up the mountain. Eventually she found a trail and followed it upward, but it was not to safety as she had hoped.

Megan's thoughts shifted back to the present. She wrapped her arms around herself. The night had grown chilly, and with the door between her and the fireplace, the cold mountain air had seeped into her room. Stiffly rising to her feet, she snapped off the lamp and crawled beneath the heavy quilt, snuggling into its comforting warmth. It wasn't enough. She was cold and alone.

With her mind still resisting sleep, her thoughts continued to stray back in time. They skipped over the pain and terror, to the gentle hands that had lifted her out of the dirt, gently brushed away the sharp pine needles, and carried her away from the nightmare. A face appeared and disappeared over and over through the blackness until she awoke to find him sitting beside her hospital bed. He came every day, and sometimes his mother came as well, a quiet, cheerful woman with brunette hair sporting streaks of gray. Her rescuer talked and told her stories; he made her laugh, and he made her feel safe.

At first she didn't tell anyone her name. She was too frightened and sick to tell the police what had happened. Then Lee and her mother came.

Doug was with her when Lee and Mama entered the room, or she might have screamed. Instead she clutched Doug's hand so tightly her fingernails left little half moons in his skin. When Lee started walking toward her, nausea rose in her throat. She couldn't look at him. Coldness crept up her arms and legs until she felt like a frozen statue, then she was sick all over the bed. Doug called a nurse, and a policeman came running into the room. She remembered the prick of a needle, then nothing.

The next few days ran together as a woman in a gray suit asked her questions over and over; two police officers, one a middle-aged man, the other a young woman, stayed beside her bed for what seemed like hours, always asking questions. Once she heard Lee shouting at someone outside her room. Doctors and nurses came and went. She couldn't talk to any of them. Her mother came to her room alone one time. She didn't say anything, only gazed sadly at her for a long time, then quietly left the room, leaving Megan to drift back to sleep.

When she awoke, Doug was beside her again and they were alone. At first she didn't understand what he was saying. Something about her father wanting to check her out of the hospital and take her home because he couldn't afford the hospital bills. Her mother, though, seemed to think she should stay a little longer. In fact, Megan shouldn't go back home at all, Doug was saying, and he had found a way so that she wouldn't have to go back to her parents, if she didn't want to.

Megan's mother had agreed to his plan, saying that she would sign the papers, Doug continued. A little crack of trust crept into her heart, and slowly she reached out to take Doug's hand. As his fingers closed around her smaller hand, she experienced a previously unknown surge of peace.

Two days later they were married right there in the hospital with a tall, silver-haired judge performing the ceremony. A friend of Doug's and his mother were the only witnesses. Doug's mother had brought her a lovely, white gown with pink rosebuds embroidered on the yoke and a matching robe. Her eyes were red rimmed with unshed tears, but she smiled as she helped Megan into the new clothing.

Doug had pinned a tiny corsage of fragile pink rosebuds to the collar of the robe. The tall judge looked unhappy as he spoke to her before beginning the ceremony, informing her she didn't have to do this. If she needed help, he could pull a few strings to have her placed in a protective facility for young women or in a foster home. Doug's friend had kissed her cheek and solemnly promised to be her friend. Doug held her hand, and she felt warm and safe as she whispered the brief words placing herself in his care.

She recalled feeling nervous and out of place when Doug carried her through the door of his mother's house and up an elegant carpeted staircase. She'd caught glimpses of dark wood and brocaded fabrics like those in the magazines she sometimes picked up at the library. It reminded her of the house in San Antonio where she hadn't been allowed to touch anything.

Her new husband left her tucked in a huge bed with smooth, sweet smelling sheets. He told her to rest, but she hadn't rested. Instead she had stared at sheer curtains the color of sea foam with darker green drapes looped across the top of a brass rod, which matched the lush green carpet on either side. A brightly flowered arm chair, a gold and white antique desk, and matching bureaus were scattered about the room.

Raising her head she glimpsed a painting of a young woman sitting in a meadow with two little girls. They wore white dresses with pastel ribbons. The little girls were placing a crown of yellow dandelions on the woman's long brown hair. A rag doll and a wide-brimmed summer hat lay abandoned in the long grass dotted with daisies and dandelions. Their apparent happiness caused a little ache in Megan's heart.

Doug and his mother brought trays to her room where the three of them had a picnic supper. The following morning Doug stopped at her door to ask what she would like for breakfast and ended up helping her down the stairs to eat with him and his mother. The days passed pleasantly as she listened to Doug's enthusiastic talk of oil exploration and his dreams of developing environmentally safe procedures for extracting the oil.

New clothes, underwear, nightgowns, loose shirts that would slide easily over her cast, casual pants, and skirts appeared as if by magic. She fell asleep each afternoon listening to the piano as it was played by Elizabeth Beckwith in the big room off the front hall.

The evening before Doug was to fly to the Middle East, Megan saw the judge who had performed the marriage. She learned that he was the father of Doug's friend who had served as witness. She thought he watched her carefully over their shrimp cocktails, followed by prime rib, baked potatoes with cheese and chives, and tiny buttered peas. Lemon pie piled high with meringue finished the meal and nearly finished Megan. She wasn't accustomed yet to food skillfully and abundantly prepared.

After dinner, the judge asked to speak with Megan alone in the study. Startled by the request she nodded her head. Nervously playing with the edge of her cast with her good hand, she led the way to the study. When both were seated in the large wing chairs on either side of the white brick fireplace, the judge attempted to put her at ease by casually telling her a little bit about Doug and his parents and the judge's longtime friendship with the family.

Gradually he brought the one-sided conversation around to the events of the previous two weeks. "Are you happy with the present arrangement?"

"Yes," she admitted shyly. It was true; she liked the big house, Doug, and his mother.

"Are you aware Doug is a wealthy young man?"

The question startled her, but she said she thought he probably was rich because she had never seen anything before like his house or the kind of food he ate every day.

The judge shifted in his chair. He appeared almost ill at ease when he spoke. "The doctor who saw you in the hospital said your injury wasn't an accident, that you were attacked by a person or persons who attempted to rape you. Do you know who attacked you?"

Sitting very still, not lifting her eyes, she nodded yes.

When the judge pressed for the man's name, she refused to answer.

"Your father thinks it was Doug and that he married you to keep you from testifying against him."

Megan's eyes flew to meet the judge's. Shock and confusion held her speechless for long seconds.

"Your father said you were separated while climbing together, that he searched for you until evening, then drove back to Salt Lake to report you missing. He didn't realize that Utah County was the county of jurisdiction. He believes you are in danger here. Do you want your parents to come get you?"

Doubling over she began to sob. "No, no, no."

"You don't have to leave unless you want to, but you don't have to stay either." He paused, his face grave. "You should also know that I am aware that your father has a prison record. He served time for theft and smuggling. However," he paused gravely, "if you are working with him to extort money from Doug, you'll be lucky if you're sent to a juvenile detention center. There's every likelihood you'll be tried as an adult, and that means prison."

Megan's eyes rounded with horror. She teetered on the edge of her chair. The judge reached toward her. She shrank from him in terror before running from the room and up the stairs where she threw herself onto the bed.

"How can he believe Lee's lies?" She sobbed. "I hate Lee! I hate him!" She pounded the pillow. "He always ruins everything." Tears ran down her cheeks to soak her pillow until she eventually cried herself to sleep.

Mrs. Beckwith found her there sometime later tightly curled in a ball. It was Doug's mother who brushed the tears from her wet cheeks, gently undressed her, and helped her into a fresh gown, then slowly patted the back of her good hand until she settled back into sleep.

Megan didn't remember the nightmare that woke her, but she did remember the man who held her easily against his bare chest. She remembered her tears running down his smooth flesh. Taking one corner of the sheet he wiped her face dry. With one hand he pulled her head against his shoulder. No words were exchanged as they sat silently. Doug's chin rested against the top of Megan's head, and one hand softly soothed its way slowly up and down her uninjured arm.

After a while Doug began to speak. "I'll be leaving before you're awake tomorrow," he told her. "But you'll be safe with Mother. I've made arrangements for her to buy you whatever clothing you need and see that you have money for whatever you need."

She leaned back against the comforting warmth of his chest. He asked if she would write to him and promised he would telephone when he could. He reminded her she could annul their marriage any time after she turned eighteen.

"I know you don't want to talk about it," Doug whispered. "But I think you need to be kept safe from your father. As my wife, your parents no longer have any authority over you. If your father threatens you in any way, tell my mother or Judge Williams."

Slowly Megan relaxed. As her body softened she became aware of the firm muscles under her hand. The hand stroking her arm was now easing the muscles at the back of her neck, before working its way down her spine. When she turned to better accommodate the comforting motion of his hand, the stroking hand faltered, then resumed its leisurely relaxing motion. Megan had never felt this way before: relaxed and dreamy, safe and loved.

Almost imperceptibly her body slowly shifted until they were lying face to face. Doug's free hand brushed her hair away from her face. One finger touched her bottom lip, moved to the corner of her mouth. Then his lips brushed hers as lightly as a butterfly's wing. Their eyes met in the dimly-lighted room, illuminated only by the moonlight shining through the wide window where the drapes had not been drawn.

"I think it's time for me to return to my own bed," he murmured.

"Don't go. I'm afraid to be alone."

"Oh, Megan," Doug whispered, "You're so young and so beautiful. This isn't right. You're too young, and I'm going away. I don't want to hurt you . . ." His voice disappeared in a defeated groan as he pulled her closer.

Momentarily frightened, she hesitated, then with all the fierce longing of years of denied love she clung to him until waves of desire overtook her, and she was lost in their thundering roar. Intense satisfaction gave way to sleepy indolence; she was warm and safe, and she slept.

Megan tossed restlessly, remembering bitterly that one night when she had trusted and believed. She remembered waking up the next morning full of hope and happiness. Feeling her cheeks redden she recalled the magic of Doug's hands pushing away the sordid memory of those other hands.

Dressing as quickly as she could in a new pair of jeans and an over-sized sweatshirt, she'd rushed toward the staircase, hoping to see her husband before he left for the airport.

Halfway down the stairs, she was stopped by angry voices. Recognizing first Lee's voice, then Doug's, she cringed against the wall. From her position on the stairs, she could see into the study where the two men stood facing each other.

"Take the money and go," she heard Doug snarl.

"Seems to me, boy, you're getting more than you're paying for anyway." Lee's sneering voice carried to the girl frozen on the stairway. "She's a hot little piece."

She didn't hear Doug's quiet response, but she sensed his anger and saw her stepfather take a step backward even as he reached out toward the thick stack of bills Doug practically threw at him. Lee thrust the money into his pocket. Megan's hand flew to her mouth, and she stumbled back a step.

A piercing scream startled them all, and Megan watched in a daze as Mrs. Beckwith rushed into the hall and collapsed in the open doorway. Her handbag, which she had been clutching to her chest, dropped to the floor, its contents scattering across the room. For a second frozen in time everyone stood in a still tableau staring at a gold tube of lipstick spinning crazily in the center of a wooden parquet square.

Pandemonium ensued as Doug rushed to his mother's side. Taking advantage of the confusion, Lee dashed toward the open window. But his jacket caught on some rough edge and in struggling to free himself, the money slipped out of his pocket to the floor just as he hurtled himself through the window to freedom.

The wail of a siren woke Megan from her dazed state. She retreated further up the stairs, then into her room. She closed the door and gingerly sat down on a chair. Through the window she saw two para-medics carry Mrs. Beckwith out on a stretcher to an ambulance. A car pulled up to the curb, and Judge Williams and his son Brad climbed out. They hurried to Doug's side as he stood by the ambulance. After talking to them briefly, Doug climbed into the ambulance with his mother, and Judge Williams and Brad followed as the ambulance pulled away.

The angry words she'd overheard kept repeating in her head. She moved like a sleepwalker about the room. She packed a few things in a plastic bag she found in the closet. Downstairs she walked, still as if in a trance, to the study. Blindly she stared at the scattered bills, coins, credit cards, a compact, lipstick, and all the paraphernalia of a woman's purse. Her eyes focused on one thing—the money she would need to escape. Looking at the lovely house now tarnished by the ugliness of betrayal, she remembered, in spite of the numbness controlling her robotic actions, to lock the front door behind her as she left.

Megan pulled the quilt tighter around her shivering form. What did it all mean? Why had Doug really married her? Why had he given Lee all that money? The questions screamed through her mind, but the answers eluded her grasp now as they had then.

Five

I'M NOT TOUCHING ANY DIRTY WORM." Megan shuddered. "Oh, Mom!"

"That's okay." Doug reached for her rod. "Baiting fishhooks is one of the few chivalrous tasks left for macho males to perform for our fair damsels. Male superiority today rests, alas, on the lowly earthworm."

Jason snickered as Doug finished baiting the hook with a flourish. Doug winked mischievously at Megan before turning to Jason. Patiently he taught the boy to look for the quiet pools on the downstream side of big rocks, the tantalizing eddies, and the deep holes where the water seemed to ebb and swirl. She followed them, intent on watching over Jason. Again and again Megan watched Doug show Jason how to cast his line into the desired spot. With feigned exasperation and a great deal of laughing and splashing, he helped Jason free his hooks from tree branches, bushes, underwater roots and submerged logs. Megan was amazed at his patience with the child. He appeared to really enjoy doing things with Jason. But of course, she reminded herself coldly, it might all be an act.

As the three worked their way downstream, Jason's skill improved, fewer hooks were lost, and gradually he drifted a short distance ahead of her. She made no effort to catch up to him, but trailed behind, occasionally dabbling her line in the water, but mostly enjoying the sun on the water. She stopped to examine the wild flowers and to gaze at the mountain peaks. Where Jason and Doug splashed through boggy places and pushed through shrubs, Megan carefully picked her way around the obstacles.

She felt more relaxed than she had for the past three days, three days in which she had struggled to be polite, friendly, and poised. Despite her fears, she had encouraged Jason to join in the activities Doug suggested to keep him busy. Still she remained on her guard against their leaving the cabin without her. In spite of her distrust, she had to admit she was beginning to enjoy being with Doug. It surprised her to see that he spent as much time trying to win her trust as he did Jason's, though she cautioned herself not to become complacent—she'd been lulled into trusting Doug once before with disastrous results.

She was glad there had been no more outbursts of temper, though Jason continued to scowl suspiciously whenever Doug got too close to her. He made it clear he resented Doug's assumption of authority if he tried to assign him tasks or correct his behavior in any way. Nevertheless Megan could see Jason was drawn to Doug in spite of his determination to keep Doug at arm's length. It was obvious they enjoyed their daily sessions shooting Jason's basketball at the hoop over the shed door, and Jason couldn't contain his excitement when Doug suggested an all-day fishing trip, gradually working their way downstream to the beaver ponds. She wasn't sure she liked how much Jason was beginning to enjoy Doug's company. She didn't want him to start depending on his father.

A loud shriek interrupted Megan's thoughts and sent her crashing through the brush to reach her son. Ahead of her she could hear similar sounds signaling that Doug was also scrambling to reach the child, and she felt an unexplainable wave of relief knowing he would get there first. Stumbling past the last tree obstructing her view, she jerked to a halt and stared in disbelief.

Jason was laughing and dancing around a small clearing waving his fishing rod in the air. Dangling from the line was his long-dreamed-of first fish. As she stood watching, Doug showed Jason the best way to safely remove the hook, before slipping the slippery ten-inch trout onto a short forked willow by inserting one tip through a gill and back out the trout's mouth. After rinsing the skewered fish off in the stream, Doug opened a small wicker basket threaded onto his belt to let Jason drop his fish inside.

"Did you see my fish?" Jason ran to throw his arms around her. "Doug said I should pull really hard when one started to bite my worm. It worked! I caught it all by myself!"

Looking down at his happy face, she laughed and hugged him back. "Yes, I saw it. It's quite a beauty." She met Doug's eye over the boy's head and exchanged a silent message of relief for the happy outcome to their shared fright.

After that the two adults were careful to stay closer to Jason, who, despite the frequent tugs on his line, didn't catch another fish until they reached the place where the beaver dam blocked the stream, forming a small pond. On a grassy knoll just above the pond, Doug removed his backpack and spread a blanket beneath a towering pine tree. His pack yielded sandwiches, peaches, cookies, and even a thermos of ice cold orange juice. Megan enjoyed their lunch, slowly savoring each bite of the simple meal, but Jason was too anxious to try his luck fishing the pond to take time to eat much.

"Mom, I've got to catch more fish than Monica. She said she caught six when her uncle took her and her mom fishing in Canada."

Only when Megan promised him he could fish again as soon as he finished one sandwich, did he reluctantly sit down beside her. As he hastily washed down the last bite with a cup of juice, Doug reached across to place something in the boy's pocket. Glancing down at the thick bulge in his shirt, Jason laughed, patted his pocket, then jumped to his feet.

Megan watched Jason hurry toward the water, pole in hand. Her curiosity made her ask Doug, "What did you give him?"

A mischievous smile spread across his face. He reached into his pack once more.

"Hold out your hand."

Tentatively she did as he instructed. Doug filled it with a mixture of nuts, dried fruits, and grains.

"Cathy's famous granola." His hand lingered, fingers barely touching hers, sending a ripple of awareness coursing up her arm. Lightly closing her fingers around the treat cupped in her palm, he teasingly admonished her, "Don't drop any. Cathy doesn't allow us to waste any of it."

Slowly withdrawing her hand she covered her confusion. "Looks like oatmeal cookie crumbs to me."

"But better," Doug agreed. "These crumbs are Cathy's special recipe." He popped a handful of the mixture into his mouth, then reached for his fishing rod.

"Coming?" He extended his hand to help her to her feet.

Glancing about, she noted she could easily see all the way around the pond. "No, thanks. I think I'll stay right here and watch."

"Okay, if you change your mind, though, I'll bait your hook for you again."

Megan watched as he walked away, covering the distance in easy strides to where Jason sat on a tree stump. An ache built low in her stomach, as she registered the smooth motion of his denim-clad hips and the easy way his long legs moved across the uneven terrain. He stirred old memories, and they weren't all bad. She thought longingly of the easy friendship they once shared.

Her brow furled and her chin lifted as she reminded herself of Doug's threat should she try to leave with Jason. *He can't bluff me out of trying to escape. He's underestimating his enemy if he thinks I don't know he only holds the advantage if he can keep Jason in Utah. Until our marriage is dissolved and a judge awards custody, I have every right to take Jason anywhere I choose.* Unfortunately, Doug also had that right and if he chose to disappear with the boy, she had no way to stop him. As soon as they were back in Montana she could file for a divorce and request custody. There she would have the advantage of being a respected, self-supporting member of the community. She should have divorced Doug years ago, but she'd been reluctant to draw attention to herself and unwilling to risk the possibility a judge might take Jason away from her.

Feeling restless, she picked up the fishing rod and walked to the water's edge. She tossed the line carelessly into the water and turned her attention to scanning the shore line until she spotted the two avid fishermen on the other side of the dam. When they dropped out of sight she felt a moment's panic, until first Doug's head then Jason's, appeared over the bushes. Soon she observed them settling down together on a fallen log with their poles extending once more over the water. She wished she were sitting there with them. No, not really. She just wanted to be certain Jason was safe.

A sharp tug on her line interrupted her thoughts. *Good grief! What will I do if I actually catch a fish!* she thought in horror. Reeling in her line, she felt both relief and regret to find it empty. Now her bait was gone. She wondered what to do. Jason would be disappointed in her if she gave up on fishing so soon. She knew for certain she wasn't putting another worm on that sharp little hook, but she would feel silly to sit dangling an empty hook in the water.

She grinned sheepishly as she acknowledged her own squeamishness. Most of the women she worked with at the station wouldn't hesitate to bait their fish hooks themselves. She wandered back to the blanket where they had eaten lunch to look for an alternative to a worm for bait. She had heard of using corn or cheese, but she had neither. Spying an interesting looking lump of Cathy's granola on the blanket she promptly jammed it onto her fish hook before returning to the water.

Her line sailed over her head in mimicry of Doug's casting demonstration. *Piece of cake!* She pretended to put the "pro" in his place.

Wham! Megan's rod bent nearly double. Her line screamed a high-pitched zing. A monster was trying to run away with every inch of line on her reel. She wouldn't let him get away with it! She gripped the little handle of the reel, tried to turn it backward, only to have the crazy beast turn and begin racing toward her. Frantically she cranked the wheel trying to regain her line. It wasn't fast enough. She remembered Doug telling Jason not to let the line go slack. She grasped the pole firmly in both hands and ran as fast as she could backward up the incline.

"Oh!" Her feet went out from under her as she stumbled over Doug's pack. Sitting down with a thump, she kept cranking the line in. Seconds later the dirtiest fish she had ever seen bumped over the ground to land by the blanket. She stared at the fish, then began to giggle. Soon tears ran down her cheeks as she hooted with laughter. She, Megan Nordfelt, had caught a fish! It wasn't just fun—it was funny. She laughed as she'd never laughed before.

She was quite aware of Doug's approach as he arrived with all the finesse of a charging moose. Jason was only a few seconds behind him. Suddenly Doug stopped short. Was Megan laughing? From across the pond he'd thought he heard screaming. He recognized a hysterical edge to her laughter and approached her carefully. She'd been so self-contained the past few days. Had something happened to cause this outburst? Did he dare touch her? He knelt beside her and tentatively spoke her name.

"Megan . . . are you all right?"

Jason abruptly threw his arms protectively around his mother. "Mom! Mom! What's the matter?"

She looked at their faces and laughed harder. "I . . . I . . ." she gasped. "I caught a fish!"

Two pairs of eyes followed her hands as she picked up the line to hold aloft the biggest, most battered trout they had ever seen.

"Wow! Must be ten pounds!"

"Well, maybe not that much, but it's certainly one of the biggest I've ever seen!" Doug's amazement was tinged by a wave of relief. Megan was all right. Maybe she had overreacted a bit, but then again, Doug had never been around a woman who just caught her first fish before. And what a fish!

Doug withdrew the hook from the trout's throat. Still firmly clinging to the hook was the chunk of granola. He looked at Megan questioningly, then it was his turn to laugh. He was still laughing when he secured the fish to a forked willow. Jason excitedly carried the fish to the pond to rinse it. He and Jason teased Megan all the way back to the cabin about her unique fishing style.

"Monica says when somebody catches a fish they have to clean its insides out themselves. She said it's a rule. Does Mom have to clean that big fish? It might be kind of messy, and Mom doesn't like messy things." Amused, Doug offered to clean the fish with Jason's help—along with the others he and Jason had caught—if Megan would do the cooking. When Jason asked her, Megan agreed with a sigh of relief.

Doug thought supper that night was the best he had ever eaten. He froze the big fish for later, and Megan fried the smaller trout to a beautiful golden brown and served them with hash brown potatoes and bowls of peaches sprinkled with sugar and nutmeg. Megan was friendlier and more relaxed, making his spirits soar. If he continued planning activities for the three of them, he'd not only learn more about them, but hopefully in time Megan would feel comfortable enough to really talk with him.

The following morning Doug woke them early and again packed a picnic lunch. He led them on a long meandering trek along rarely traversed mountain trails. He was glad Megan had taken his advice to dress in blue jeans and a long-sleeved shirt to protect her arms and legs from mountain brush. In jeans and hiking boots she still looked fragile and beautiful. He wanted to put his arm around her, but he knew she wouldn't welcome the action.

As the three of them followed a trail leading up the mountain, Doug took time to identify patches of pink Monkey Flowers with their sticky, hairy stems and brilliant rosy blooms. He made up stories about a magic rabbit as he pointed out the lilac blue harebell, and joked about Elephant Head and creamy Ram's Horn. He showed them meadows of wild geraniums and clumps of scruffy goldenrod.

"Monica says that kind of flower is a grandmother flower," Jason volunteered, pointing to a delicate pale yellow columbine.

"Now what is a grandmother flower?" Doug asked in bewilderment. He thought he knew the common name of every wild flower in the Rocky Mountains.

"Monica says grandmother flowers are the kind of flowers grandmas grow in their gardens. They don't come in boxes from the greenhouse like petunias do, and you have to work hard to get them to grow out of the dirt in the same place every year."

Doug chuckled at this explanation. Jason was enjoying this outing and opening up more with each thing they did together.

A tiny shiver shot down Megan's spine as Doug laughed. She had difficulty moving her gaze from the rippling motion in his tanned throat. Slowly her eyes traveled down the column of his neck to where his partially buttoned shirt gaped open, revealing dark hairs curling against bronze skin. Raising her eyes, she became aware Doug no longer laughed. He was watching her. Feeling a flush climb her cheeks, she quickly looked away.

"I wish I had a grandmother." Jason said as he stole a peek at her from under his eyelashes. He didn't see the suddenly taut expression on Doug's face nor hear his muttered words, "And I know a grandmother who would like to know her grandson."

But Megan heard. Quickly she turned away, not daring to think about the woman who had mothered her those days so long ago. She didn't want Doug to glimpse the sadness she suspected her eyes would betray. He'd never know how much she had missed his mother. There had been such an immediate closeness between them—or had she imagined it because she'd wanted it so much?

Lunch time found them spreading Doug's pack on a wide flat rock that served as both a table and a lookout point. Two gray squirrels scolded from an overhanging tree. As though daring each other, they raced down the tree, approached the picnickers without getting too close, then scurried away, only to repeat the process a few moments later. Megan was amused by Jason's determination to coax them closer. He laid a trail of potato chips from the toe of his boot to the edge of the rock. He placed a finger over his lips to caution the adults to be quiet. They sat still and waited for the busy little animals to venture closer and closer, gobbling and running, until finally, one braver than the other, snatched the last crumb from Jason's boot and scurried out of reach. Unable to keep his delight to himself, Jason burst into laughter. Doug and Megan joined in.

They sat in peaceful silence slowly absorbing the lazy hum of summer. The meadow stretched before them in varying shades of green, sprigged with a multitude of wild blossoms. A tinkling whisper floated on the breeze from nearby quaking aspens. Doug's eyes shifted to soaring mountain peaks. Above them he could see the wings of a hawk climbing and drifting with unseen air currents in the brilliant blue of the sky. Doug wanted it to be like this always. He was ready to be a husband and a father.

"Mom, is that where God lives?" Jason's voice held a note of reverent awe as his eyes scanned the lofty mountain spires.

"Maybe." Megan's voice was hushed. "I think he lives on mountain peaks, and oceans, and cities, and in churches, but most of all he lives wherever people stop to look for him."

"Do you think God is up on that mountain?"

Doug was startled to realize Jason was addressing him. A prickle of moisture dampened his upper lip. He didn't know how to answer, but he felt a compelling need to not let his son down. Suddenly a long ago conversation with his own father flashed into his mind, and he found himself repeating his father's words.

"The Indians believe everything has a spirit. They believe in strong spirits of the mountains, gentle spirits of flowers, and brave spirits of eagles and bears. They worship a Great Spirit over everything. My good friends, the Williamses, are Mormons. Their beliefs aren't too different. They believe in a Father God, who with the help of his Son, created this whole world and even the universe. Because he created the mountains and animals and plants, we should treat them with respect. Yes, I think it's quite likely God is on that mountain, and like your mother said, wherever we need him."

Doug didn't feel satisfied with his answer. He wasn't certain what he believed about God, so how was he supposed to explain God to a nine-year-old kid? He would be better prepared to answer Jason's questions next time, he decided—if he got a second chance.

He turned Megan's words over in his mind, and it occurred to him that if ever someone needed to look for God, he did. He certainly could use all the help he could find. As a boy he used to go to Primary and Sunday School with Brad. While he didn't disbelieve what he heard there, it just hadn't seemed important—not as important as scouts or ball practice anyway. He wished now he'd paid closer attention.

Once they left their table rock behind, Doug led the way again. "We'll come to a stream in a few minutes," he told them. "Then we'll start back on a trail on the other side."

On the bank of the stream he knelt near a narrow spit of sand to point out tiny hand prints in the damp sand. Quickly he assured Megan and Jason that the prints were not made by a lost child, but by raccoons who had brought their food to the stream to wash before eating. He stood again and pointed out the stepping stones the three of them would have to use to reach the opposite shore. Jason began leaping from rock to rock and was safely across in no time. Megan looked dubiously at the stones. She approached the edge of the stream and peered into the water. Tentatively she stepped to the first rock, then slowly pointed a toe toward the second. Seeing her hesitancy Doug stretched out his hand.

"Here," he urged.

Doug held his breath while Megan glanced at his waiting hand then at the rushing water. Panic flickered in her eyes, then slowly she reached out to clasp his fingers. She never lifted her eyes from his arm as he led her from stone to stone until she safely reached the opposite shore. When she stood with both feet firmly on solid ground again, she took a deep breath then released her grasp on his hand. She nearly stumbled in her rush to move away from him. He stood still, his hand warm from her touch, wishing she'd left her hand in his.

It was time to begin the trek back down the mountain. The sun didn't shine so brightly anymore. A touch of melancholy tinged his thoughts as he dwelt on how quickly Megan had dropped his hand and moved away. She was quiet and Jason seemed to have run out of questions. Perhaps they were just tired. As they hiked along Doug's spirits slowly rebounded. At least she had touched him of her own free will, no matter how brief the contact.

Back in the cabin after supper, Megan curled up in one corner of a love seat with a book in her hands. Her body ached with the fatigue of unaccustomed exertion. Still the day had gone well, and there had been only one uncomfortable moment when Doug helped her cross the stream.

She'd enjoyed Jason's delight in their hike. Doug had seemed to enjoy it too. She'd never known a man before who took pleasure in simple things like flowers and silly stories. She glanced up to see Jason and Doug hunched over a game board. Jason was happy and not demanding her attention. Maybe she wouldn't search for Doug's truck key tonight. Turning back to her book, she felt unexpectedly relaxed.

She felt a gentle nudge to her elbow. She'd been asleep. Surprised she looked up to find Doug occupying the other half of the love seat and Jason sprawled out sound asleep on the rug.

Doug whispered, "Let's not wake him. I'll just carry him up to bed." He scooped up the child and carried him up the stairs. When he returned, he found Megan in the kitchen stirring chocolate powder into hot milk. She handed him a cup before making her way to a cushioned seat before the fireplace.

"You've done a great job with Jason, Megan" Doug unfolded his length beside her. "I'm sorry I've missed knowing him and watching him grow."

The softly spoken words made Megan uneasy. She didn't want to discuss the reasons she'd kept quiet, and she wasn't going to admit he had a right to any part of her son's life.

"It's hard for me not to feel angry and cheated because you decided not to tell me about him." He paused as though expecting a response. She didn't know what to say. She didn't want to have this conversation. Doug's every reference to Jason was a threat to her security. When she didn't attempt to defend herself, he went on. "My head tells me you didn't know me well enough to trust me. It boggles my mind to even imagine how difficult it must have been for you, when you were so young, to take care of yourself, give birth alone, then keep him. How did you manage?"

"I did what I had to." It wasn't fair of him to make her feel guilty for not telling him about Jason. If he'd known, he would have taken the baby from her or forced them to stay with him. He had money and power, she'd had nothing. He might have sent her to jail for taking his money, too. She hadn't been willing to take that risk.

She thought of the nights she'd fallen asleep studying, the days she'd walked to school crying because she'd had to leave her baby with strangers. She'd gone without a coat or boots so she could buy diapers and make the money last until she could finish school and start earning enough to take care of her baby properly. She was the one who'd faced the long terrifying nights when she dreamed Lee had come to take Jason away.

Almost as though he read her mind, he told her, "If I'd known, I would have helped you." Megan saw the sheen in his eyes and heard the catch in his voice. "I can't put into words how much it hurts to know you were pregnant with my child, practically a child yourself, and too scared of me to ask for the help you had a right to expect from me." He paused briefly before continuing in the same earnest vein. "I know I owe you an apology for the things I said the other night. I really am sorry I lost my temper, but please understand I won't let either of you disappear from my life again."

Megan stared into the fire saying nothing.

"I don't think you're indifferent to me," he continued. "You pretend indifference, but you're as aware of me as I am of you. We could have a good life together. We could share Jason."

"No, Doug . . ." Panic laced her voice.

"Hush." He laid one finger softly against her lips. "Don't say anything yet. Please just think about it."

Megan trembled at the feel of that one finger touching her mouth. There was no pressure, but still she felt a threat to the safe world she had constructed for herself and her child. There had to be a way to leave. If only Doug would leave them alone for a couple of hours.

Mesmerized she stared into his deep blue eyes, then shaking herself back to reality she clumsily rose to her feet. Doug followed her.

"I'm going to shower and go to bed." She struggled to keep her voice steady. "If you want the bathroom first, please go ahead." Turning she hurried from the room. She couldn't think about losing Jason. He was everything to her. She remembered the last big story she had done in Missoula. Jasper had had custody of his children. He'd taken them from their mother and look what happened. Doug said share, but she knew he meant more than that. When Mama had married Lee she said he was going to be her daddy, but after he came she always had to do everything he wanted. Mama did too. She wouldn't let that happen to Jason.

She emerged into the tiny hall a short time later with her robe over one arm. She stopped when she saw Doug coming toward her. His hair was wet and he wore a towel around his waist. Damp curls formed a springy mat across his chest. She averted her eyes and sucked in her breath. Squeezing against the wall she made room for him to pass.

But he stopped in front of her. For long seconds she stood staring at the floor. When he made no effort to move on, she lifted her eyes to his face. Slowly he bent forward until his lips barely brushed against hers. Neither his hands nor his body sought closer intimacy. The kiss ended almost as quickly as it began.

"Good night, Megan." He walked away.

Torn between a desire to run and the inability to move, Megan stared blankly at the spot where Doug had stood, then stumbled into the bathroom. After locking the door, she stood for a long time under the spray of the shower. She touched her fingers to her mouth. She wanted to believe in Doug. She still held those childish dreams of years ago. Could she trust him? Mama trusted Lee, and look what had happened. Leaning her face against the tile wall, she became aware that not all of the water sluicing down her cheeks had come from the overhead fixture.

Six

SQUEEZING AGAINST THE CUPBOARD, MEGAN MADE
room for Doug to open the refrigerator door without brushing
against her. It was the first time she'd worn shorts since he arrived.
She wished she had put on jeans. His frankly approving glances
toward her long, bare legs made her feel self-conscious. She had skit-
tishly avoided any physical contact with him since the night he'd
kissed her although she hadn't been able to shake the memory of that
brief contact. That, added to his present blatant perusal of her legs,
made her feel uncomfortable. Lee used to watch her like that. He
would watch her, then he would try to touch her. She shuddered. A
drawer handle gouged into her hip as she made herself smaller.

Doug's jaw tightened, ominously betraying his irritation over her
efforts to avoid touching him. Their hands were kept busy packing a
more substantial lunch than was their usual fare for their daily hiking
and fishing forays. But Megan found that the work served neither to
keep her mind busy nor to ease her intense awareness of the man
sharing the task.

She reached for a pickle jar in the depths of the refrigerator. Above
her, Doug suddenly opened the freezer compartment. Abruptly
drawing back to avoid bumping her head against the door, she
crashed into the solid male chest behind her. His hands shot out to
grasp her shoulders. The jar slipped through her fingers and shattered
onto the floor. Glass bits and pickle juice flew in every direction.

Megan stared at the floor then at the man hovering over her. He
held her by the shoulders. Her legs felt wet and sticky. One part of

her mind struggled to assure herself she was safe and no one was going to hurt her, but the other part shouted louder. She couldn't breathe. A kind of numbness began taking over her brain. She had to fight the panic. She jerked free of Doug's hold and stooped down. Mechanically she reached for a large piece of glass that lay at her feet.

Doug grabbed her wrist, "Don't touch that! All we need is a little blood to add to this mess!"

"Let go!" She tried to shout. The familiar dark, panicky sickness rose inside her. She struggled harder to free herself. Her teeth gashed the side of her tongue.

Without warning Doug swept her up in his arms. "Hold still." Wrapping one arm firmly around her arms and using the other to clasp her legs together, he pulled her tightly against his chest to keep her from flailing about. "This never would have happened if you weren't so childishly determined to avoid me."

Her mind shut out the familiar voice. She heard only Lee's obscene threats. Her body remembered being unable to move, male hands on her legs, pressure and blood, the incredible pain as her arm snapped, and the blow to her head that sent her tumbling into blackness.

Her long, high-pitched scream shattered the stillness of the early morning air. Doug stood still, absorbing her fear. For agonized seconds he stood rooted. What could he do? The cabin door slammed loudly against the wall. Jason! Doug had to move quickly before Jason ran to his mother across the sticky, glass-littered kitchen.

Without loosening his hold on the struggling woman in his arms, Doug stepped into the living area. Megan hadn't made a sound since her unexpected scream. Now her breath came in shallow gasps as she twisted and turned. By the time he settled himself on the sofa, the boy was upon him, not biting and kicking or uselessly raining blows this time, but pulling at his shirt sleeve and begging him to let his mother go.

"Jason," Doug spoke to the boy. "Your mother is all right. She dropped a bottle of pickles and it made a big mess, but she isn't hurt."

"But you're hurting her." Tears threatened to overflow Jason's troubled eyes.

"No, I'm not. Look, I promise I won't hurt her. I'm just going to hold her until she calms down."

"Don't! You promised. Please, don't hold her tight. She hates not being able to move even worse than she hates being dirty or messy."

Freeing one hand Megan struck out blindly, catching Doug a stinging blow to his mouth that left blood trickling from his lip. He recaptured her arm, tucking it firmly between their bodies where it could do no damage. The cut lip didn't matter. He had to keep her from hurting herself.

Forgetting the wide-eyed boy leaning against the adjacent love seat, Doug began talking to Megan. He wanted to stroke her hair off her face, kiss away the fear, and gently love her until she was relaxed and calm. He struggled to put into words all the tenderness he longed to show her. He was painfully conscious of his arm pressed against her softness and her frantic struggles to slide off his lap. Her body was warm and real, but her mind was somewhere else—in some hell he couldn't fathom.

At first she neither heard nor understood as his voice rumbled slow and steady in her ear. Gradually the soft words began to penetrate the haze obscuring coherent thought. *He isn't Lee. This is Doug.* She finally understood. He was bargaining with her. He interspersed his soothing words of comfort with the promise of release, if she would sit still and stop fighting him. It took longer for her mind to convince her body to cease struggling. She continued to tremble long after Doug released her arms and legs.

Sitting on Doug's lap with his arms loosely wrapped around her, a sense of warmth and security slowly replaced her fear. She fought an unwelcome urge to settle her head against his chest. She couldn't surrender to this or any other man. She knew from painful experience men couldn't be trusted—not even Doug. She'd made that mistake once before. She reminded herself that he wanted Jason and that he conspired with A.J. to keep her a prisoner here.

Squeezing her eyes shut to block out the memory along with the light, she saw Doug give a thick stack of bills to her stepfather and she felt the crushing humiliation of knowing that the gift she believed she had freely given had in fact been purchased. The childish dream of marriage to a wonderfully kind man and of a family of her own shattered at her feet, just like the pickle jar. *It was a pickle jar, only a broken pickle jar. Nothing happened. Nothing is going to happen.*

Doug felt the exact moment when the woman in his arms changed from a frightened child to a cool adult.

"If you'll excuse me," Calmly she slipped from his lap. "I need to wash and change. The kitchen floor needs to be cleaned also."

Feeling perplexed Doug watched her leave the room. How was he ever going to reach this woman, he asked himself. Ruefully he admitted to himself he had envisioned cuddling and comforting her, as he had once before. He had a momentary fear that Megan might not be completely sane, but Doug immediately dismissed it. Then his eyes met the accusing eyes of her child.

"Have you seen your mother like this before?"

Jason's head moved up and down in a hesitant affirmative nod.

"Often?"

This time the boy's head moved back and forth. "Just a couple of times. One time when I was really little a man was in our house. When he was walking out the door, he started kissing Mom and she screamed. He ran away, but she just sat on the floor and it didn't seem like she could hear me for a long time. The other time was before A.J. knew Mom didn't like to be touched. He sneaked up behind her to surprise her. Mostly when she's scared she just stands really still till she isn't scared anymore. Sometimes she moves and talks, but she's still kind of frozen. I hate it when she goes away like that; sometimes I think she'll never ever come back."

Looking into the child's worried face, Doug caught a glimpse of Megan's fear mirrored in her son's eyes and sensed an unnatural maturity beyond his nine years. It wasn't right for a child to feel so responsible for a parent. *Why hasn't she gotten some counseling or done something to help herself?* he questioned angrily, but his anger was swiftly followed by a wave of guilt, guilt for carelessly impregnating Megan all those years ago and guilt for not being there when she was scared and alone. Was he to blame for her irrational fears?

"You don't have to worry anymore," he attempted to reassure the boy. "From now on I'll take care of both of you."

"You're my dad, aren't you?"

Torn between a deep desire to claim the child he ached to acknowledge as his own, and his fear of the consequences to his shaky relationship with Megan if he did so, he hesitated.

Shrugging his shoulders the boy continued, "It's okay. You don't have to tell me, if you don't want to. I heard you talking about being married to Mom, and she told me a long time ago I looked like my dad. You know, the same color hair and stuff like that. She said you didn't know about me because you had to go away to a faraway country. She said my dad liked to climb mountains too, so I just figured it out."

"You're right." Doug decided he owed his son honesty. "I am your father, and though I haven't known you long, I'm proud to have you for my son. I wish I had known about you when you were a baby. I wouldn't have gone away if I had. We could have done so many things together right from the start. Instead we'll have to begin right now."

Holding out his arms he gently drew the child into their shelter. With a sob Jason buried his face against his father's chest. Awkwardly Doug patted the boy's thin shoulders and for just a moment the memory of his own father holding him and offering comfort over some childish problem flashed through his mind. His chest hurt with the volume of love he felt for the crying child in his arms. After the tears subsided, Doug wiped a tear from his own eye, and Jason looked up as though pleading for understanding. His words surprised Doug.

"I wish you weren't my dad or that you had stayed lost."

In spite of the hurt Jason's words caused, Doug spoke softly, "I thought we were friends, and I was hoping someday you would love me the way I already love you."

"It's not that. You're a super dad, just like I always wanted. It's Mom. I don't think she likes you very much, and you keep grabbing her and bossing her around. When she gets away from here, she won't ever come back. I just know it." Tears threatened again.

"Maybe we could work out a plan so your mom will want to stay," Doug suggested. Privately he examined Jason's words. Was that what he had been doing? Grabbing and bossing? If that was how Megan saw his actions, no wonder she resisted him. But no, he didn't think so. He came from a physically demonstrative family. People show loving and caring by kissing, hugging, and touching. He suspected Megan hadn't known much love in her family. It was something she and Jason needed to learn about.

"In the meantime," he suggested. "We ought to start cleaning up the kitchen since your mom is still in the shower, and her showers tend to be rather long." Doug and Jason's eyes met in a watery conspiratorial smile.

Megan stepped into the spotless kitchen to find a lunch packed in an old-fashioned wicker basket and a spotlessly clean floor so she couldn't use cleaning the kitchen for an excuse to avoid the excursion Doug had planned. Her faded blue jumpsuit completely covered her legs and arms, but she still felt exposed, although not so much physically as emotionally. She'd made a fool of herself.

Without meeting Doug's questioning eyes, she let Jason take her hand to lead her toward the Bronco. Halfway there he dropped her hand to run ahead. He scrambled onto the back seat then leaned forward to offer her a helping hand. She grasped his hand and the side of the seat to pull herself into the bucket seat. She'd rather sit in the back with Jason, but she suspected Doug would demand an explanation if she did. She wasn't ready for a confrontation of any kind right now.

Doug placed the picnic basket in the back then stepped easily into the driver's seat. Megan couldn't force herself to look away as he inserted the key into the ignition. She had hunted for his keys more than once during the past week and finally concluded he must keep them with him all of the time. This was the first time he'd suggested they take the Bronco on one of their outings, so she was disappointed to discover it had a standard transmission. She probably couldn't drive it even if she did manage to get her hands on the key.

The big vehicle moved smoothly over the rough road that had been such a challenge for A.J.'s rental car. All three occupants were subdued as they passed beneath stately pines. Megan couldn't stop thinking about what had happened earlier. She wished neither Jason nor Doug had seen her like that. *If Doug wasn't constantly around, always trying to touch me, making me remember the past, it wouldn't have happened.*

When they reached Park City, Jason's natural curiosity erupted in an endless stream of questions about the old mining town turned modern tourist attraction. Under other circumstances Megan would have been charmed by the inviting frontier store fronts and enticing curio shops, but today she saw it the way a thirsty desert traveler envisions tantalizing mirages. Among people who moved about freely, Megan bitterly accepted the futility of reaching out to share their freedom. Her words would be lost in the rumble of traffic, and a plea for help would result in the loss of her son. Doug didn't care that her home and her job were in Missoula; he'd made it clear he intended to keep Jason in Utah. Precipitating a struggle over Jason while still in the state was not part of her plan. She would have to wait until she found an opportunity to get them both safely out of state.

Reaching the highway, Doug turned south. They passed swiftly through sagebrush-covered hills. She scarcely noticed when they began moving east into pine-covered mountains again. She was vaguely aware of Jason and Doug conversing with each other. Jason's animosity toward Doug had melted away to be replaced by something resembling adulation. She supposed it was only natural for a boy to be drawn to his father, especially when that father played basketball, drove a truck, taught him to fish, and did all the things a small boy considered important. How could a mere mother who dropped him off every day at a hated day-care center begin to compete?

With a squeal of brakes the truck slammed to a stop. Only the straps crossing her shoulder and waist prevented her from flying into the windshield. Even before she caught her breath she turned to check on Jason.

"Wow! Did you see that, Mom?" an awestruck Jason asked. "Wasn't he beautiful?"

"See what?" Megan felt confused.

"It was a buck, wasn't it? Gosh, you saved his life, Dad."

Dad! Dad! Dad! The one syllable word echoed endlessly through Megan's head; it screamed in her ears, and vibrated from window to window. Jason clapped one hand over his mouth staring at his mother in horror. Fury rose in Megan's breast, fury and a sense of betrayal left her speechless as she turned accusing eyes toward Doug.

Doug met her eyes squarely, but at the rage that burned through her, his eyes turned away and his shoulders sagged until his forehead met the steering wheel still gripped tightly in both hands. How long they sat there she didn't know.

"He is my dad," Jason muttered defensively.

Megan's shoulders shook as she struggled to control the sob rising in her throat. She said nothing. She couldn't speak.

"Are you mad at me?" came the boy's uncertain query.

"No, I'm not angry with you."

"Are you mad at Da—Doug?"

"We'll talk about it later."

Without a word Doug put the truck in gear and started forward. A few miles further down the road he pulled off into a small clearing overlooking a tiny jewel-like lake. Jumping out he slammed the door behind himself, then promptly reopened it to jerk the keys out of the ignition. His face was grim as he pushed his seat forward and reached for Jason. She sucked in her breath.

Megan's heart contracted painfully as she saw the big man embrace the boy tightly before setting him on the ground. She released the breath she had been holding. Of course, he wouldn't hurt Jason. When Jason would have run to her, Doug prevented him by steering him to the back of the Bronco where the fishing rods were stored. Her first impulse was to go after him, but her childhood conditioning urged caution. It might be best if Jason stayed out of sight until Doug calmed down. With only a fleeting guilty glance toward her, Jason was soon on his way toward the water, fishing pole in hand.

"Get out of the truck!" Doug stood a few feet from her still-closed door and shouted through her open window.

Megan glared back mutinously, but didn't move.

Opening the door Doug repeated, "Get out, or I'll haul you out, and I know how much you'd like that!"

Megan obeyed reluctantly, cringing as her arm brushed his.

"Well, excuse me!" He stepped back mockingly, indicating she should precede him down the path to the water's edge. For a moment she wondered if he meant to drown her; he certainly seemed angry enough. Fighting desperately to keep back the tears, she concentrated on gathering her composure. If she started screaming at him, she would be lost.

Raking his fingers through his hair, Doug indicated she should seat herself on one of the large rocks littering the shore of the small lake. Long minutes passed as they both sat quietly staring at the clear blue water. Megan's apprehension increased as she waited for him to speak. Unable to bear the silence any longer her words began to spill out.

"You couldn't wait, could you? You think you can just walk into my life and take it over, take my child, keep me a prisoner, hurt and humiliate me. I'm sick of being pushed around. I've paid you back every dollar I took twice over. . . ."

"Megan!" He cut her off abruptly. "I didn't tell Jason I am his father, but I couldn't lie to him when he asked. The other things you accuse me of aren't true either."

"Liar! You and A.J. planned this whole thing. He tricked me into coming here, and made certain I would be isolated without transportation or anyone to turn to for help. You wanted me to be completely at your mercy!"

"I didn't know you were here until the day of the storm. I had just returned from six months of fighting oil well fires in Kuwait when Allen showed up at my house unexpectedly. We hadn't seen each other for three or four years. I was surprised to see him, and even more surprised when he told me where you were. I dumped my gear in the house, kissed Mother hello and good-bye, then drove straight up. I thought you might be scared of the storm." He laughed without humor. "Stupid me. It never occurred to me you might be ten times more terrified of me than you were of the thunder and lightning."

Megan didn't respond. She clenched her jaw tightly while her eyes automatically followed the shoreline, seeking the bright red stripes of Jason's shirt. She spotted him not too far away on a small sandbar trailing his line in the water. Doug heard Megan's sigh of relief.

"He's safe. I wouldn't let him wander off where I couldn't keep an eye on him. I care about him, too."

"Do you? I suspect you just like to think you own him."

"That's not true, Megan. I haven't known him as long as you, it's true, but I love him. I didn't even know he existed until the other night. Then it took almost a whole day before it occurred to me he was my son. Would you have ever told me if I hadn't guessed?" He rubbed a hand across his eyes. "I doubt it." He answered the question himself. "He's really something, so bright and anxious to learn. He's going to be an athlete too, I can tell. It's in the way he moves and the way he's anxious to test his physical ability, and he really does have ability. I can't wait to see him play ball."

"Already planning his life? You must be awfully sure you can take him from me." She abruptly stood up.

"Megan, I don't want to take him from you. I want to share him with you."

"Oh, I can see it now. You choose his schools, you decide every sport he should play, you decide what he should think and where he lives. And if he is foolish enough to miss his mother maybe, just maybe, you'll let him come to Montana two weeks every summer and every other Christmas. Thanks, but no thanks!"

"That isn't what I said. You put your own interpretation on everything I say. Of course Jason needs his mother, but he needs his father, too. You've had him to yourself for nine years and in most respects you've done a fine job raising him, but he has problems I think I can help him with."

"Problems? He doesn't have any serious problems. Sure, you could probably teach him how to play ball or climb mountains better than I can, but somehow I don't think those are problems he desperately needs your help to deal with."

"You don't think he has any problems? Megan, be honest. He has some problems that really worry me and should scare you, too. To begin with, he has a terrible temper."

"Look who's talking."

Doug went on as though she hadn't interrupted. "In addition to learning how to control his temper, it certainly isn't normal for a nine year old to be so protective of his mother. He's terrified to let you out of his sight, and your violent reaction to being touched in any way has dumped a king-size load of responsibility on his shoulders. A child shouldn't be responsible for a parent's emotional well-being. He's afraid you're just going to withdraw from him completely someday, disappear, and he won't be able to save you."

"You're even more vicious than I thought." Megan's face was pale as she faced her tormentor. "You'd like that wouldn't you? If you can convince Jason I'm crazy or the courts that I'm an unfit mother, then he'll be all yours." Megan turned away to stumble back to the truck, hurting too badly to even cry.

Doug followed her. He reached her side before she could climb inside. Placing both hands on her shoulders he turned her around. She stiffened beneath his hands, but he didn't let go.

"All right, Megan. You've deliberately twisted everything I said. I don't think you're crazy, and I don't believe you're an unfit mother."

He paused, "I'll make a deal with you. You give me the rest of the summer. We'll share the cabin and try—really try—to get to know each other. You'll stop freezing me out or getting hysterical every time I happen to touch you." Seeing the expression on her face, he ground his teeth together before continuing.

"I give you my word, I won't hurt you. We'll continue to do things together, and neither one of us will try to influence Jason against the other. If you still want to leave and take Jason with you at the end of the summer, I'll let you go and agree to see my son only when it's convenient for you."

Megan shuddered.

Doug winced and withdrew his hands. "Is it a deal?"

"What about the money?"

"What money? Sure I paid the hospital bill, but you don't owe me for that."

"The money you paid Lee. You know I took it, but I also paid it all back."

Stunned, Doug stared at her. "You knew about that?"

She nodded her head. "I was on the stairs. I saw you give him the money. I was never certain whether you were buying me or paying blackmail. He dropped it when he left so I took it. At first I wasn't going to use it, but when I found out about Jason I had to." She didn't want to ask but she knew she had to. "Why were you giving him money?"

"He threatened to take the story to the newspapers, that I had attacked you and married you to keep you quiet. . . . And he said he would tell them things about you—terrible things—I knew they weren't true, but I wanted to protect you."

"And you really didn't know I took the money?"

"I didn't even know if you were alive, until I received a cashier's check in the mail from some bank in Chicago with your name on it. I had no idea why you were sending me money."

"Well?"

"Forget the money. Like you said, you've paid it back. You can have it, if you want it, or put it in a trust fund for Jason. I don't care. How about our deal?"

Pale blue eyes stared into space. Her thoughts were too much in turmoil to settle on all the doubts and questions flying through her mind. "I don't know if I can," she whispered.

"Will you try?"

Slowly she nodded her head.

"Seal it with a kiss?" He pressed his luck. Not giving her time to refuse, his hand gently cupped her chin. Lightly he pressed his lips to hers. Her body tensed. Disappointed, he quickly let her go. He had to be patient. Everything would be all right, he had the rest of the summer to win her over. He smiled softly before he surprised her with a quick boost into the truck.

"I'll get Jason," he called before disappearing up the trail in the direction of the lake.

Seven

MILES PASSED IN A HAZE AS MEGAN STRUGGLED TO appear natural to Jason. She schooled herself not to show any reaction each time her son called Doug, "Dad." They stopped to fish in another small lake, and she complimented Jason on the two beautiful rainbow trout he caught, but it hurt that he showed them first to Doug and that he turned to Doug for answers to his questions.

It took all of the self-control she could muster not to pull away when Doug took her hand, touched her elbow, or helped her in and out of the Bronco. She would stick to the deal. She'd given her word. Besides, as long as he thought she was cooperating, she'd have time to decide what to do if he changed his mind.

Shortly before noon Doug parked the truck in a clearing a short distance from the road. He rushed to assist Megan out, much to her annoyance, then lifted the picnic basket from the truck. Megan watched as Doug transferred their lunch to his backpack.

"Are we going to hike now?" Jason asked.

"There's a place about a mile up this trail where I used to go with your grandfather." Doug spoke to Jason, but his words conjured a picture in Megan's mind of the old man who had played a prominent role in her early life. There had been no special places the two of them had shared.

"Would you like to eat our lunch there?" Doug asked.

"Sure," Jason grinned. "Should I bring the fishing gear?"

"No," Doug glanced briefly toward Megan. "I think maybe we've fished enough for today. Besides the trail gets a little rough. We may need to keep our hands free."

Jason darted toward the well-worn path. Megan followed more slowly. Doug brought up the rear. It didn't take long before Megan had a pretty good idea why Doug had selected the trail. It was extremely steep, and he never missed an opportunity to put his arm around her waist to help her up a steep wash or to lift her over a boulder, whether she needed help or not. Each touch left her feeling more confused. Panic would assail her, leaving her consciously struggling not to flee each time she felt trapped against Doug's side. At the same time his strong arm around her waist or his thigh brushing against her hip stirred an awareness of an intimacy she had barely begun to explore so long ago and didn't want to think about now. By the time they reached their destination Megan felt like a jittery wreck. Hastily she put some space between herself and Doug as she spread out the plastic tablecloth Doug handed her.

They ate their picnic lunch in a little glen where a slender waterfall streamed from the rocks high overhead. The sun shining through the boughs of giant firs formed a rainbow to dance and flirt with the silvery spray. A few clouds gathered to the west.

Megan knew Doug deliberately brushed her fingers each time he asked her to pass him a piece of chicken or another cookie. Each touch took her back to that awful time when Lee was always finding excuses to touch her. She steeled herself not to react. She told herself a person could get used to anything if the stakes were high enough, and she was fighting for her son.

Jason and Doug laughed a lot, and Jason asked questions about his grandparents. Doug told the boy stories about the camping trips he had enjoyed with his father and how he had felt when his father died. Listening to him reminisce about memories of his childhood, Megan felt left out and envious. Worse, she became aware of the father-son relationship she had denied her son, and guilt ate at her conscience.

Megan's plate sat untouched in her lap as she listened to Doug's stories and unconsciously compared them with her own memories of Lee and her grandfather. Had she cheated Jason out of a happy relationship with his father or was all Doug's talk just stories?

Jason was happy and excited to discover he had a real grandmother. Turning to Megan, he demanded to know when they could meet her.

"I . . . I don't know," Megan stammered as she shot Doug a black glare.

"Monica has a grandmother." Jason happily informed both adults. "Sometimes she comes in her pink VW bug to visit Monica and her mom. She has to sleep on the couch, and she calls Uncle Greg a worthless bum, but I think she likes him anyway because she hugs him and sits on his lap. She has really long, fuzzy hair, and she wears funny, shiny clothes that sparkle. Monica gets mad because she always brings her a new dress with lots of lace and ruffles and stuff and she'd rather have jeans. Monica's grandmother is really nice and lots of fun, but she won't let Monica call her Grandma. She has to call her Sandi. Monica says she loves her grandmother, but sometimes she wishes she had a grandma like Coach Jenson's grandma. She digs in her garden and bakes cookies. What's my grandmother like?"

Doug roared with laughter as Jason finally wound down to ask his question. "I can't wait to meet Monica," he muttered under his breath before attempting to answer his son's question.

"Your grandmother's a nice lady, very gentle and kind." Megan joined the conversation for the first time, much to Doug's surprise. "She wears beautiful clothes and has a rose garden. What I remember best about her is her music. She plays the piano for hours every day, and her music fills her lovely house with peace and sunshine."

"Do you know my grandmother?" Jason looked at his mother, astonishment and bewilderment on his face. "Why didn't you tell me or let me see her?" There was an angry, accusing edge to his voice.

Seeing the anguish on Megan's face, Doug quickly stepped in.

"Jason, your mother didn't deliberately keep secrets from you. She thought she had good reasons to stay away from me. She didn't know I would love and want both of you. Remember, your grandmother is my mother, and most of my life we have lived in the same house. How could you visit my mother and not see me too?"

Jason continued to scowl. "Well, it isn't fair!"

"Now look, Jason." Doug looked his son straight in the eye. "Your mother always has done what she thought was best for you and she always will. Sometimes decisions parents make don't seem fair to their children, but I promise you this, both your mother and I will always do what we think is best for you. When you think we're wrong, you can tell us, and we'll talk about it. We'll try to be fair, but until you're older you'll have to accept our decisions, even when you don't like them."

"I'm sorry, Mom." Jason threw himself in his mother's arms. "I just want to be a whole family with you and Dad and a grandma and cousins and a brother and everything."

Doug arched one eyebrow. "You left out sisters. Wouldn't you like a couple of sisters?"

He grinned when Jason raised startled eyes to his face. Laughter rang through the glen as Jason reached out to hug his dad, too. "Monica wants a little sister. She told A.J. and me she wants a sister more than anything else in the whole world. She'll really be mad if I get one first, but that's okay. I think I'd like a little sister too, the sooner the better!"

"I'll second that," Doug whispered watching Megan's face turn scarlet.

Megan worried that Jason would be hurt when it was time to go home—if they were allowed to go home. She was still uncertain whether she could trust Doug to keep his word. She wished he wouldn't hold out promises of a life together that would leave them all hurting when he finally had to accept there was no future for them as a family. She wondered if he was following a carefully calculated plan to gain Jason's trust and leave her looking like the spoiler.

"What's up there?" Jason pointed to the cliff behind the waterfall.

Doug strolled toward the falls. A fine spray misted his face as he glanced upward. "I haven't been up there for a long time, but as I remember, it's a long narrow canyon."

"Can we climb up there?"

"It's pretty steep, but if your mother's willing . . ." They both turned questioning eyes toward Megan.

"Oh, all right," she reluctantly consented. "It would be hard to get any grubbier than we already are."

Before she could gain her feet, Doug was there to assist her. He kept her hand until they actually started the climb. She wanted to snatch it away, but she'd agreed, and Jason certainly didn't need to witness another scene.

There was no real path, but there were indications that others had used the large boulders at the base of the falls as a clumsy stairway to begin the climb. Several times Doug had to boost Jason, then Megan, from one level to the next. She stumbled when he placed his hands on her hips to steady her as she climbed upward. When her feet were once more on solid ground he gave her fanny a light pat. She resisted the urge to turn and shove him backward. Mumbling imprecations to herself for letting him get away with such familiar behavior, she hurried to catch up with Jason. She didn't want to face the conflicting emotions Doug's touch evoked.

A faint trail angled away from the falls, zigzagging back and forth across the steep incline. By the time they reached the upper canyon floor, perspiration ran down Megan's neck. Sinking to rest on a fallen log, she fanned her flushed face with her hands. Doug removed his cap as he walked to the small stream. In minutes he was back with the cap dripping a stream of cold water. She eyed it warily. Solicitously he patted the cool water on her face and arms. She scooted back. Doug grinned and dripped a fine stream down her neck. A tiny shudder shook her slender shoulders. Whether it was caused by the cold water or Doug's lingering fingers was hard to tell.

"Mom, is it okay if I wade in the water?" Jason called from where he lay on his stomach, splashing his hands in a small pool.

Unconsciously Megan turned to Doug with a question in her eyes. Realizing what she'd done, she quickly looked away. This was a decision she could make herself.

"Take your shoes off and soak your feet in the water if you like, but the rocks are too sharp for wading," she called back to Jason.

"You should keep an old pair of canvas sneakers for wading in creeks," Doug added. "And don't drink out of the stream. It looks clean, but almost all mountain water now has little parasites that can make a person terribly sick."

Megan and Doug sat side by side on the log. Both were silent. She welcomed a stray breeze that lifted the sweat dampened curls on her neck and cooled her flushed skin. Doug brushed away an irritating deerfly. Reaching across Megan's lap, he picked up one of her hands. He carefully laced her fingers through his. Her muscles tensed.

"Do you really hate me touching you?" he asked softly.

"I hate any form of sexual harassment," she answered bluntly through clenched teeth.

"Harassment? You think I'm harassing you?" He seemed genuinely puzzled.

"It's a domination game men play. Touchy! Touchy! Remind stupid females they're smaller and weaker and that ultimately they must surrender to the larger, stronger male."

"Now that sounds like a lot of feminist hype to me. Surely you're not serious?"

"I'm completely serious!"

"Megan, listen to me. I touch you because I care about you. You're beautiful, and I desire you. I don't want to dominate or subjugate you; I just want to love you."

"I don't believe you. You're a man. You want to dominate and control. You'll notice, you're the one calling all of the shots around here."

"Honey, talk to me. Who made you so cynical about men? I know so little about your past. I am aware now of the part I played in hurting you, but I don't believe I ever did anything to merit having you cringe every time I come near you the way you do. In fact, my memories of the one night we spent together are pretty special."

Placing both hands against her cheeks, he lifted her face to look deeply into her eyes. Silently she shook her head, and when one teardrop leaked slowly down her cheek, he lifted his thumb to gently brush it away. Her eyes widened. She tried to pull away.

"I won't hurt you," he whispered. He hesitated briefly. Her uneven breath sounded harsh in her ears. Ever so gently his mouth covered hers, coaxing, promising. She didn't resist. She felt no anxiety. The slight pressure felt almost pleasant.

When Doug lifted his head it was to smile at her. "Each time I touch you, every kiss we share, is a message of love and my desire to spend my life with you. Please don't read negative messages as my motive. I want to give you happiness, not pain."

"Mom? Dad?"

Megan jumped. She had been so intent on Doug and the feelings he had aroused in her she had momentarily forgotten her son. Glancing up guiltily, she noticed the confusion mirrored on his face. He had never seen anyone kiss her before, and he evidently wasn't sure he liked it.

"Are you okay, Mom?"

She heard the wariness in his voice.

"Yes, I'm fine." She swallowed hard trying to subdue the pounding pressure she felt beating in her chest.

"Do you like Dad kissing you?" He sounded both skeptical and jealous.

"It's . . . it's okay," she finally stammered.

"It's more than okay," Doug added with a grin. "In case you're interested, *I* like it a whole lot."

Jason dragged his heel in a half circle through the dirt intent in thought. Megan watched him closely. After a pause he lifted his head.

"Is it okay if I hike up the trail for a ways?"

Megan didn't look at Doug. Scrambling to her feet she hurried to join the boy. "I'll go with you."

Doug was quiet, but Megan was aware he trailed behind them as they set off following the tiny stream. Twice they spotted a deer in the distance and Jason halted several times to peer more closely into the water. Megan didn't bother to ask if he had seen a frog or a water snake. A low grumble sounded unnoticed in the distance as she struggled with her confusing thoughts.

Even though Doug was behind her where she couldn't see him, she was constantly aware of his presence. For almost ten years she had rarely thought of him, but now she couldn't stop thinking about him. Maybe she hadn't forgotten him at all but only suppressed his memory to retain her sanity. He excited and scared her. She felt longings toward him she had long ago convinced herself she was immune to. She swore she would never trust any man as long as she lived, but there was something about this man that drew an instinctive trust, and that worried her. She jumped when a hand settled on her shoulder.

"We had better start back."

"Aw, Dad. Can't we go just a little further? I want to find the place where this stream starts."

"There are little pockets of snow higher up. This stream comes from there."

"Snow! Let's find it!"

"Not this time. It looks like rain, and a narrow canyon is no place to get caught in a rain storm in these mountains."

Startled, Megan glanced around. She had been so intent on her thoughts, she hadn't noticed that the canyon had narrowed so greatly that they now stood between two steep rock faces. She had to crane her neck to see upward to where dark clouds had replaced the bright sunshine. A distant crack of thunder sounded a warning.

"Come on, Jason. Doug's right. There's too much danger of a flash flood catching us here." Megan reached for Jason's arm to start him moving back down the trail.

Doug set a blistering pace, but Megan didn't complain. A misty sprinkle of rain cooled the air. Several times she caught Doug's hurried glance at the sky or a quick turning of his head as though he were listening for a sound behind them. They were almost to the mouth of the gradually widening canyon when Doug suddenly shouted.

"Run for those rocks!" He pointed to a steep mound of boulders and brush nearly twenty yards ahead, off to the side of the trail. Without hesitation they began to run. Doug suddenly gripped Megan's hand urging her to hurry. Jason was slightly in front of Megan and Doug when one of Jason's feet came down on a badger burrow, sending him catapulting forward. Desperately he clutched at the brush trying to save himself. Before he hit the dirt, Doug's arm was around his waist, lifting him off the ground. Without breaking stride, Doug swung the boy to his shoulders and continued running.

Megan's chest felt like it was going to explode. A sudden flash of lightening was followed immediately by the deafening crash of thunder. The long hike had tired her; the run might finish her off, and her son's fall had scared away any reserve of strength she might have. The roar in her ears made her wonder if she might be blacking out. They had reached the rocky outcropping and Doug released her hand with a shouted order to climb when she realized the roar was not in her head, but was coming from the canyon behind them.

Doug still held Jason in one arm as he scrambled up the rocks with Megan beside him. The roar was getting louder and rain was now pelting them as they climbed, making the rocks slippery. Doggedly they persevered, though Megan doubted her ability to take one more step. Doug's free hand reached out, over and over, to steady her.

When they had climbed as high as they could go, Doug settled Jason on a small ledge with his back against the canyon wall. Reaching out he pulled Megan into the protective shelter of his arms. Together they turned to face the way they had come. They were in time to watch a wall of water shoot around the bend, tossing small trees and boulders before it. From their perch high above the crazed, muddy water, they watched in awe as it plunged the remaining distance down the little canyon, then rolled and tumbled in widening waves across the open ground. A lake appeared where a short time ago a tiny trickle wandered across a lush meadow.

Megan shuddered. She reached for Jason, hugging him to her side. She could have lost him. They might have all been killed. If it hadn't been for Doug.

As the roar diminished, Jason shouted to be heard, "How are we going to get back to the truck?"

Doug settled Megan beside Jason before answering. "We'll have to stay here for awhile. When the water recedes we'll be able to hike back. It'll be muddy, but once we're out of the canyon, there's another trail on higher ground we can follow back." He settled himself beside the other two wet, bedraggled hikers.

By scooting to the back of the ledge, they found that the cliff side provided some protection from the storm. Doug checked Jason's ankle to assure himself it wasn't broken or badly sprained, although Jason insisted that it didn't hurt and he would be able to hike down by himself. Megan shivered as she glanced down at the swiftly flowing river then back at her son. Seeing the movement Doug asked if she was cold. Ignoring the negative shake of her head, he sat beside her and wrapped his arms around her in an attempt to warm her and take her mind off the near-disaster. She didn't resist.

The summer squall ended as abruptly as it had started, and the sun came out, lending a sparkling brilliance to the rain-washed world. Nearby a small bird landed on a clump of brush to trill a joyful tune. The whole world seemed washed and new. For the moment Megan felt safe. In response to Jason's questions, Doug explained how the flood had started higher in the mountains when the storm hit there first. Then, when the rocky, thin-soiled ground could not absorb the sudden deluge, the water had concentrated in the narrow canyon to rush down the mountain.

Megan glanced in Jason's direction and smiled slightly to see him curled against his father's thigh, breathing deeply in sleep. Her eyes lifted slowly to the man beside her. She became aware that he was watching her. When he caught her eye and smiled, Megan's heart leapt. Shyly she turned her head away, but Doug wouldn't allow it.

Lifting one hand, he touched her face, turning it toward him. Very gently he brushed a kiss across her lips.

Megan stared into his eyes for a long minute, then dropped her eyes to her hands, which were clasped in her lap. She examined her dirty, broken fingernails while her mind drifted far away. Lee had been kind to her and to Mama at first. But Doug's arm weighing heavily on her shoulders reminded Megan that even though it warmed and comforted, it also restrained so that she could only move if he allowed it. Even if Doug was never cruel or abusive, she knew she could never tolerate him or any other man controlling her life. That thought stirred resentment.

"Doug, I appreciate what you did for us today. You probably saved our lives, but it doesn't really change anything. Please move your arm."

She was beginning to think he wasn't going to respond or that he was angry. Nervously she tried to edge away. His arm pulled her snugly back against his side.

"We still have a deal." His voice sounded harsh to her.

Megan stiffened. Doug's hand cupped her shoulder, moved coaxingly up and down her arm, urging her to relax. She couldn't relax; she was too conscious of his strength holding her in place. Her body was trembling, and she felt the urge to scream.

Becoming aware of the panic Megan was fighting to control, Doug cleared his throat. "It's going to be dark soon. We ought to see if we can reach the trail." He released Megan and gently shook Jason awake. Jason's eyes automatically searched his mother's face as he awoke. Frowning, he turned suspicious eyes toward his father.

It was a difficult climb down the muddy rocks to where the water still completely covered the canyon floor. Insisting they join hands, Doug led the way using a heavy stick to probe the way along the water's edge until they left the canyon behind. Once out in the open, they waded across the meadow until they came to a trail some distance from the waterfall where they had ascended.

The trail was rough, slippery with mud in places, and littered with sharp rocks in others. Once Doug had to help Megan and Jason over a fallen tree that blocked their path. They were all relieved when they finally turned a corner and saw Doug's Bronco a short distance ahead.

During the long drive back, Megan stifled her irritation as Doug's hands repeatedly brushed the rain-stiffened denim covering her leg as he reached for the gear shift between their seats or adjusted the heater. Gritting her teeth she vowed not to react to the crawling sensation of Lee's hand on her leg as he drove. Still a whimper of fear passed her clenched teeth. She scuttled across the seat to huddle against the door.

Before they reached Park City, she drifted into an uneasy slumber, unaware of the change of tactics as Doug, resting his hand on the gear shift, suddenly became extremely careful not to bump her. He had no desire to startle her while she slept.

A twinge of remorse twisted a wry smile across Doug's face. He knew he had pressured Megan to the limit of her endurance. Perhaps pushing her to accept being touched was too much. But she had responded to him in spite of herself. She had accepted the bargain he offered. They had cleared up some of the misunderstandings separating them, and appreciation for her quick mind and courage filled him with a sense of pride. In the canyon she had trusted and followed his lead without question. And he'd kissed her. For the first time, he felt optimism surge through his veins.

"Who's that?"

Megan jerked awake as Jason shouted his question practically in her ear while pointing straight ahead. Turning her eyes forward, Megan saw the cabin sitting in its little clearing. For just a moment she felt strangely as though she were returning home. Then she spotted two vehicles parked in front of the wide porch. They looked like a large custom van and a smaller red Jeep.

Because sleepiness slowed her thought processes, Megan stared, not understanding the significance of visitors. An idea began to surface. Hope started to rise in her chest. Perhaps they could get away! Hope died a sudden death as Doug's large hand closed over her small fist.

"Don't even think of running out on our deal." He lowered his voice so Jason wouldn't hear. "If you try to leave with either of them, I'll make certain you never see Jason again."

Eight

HEY, A.J.!" JASON LAUNCHED HIMSELF INTO ALLEN'S arms. "Now you've really done it. You're in big trouble!"

Jason stopped, bewildered. Behind A.J. stood a toddler with her thumb in her mouth and red curls shimmering in the firelight. A smaller one snuggled in the arms of Doug's friend, Brad, who was ensconced in one corner of the nearest love seat. The baby stopped sucking on her bottle to stare wide-eyed at the newcomers. Two more little girls lifted their curly red heads from the coloring book they were sharing in front of the fireplace and a fifth girl—tall, with stray curls struggling to escape the confines of two waist-length braids—appeared to be almost Jason's age. She sat on the stairs dribbling his basketball. A pretty lady with more of the bouncing red curls stood with a ladle in one hand before a large bowl she had just placed on the table.

Hugging the boy tightly, A.J. avoided meeting Megan's eyes. More than once he'd called himself a fool for thrusting her and Doug back together. It was one of the hardest things he'd ever done, but he felt he owed Doug and was convinced it was best for Megan too.

"May I introduce you to Barbara, who is over there thumping your basketball, only she likes to be called Bobbi. Michelle and Ashley," he pointed, "are on the floor. The man is Brad Williams and he is holding Kelly." Stooping down he scooped up the wide-eyed three-year-old he introduced as Heidi. "That's Cathy Williams, these monsters' mother." He continued the introductions. "Come on over here and meet Jason," he called to the girls.

Finally steeling himself to face Megan, he sat Heidi on the floor and walked toward her. "This lovely lady is Megan Nordfelt." His eyes met Megan's and widened in shock at the hurt, little girl vulnerability he saw there.

"Megan Beckwith," Doug corrected placing one hand on her shoulder. Megan concentrated on not pulling away, tried to smile, but couldn't. Who were all these people? Her eyes darted around the room with a panic bordering on hysteria. Was it another trick A.J. had concocted? Feeling a need to get away she tried to ease away from Doug's restraining hand only to feel his grip tighten. *Don't do anything stupid*, she ordered herself fiercely. But her whole body trembled.

Cathy gave Doug a resounding kiss of congratulations and suddenly Doug needed both arms to hold the avalanche of females who were trying to hug him simultaneously. Heidi demanded to be held, and the other girls were clamoring for kisses too. Megan carefully edged away from him.

A.J. slowly approached Megan's side. She looked tired, dirty, and disheveled. Dark smudges showed beneath her eyes, eyes that indicted him for his betrayal and glittered with a confusing array of emotions. The two moved away from the happy bevy of females surrounding Doug.

"Are you all right?" he whispered. Megan shot him a look of contempt and loathing.

"Megan—"

"You stinking pig!" Her hoarse whisper cut him like a knife. Turning her back on him she began to walk away. A.J. felt as though he'd been kicked in the solar plexus. He stood statue-still watching her leave. Pain, anger, pity raced through his heart.

"I wanted to set the ice princess free, not do this to her." His murmur barely reached Brad, who cast a questioning eye toward Megan before turning his eyes to Doug. Watching Allen's downcast face, he wondered, *What's going on here?* He moved to intercept Megan.

"Megan, I'm glad to see you again." She looked startled. Brad could tell she saw something vaguely familiar in his face, but didn't know who he was. She ignored his outstretched hand, even took an involuntary step backward. Her eyes frantically searched the room like those of a cornered animal.

"I—I'm sorry, I don't . . ."

"It's all right." He smiled gently. "After ten years it's not too surprising you don't remember the best man at your wedding."

She winced. He didn't think she appreciated the reminder. Taking in the shattered look in her eyes and the fierce struggle she was making to maintain her composure, he ventured a little unsolicited professional advice.

"It was rude of us not to warn you we were coming. You look like you've just come in from a long, hard hike. Why don't you go take a nice hot shower, then jump into bed. I'm sure you're tired and don't need all the noise and confusion of this bunch."

Megan's eyes darted toward her son and back. Nervously she bit her lip. Jason lifted his head, and as though obeying some silent summons, quickly made his way to her side.

Brad noticed the slight relaxing of tension in his friend's wife when she took the boy's hand.

"Jason," he turned to the boy. "Your mom is going to go take a shower and get into bed. Why don't you fill a couple of bowls with soup from that big kettle on the stove and take them into the bedroom. I think she needs a little quiet supper before she goes to sleep."

"Go wash first," Megan reminded her son as they left the room together.

Brad watched them go. There was definitely something wrong.

Megan was sitting up in bed finishing her soup with Jason perched on the edge of the mattress, beginning to feel more relaxed when the door opened to admit Doug. Brad strolled in behind him. Pulling the quilt higher, Megan peered warily at them.

"Brad tells me you don't feel well." Megan read skepticism in Doug's voice.

"I'm not sick, just tired."

Doug sat down beside her. His eyes were haunted and shadowed. His shoulders slumped, and he too, looked exhausted. He picked up her hand. He held it loosely while he spoke to Jason, "Son, go get your pajamas on, then come back here. Then you can curl up here beside your mom for tonight. I think she needs you."

Jason slipped quietly from the room while Doug continued to hold his wife's hand. *Wife!* he thought in anguish. *Will she ever really be my wife?*

Brad stopped at the door. "I could give you something to help you sleep if you'd like, Megan. I'm a doctor and I always carry my little black bag," he offered. She looked at him, seeing a man as tall as Doug, but heavier, with a little boy smile and the calm air of authority that had surrounded his father. It would be easy to trust him; she wished she dared.

"No, thank you," she responded politely. Brad frowned slightly before turning away.

"Good night, then." He left the room, leaving her alone with Doug.

"Honey, I didn't know they were coming. Unfortunately I don't even know how long they plan to stay. The cabin belongs to them too, so I can't just throw them out. I'll try to make it as easy for you as possible, but I won't call off our deal. Jason can stay with you tonight. Even I'm perceptive enough to see you're exhausted. I doubt you've really slept since I got here," he added with a touch of self-mockery. "If he's here with you, you won't be worrying about him being with me."

Megan flushed guiltily.

"Dad?" Both adults turned. Megan could see Jason standing in the doorway with a puzzled look on his face. "How do I make her let go?" he asked. A little girl in pink, fuzzy pajamas clung to his leg with one tiny clenched fist. She was gazing up at him with adoring green eyes, her other fist pushed her thumb into her rosebud mouth.

Bending forward, Doug kissed Megan swiftly on her forehead before rising to his feet. "Good night, love." He spoke the words softly before turning to the two children standing in the doorway.

"I wish I had your problem," he told his son as he disengaged the small fist. He pretended to toss the giggling toddler in the air. Faking an exaggerated catch, he firmly tucked her wiggling, chubby body into the crook of his arm. "Good night, Jason." He left the room, firmly closing the door behind him.

Megan fell asleep still feeling the tingling touch of Doug's lips; strangely his kiss lingered comfortingly rather than as a threat. Perhaps it was the picture of his tall form leaving the room with the happy, trusting little girl snuggled against his chest that soothed her way to slumber. Perhaps it was the steady reassuring rhythm of her own sleeping child breathing in the dark beside her.

Brad reached for Heidi as Doug emerged from the bedroom with the child in his arms. "I'll put her to bed. You look bushed." Doug could read the questions in his friend's eyes before he turned to carry her up the stairs to where Cathy was settling the other children.

He sank gratefully into the thick cushions of the sofa. His hands covered his eyes, then raked back through his hair. He wasn't ready to answer questions. He still had too many of his own. Megan's tortured eyes haunted him. What was he doing to her? She was hurting, and he didn't know what to do.

"Doug?"

He swiveled his head sharply. He hadn't even been aware of A.J. sitting a few feet away watching him.

"What happened? You both look terrible, especially Megan."

Doug's hand rubbed across his face. With a sigh he lifted his eyes to meet Allen's. "We got caught in a storm and had to outrun a flash flood."

Allen's eyes held his for long seconds. Doug was the first to look away.

"Don't give me that," Allen said clearly. "There's something a whole lot more than a brush with a flash flood bothering her."

"You're right. She's scared. But I can't explain it. Sometimes I feel as though she looks right through me and sees someone else."

"You know she's been knocked around a lot in her life."

"Are you suggesting that I—"

"No! No, I don't think anything like that." He looked away, then squared his shoulders. "Look, Doug, you've had a pretty good family. I remember your dad. He used to take you everywhere, and he talked to you. Your mom, too. I used to envy you. You know my family isn't like that. Remember I stayed at your house for three days once, and no one even missed me? My dad played golf the day I graduated from the U. Well, Megan doesn't come from a family like yours—nor a merely neglectful one like mine. And she didn't have friends to see her through the hard times. She's been hurt—hurt badly. I think she's afraid to get close to anyone."

"Do you think I can ever forget what she looked like the day I first found her? I know she's been hurt, and I'm afraid I hurt her more."

"Her hurt goes far beyond physical pain. That little scene you stumbled on ten years ago is only the tip of the iceberg."

"I really want to make her forget all that. I want to make her happy. I love her, and there isn't much I wouldn't do to take away the hurt.

Something happened the first time she looked at me, and the feeling is still there. It's like I'm not complete without her. I lost her for ten long years; I have to make it work this time."

"She deserves to be happy." Allen's voice was gruff. He stood with his back to Doug. After a moment he reached for a denim jacket folded over the arm of the sofa. Without looking back he walked out of the door into the night.

"You need some rest." Doug started at the sound of Brad's voice. He hadn't heard him reenter the room.

"I'm not sure I can sleep."

"You know, when I can't sleep, I find it helps to get on my knees and spend a few minutes talking my problems over with someone who knows the answers."

"I wouldn't know how."

"When the need is there, it's surprising how much we remember." Brad turned toward the stairs.

The fire had burned to gently glowing coals and the cabin settled into silence, when Doug slipped slowly to his knees.

"Father . . ." His knuckles turned white where he clasped his hands together. Slowly at first, then gaining momentum, the words poured from his heart. "For ten years my deepest desire has been to be reunited with Megan. On quiet mountain tops, in the midst of oil fires, or just beyond the next traffic light, I've glimpsed her face and felt her waiting for me. I didn't know whether she was alive or not, yet I felt we belonged together. Now she's here and wants nothing to do with me. She rebuffs every gesture I make to show her my feelings. Why do I feel such a strong bond if she doesn't? I've loved her so long, and you've given us a child. I want to be Jason's father and Megan's husband. Please help me to know what to do and say to make us a family.

"I'm not saying this right. I don't even know how to pray, but I believe in you, and deep inside I know you wouldn't have brought us back together if it weren't right for us to stay together. Megan needs your help. . . . And Father, so do I."

It felt late when Megan awoke. The sun was shining through the window, and she could hear childish laughter mixed with the deep rumble of men's voices. She knew without looking that Jason was no longer beside her. He must have awakened early and gone searching for breakfast. Slipping out of bed she pulled back the curtain to peek outside. Reassuring herself that all three vehicles were still parked in front of the cabin, she relaxed a fraction.

She took her time dressing, recognizing that when she dressed well, she felt more self-confident. Most of the clothing she had with her were smooth-fitting jeans or shorts and casual cotton blouses and T-shirts, though she had brought a couple of dressy pants suits. She pulled on a pair of dusty-green jeans with a loose-fitting green and rose knit top that had a wide band of cream lace decorating the square neckline and circling the bottom hem. Turning carefully before the small mirror, she checked whether bare skin showed beneath the short top. Startled at the picture she suddenly saw of herself in the snug-fitting pants, she stopped to stare. She felt suddenly foolish to think how many years she had been dressing and undressing in front of mirrors, yet still pictured herself as a skinny unattractive child. She raised her eyes to where the mirror faithfully duplicated the definite fullness of a grown woman. Why hadn't she really noticed her appearance before? She wasn't sure she liked the image she saw. Anyway, she didn't want to think about herself as a woman. Hastily she opened the closet to rummage for her white tennis shoes.

She meticulously applied her makeup, then brushed her short, gleaming curls into place. Suddenly her hand paused in midair, still holding her brush. Once again she found herself staring into the mirror. This time it wasn't herself she saw. She found herself remembering the chubby little girl nestled in Doug's arms the night before with her riot of red curls spilling across his arm.

Smiling at the memory she felt a tinge of jealousy. Recognizing the emotion, she tried to deny it. But she really did feel a bit jealous of the little girl. She tried to analyze why. Was it because it was Doug's arms the baby snuggled into so comfortably? Or was it because somewhere in the back of her mind she resented the fact that no daddy, or grandfather, or even an uncle, had ever held her like that? Shaking off her strange introspective mood, she finished brushing her hair.

A few minutes later she entered the kitchen to find Cathy stirring some kind of mixture in a huge metal bowl. The baby was strapped into the high chair, happily stuffing oatmeal into her mouth. More seemed to be covering her face, running down her arms, and dripping onto the floor than actually getting inside her mouth. Brad was leaning nonchalantly on the counter watching Cathy. They seemed to be locked in some kind of good-natured argument.

"Go feed Kelly. She's making an awful mess." Cathy told her husband.

"She's doing fine. Has to learn sometime." He grinned, scarcely glancing at the baby.

"Good morning," Megan said shyly.

"Feeling better?" Brad asked casually.

"Yes, thank you."

"Hi!" Cathy wiped her hands on a towel before approaching her. "We didn't really get a chance to meet last night. I'm Cathy."

"I guess you already know my name is Megan." Out of the corner of her eye she saw Brad dump something into the bowl Cathy had been stirring, something that looked suspiciously like a large bag of chocolate chips.

"I owe you an apology," Cathy continued, unaware of her husband's action. "We shouldn't have just dropped in without any warning."

"But," Brad came to give his wife's waist a squeeze. "Cathy has been trying for years to pair Doug off with every single female of her acquaintance, without any luck I must add. When we finally told her last week that good old Doug has been married for ten years she nearly killed me. Her curiosity got the better of her, and she just had to come see you for herself."

"Can you forgive us?" The redhead's winsome smile was hard to resist.

"Doug and I aren't really married," Megan started to explain.

"Legally we are," Doug said from behind her. She hadn't noticed Doug's approach. "And we have a nine-year-old son."

Throwing Doug an exasperated frown, Megan continued, "We haven't been together for ten years. We each thought the other had terminated the marriage years ago."

"Oh, Doug." Cathy turned a dazzling smile on him. "I'm really sorry. If this clod had told me you two were having a second honeymoon, I would have waited another week. Reconciliations are so romantic!"

"Really, I am sorry." She turned to include Megan. "I was being selfish. All I thought about was meeting you and none of us have even seen Doug since last Christmas. He went to Saudi Arabia right after that, then on to Kuwait when the war ended. But I guess you know that." She paused to catch her breath.

Before Megan could correct Cathy's misconceptions, Jason burst into the cabin followed by Bobbi.

"Come on, Dad. Bobbi and A.J. want to play again. They think they're going to beat us this time."

"We will!" Bobbi grinned. "You just got lucky last time."

"It wasn't luck!" Jason defended their previous win. "We can do it again, can't we, Dad?"

"Brad! You've ruined my granola," Cathy yelped.

"You're the lady who makes the granola?" Jason turned to her with a grin splitting his face.

"You know about Mom's granola?" Bobbi asked.

Jason and Doug exchanged glances before turning to Megan. She attempted to stare them down until a giggle betrayed her. Soon all three were roaring with laughter.

"I didn't think my granola was that bad," Cathy pouted in mock offense.

Suppressing his laughter Doug marched to the refrigerator. Opening the icebox he pulled out the monster fish frozen solid in a block of ice. Between bursts of laughter he and Jason explained how Megan caught it.

Taking one look at Megan's embarrassed face, Cathy ordered everyone out except Megan.

"You eat some breakfast," Cathy told her. "I think it's time this fish becomes lunch. It's taking up too much room in the freezer, and if it hangs around much longer those guys will have it mounted and hanging on the wall, and we'll have to listen to them entertain their friends with that story for the rest of our lives."

Cathy resumed mixing her granola with a vengeance. Megan smiled as she caught more than one complaint about Brad undermining her efforts to provide their children with nutritional snacks, and that a doctor should know better than to add chocolate chips to a health food.

As Megan ate her breakfast she accepted the friendly overtures of Kelly who laughed and clapped her hands in glee each time Megan looked her way. Finally seeking more attention from her new friend, the high-spirited infant dumped her bowl over her head, then used it to play peek-a-boo. It was apparent the happy baby was more interested in splashing in her bowl than eating from it, so when Megan finished her breakfast, she cleaned up oatmeal from the chair and surrounding floor. She picked up the giggling little girl to carry her to the cupboard where Cathy had prepared a sink full of warm water to serve as a bath. Both women were laughing and thoroughly soaked by the time they finished cleaning up the baby. Once Kelly was powdered, diapered, and dressed in a fresh sunsuit, Megan offered to carry her out into the sun to brush out her tangled curls.

As Megan snuggled the baby in her lap, she slowly set the porch swing in motion.

"You might have your mother's flaming red hair and electric smile," she told the baby, "but you've definitely inherited your daddy's solid build and easy-going style."

Big green eyes blinked back at her, a hint of a smile curved her tiny puckish mouth, and one miniature fist tightened around Megan's finger. Fleetingly she recalled Doug and Jason's teasing comments about a little sister. She cuddled the baby closer and began to sing a silly little song she used to sing to Jason.

"She's asleep," Cathy spoke softly a few minutes later. "Just lay her down in the playpen."

Megan felt reluctant to put the sleeping cherub down. It seemed such a long time since she last held a baby. It felt so right to cuddle that surprisingly heavy little body against her breasts. Sensing Megan's reluctance to put Kelly down, Cathy grinned and let her enjoy a few more moments with her. Then she lifted the sleeping child from Megan's arms to place her on her tummy in the playpen.

"Somebody's baby-hungry," Cathy teased. "Maybe you and Doug should work on a little sister for Jason."

Megan blushed furiously, but before she could explain or deny anything, Brad showed up to drag them both out to the little meadow where an impromptu baseball diamond had been set up.

"Come on, Mom. We need everybody." Jason called. "It's going to be the Williamses against everybody else. There's more Williamses than us, but they're mostly girls."

"We'll skunk ya!" Bobbi yelled indignantly, suspecting a slur in his comment.

The Williams family was up to bat first. When little Heidi stepped up to the plate dragging the bat in the dirt behind her, A.J. signaled Jason to pitch a grounder. When she tapped it a few feet back toward the pitcher's mound, A.J. made an elaborate pretense of chasing the ball. Jason ran forward. Each time Jason reached for the ball, A.J. managed to kick it a few feet further away. Finally grasping the ball, Jason threw it to Doug who was covering first base. Doug batted the ball about in the air as though he couldn't quite get a hold on it until Heidi was safely on base. Similar antics soon placed Michelle and Ashley on bases too, and with the bases loaded, Bobbi picked up the bat.

Brad joined Heidi on third, ostensibly to coach, but when Bobbi sent a ball flying past second base, he scooped up the little girl and ran with her for home. Megan retrieved the ball and tossed it to Jason. Jason, not trusting A.J., dived for home, beating Ashley to the plate.

"Out! You're out!" Jason screamed.

Ashley stuck out her tongue before she flounced to the sidelines.

Cathy gripped the bat tightly, gave a little practice swing, then wiggled her fanny to indicate she was ready. Laughing, Jason pitched a good one right across the plate and stood with his mouth open as Cathy slammed the ball in a beautiful smooth arc straight out into left field. As Megan scrambled to get it, Bobbi nearly passed Michelle as they raced for home plate. Grasping the ball, seconds after it hit the ground, Megan heaved it to Doug, and Cathy decided to stay on second base rather than try to beat Doug's toss to Jason, who was now covering third.

With only one out and three runs in, Jason let go with a high fast ball to Brad. Brad barely connected, and the ball rolled down the base line toward first. As Doug retrieved the foul ball, he signaled to Megan to stay close to second base. Brad hit the next pitch high into right field, but Doug was right under it. Catching it smoothly, he immediately sent it flying to Megan on second.

"Way to go!" Jason whooped with delight when Megan caught it, putting Cathy out before she got to third base.

With three outs, Jason's team was at bat. With a mixture of silliness, giving the little girls an advantage, and a test of skill for Bobbi and

Jason, the game continued until indignant screams from baby Kelly let everyone know she was awake and feeling left out.

Lunch brought more teasing about Megan's fish and Cathy's granola. They both joined in the laughter, but when their eyes met, Megan knew Cathy was right about getting rid of the fish as soon as possible.

Watching Jason out of the corner of her eye, she was pleased to see the happy sparkle in his eyes. Being in the middle of a large noisy family was a new experience for both of them, but one Jason seemed to thrive on until Cathy handed him Kelly's bottle and suggested he feed the baby while the girls did the dishes.

"Me?" Startled he looked to his mother for help, which she was only too happy to provide. Together they sat at one end of a love seat with Jason's arm on the armrest. Megan settled Kelly in the crook of his arm and placed the bottle in his other hand. From there Kelly took over and eagerly let him know he was doing just fine. Mother and son exchanged smiles over the baby's head.

From across the room Doug watched them. Megan looked up to see the longing on his face.

"Megan isn't the only one who is baby hungry." Cathy nudged him in the ribs, interpreting his hungry look her own way, much to Megan's embarrassment. Smiling sheepishly Doug left the cabin to catch up with Brad and Allen. Megan wondered if she should try once more to explain her situation to Cathy.

They spent most of the afternoon playing in the creek making their way downstream to a long stretch of shallow, swift water. Bobbi and Michelle went first, demonstrating how to sit in the water at the top of the long steep incline, then let the swift water carry them along the slippery, pebbled stream as though shooting down a water slide. Soon even the adults were sharing in the water games, laughing and splashing with the children.

Megan held back until Doug took her hands in his and tugged her toward the water, threatening to throw her in if she didn't try it willingly. For the first time all day she felt fear coil its way up from her stomach.

Sensing her alarm, Doug cursed himself for starting something which might prove too much for her. He didn't want a repeat of yesterday. Closing his eyes he breathed a silent plea for help.

Suddenly Jason was beside them.

"Mom, you can do it," Jason whispered. "I'll sit down and Dad can sit behind me with his arms around my waist. You can be behind Dad with your arms around him. Okay, Mom?"

She nodded hesitantly.

Doug felt a jolt go through him. Whether he consciously knew what he was doing or not, Jason was showing him the way. Suddenly he remembered Megan reaching for his hands to cross the stream during their long hike, her grip on his hand as they raced ahead of the flash flood. Megan would accept his touch only if she did the reaching, and felt free to break the contact. She associated others' reaching for her with the nightmare in her past when she was held against her will. Suddenly Doug understood. *In her mind, touching and holding are precursors to rape!* Why hadn't he seen that before? Megan could be touched, but she couldn't be restrained.

Testing his newfound theory, he sat down and wrapped his arms around Jason. Holding his breath, he waited. Then to his relief, he felt two slender arms wrap around his chest, and two long, slim, denim-clad legs slide alongside his.

Amidst clapping and cheering they began their wild ride. As he turned his head to see Megan open her mouth to scream, she got a mouthful of water. He felt her slipping, but resisted the urge to reach for her legs to steady her. He breathed a sigh when she sought a tighter grip on his shirt and wrapped her legs tighter around his. He could hear Jason whooping and yelling and feel his own heart pounding as they swooped down the natural slide. He felt he was flying on a giddy high. At the end of the ride they sat still for a moment, then Jason bounded to his feet.

"I knew you could do it!" Jason grinned proudly at his mom, then lunged to his feet to dash back to the top of the run. Slowly Megan loosened her grip on Doug. He rose as though moving in slow motion, then turned to offer his hand to her. Shyly her eyes met his, then she accepted his help.

Doug's heart slammed against his ribs. His theory was right. He held the key!

The men took over grilling hamburgers for supper while Cathy and Megan helped the children get clean and dry. Megan shivered. The sun was slipping out of sight and the sharp mountain air was turning cold.

"Anyone want a mug of hot cocoa?" Brad's offer was met with a chorus of approval. Instead of marshmallows he found a can of whipped cream to add a foamy white cloud to each warm cup.

Once dinner was over, Heidi crawled onto A.J.'s lap and promptly fell asleep. Ashley and Michelle rubbed their eyes. Megan knew she should send Jason to bed. She would in a minute. She was just so tired.

When Brad stood and invited them all to join his family in prayer before the children scooted off to bed, Megan didn't know what to say or do. She caught Jason's doubtful glance from across the room. Her eyes followed his as they moved questioningly to his father's face. Doug smiled reassuringly at them both. Hesitantly she followed Doug's lead, turning to face the seat and slowly bending her knees. Jason slipped between his parents. It felt right when the child placed his hand in hers and Doug's larger hand slid beneath their joined hands.

Brad spoke softly and easily. His words were plain and simple, yet they evoked a haunting emotion, both strange and familiar, in Megan. She felt a tremor in Doug's hand, or maybe it was her own, when Brad asked for a blessing of peace and understanding for Doug and her.

After the prayer ended, she sat beside Doug in bemusement. She hadn't known adults prayed outside of churches. She had taught Jason a simple bedtime prayer years ago that she had found in a poetry book. She was determined to be a good mother and in all of the books she read mothers listened to their children's prayers each night.

Before Megan was quite aware of what was happening, Cathy had all six children tucked in bed upstairs in the loft. At some time during the day, she had even managed to get the cradle moved upstairs for the baby. Worn out from the day's activities, they quickly settled down to sleep. Megan's muscles ached from the strenuous activity of the past few days; she found her head nodding and realized she was almost asleep too. Sitting beside Doug, she found herself drowsily contemplating how nice it would be to just lean her head against his shoulder. Catching herself as her cheek brushed his soft flannel shirt, she blinked rapidly, trying to wake up enough to understand what Cathy was saying. Something wasn't quite right. Cathy was talking to A.J.

"Allen, I've put all the bedding on the beds. You have your sleeping bag with you, so you can just pull out one of the love seats and spread it out there. We'll let the honeymooners keep the bedroom."

Nine

I DIDN'T . . ."

"We can't . . ."

Doug stared at Megan as they each came to a stumbling halt. How did they come to be together behind a closed bedroom door? Doug wanted to strangle Cathy. Everything had been going so well all day. Megan seemed more relaxed and willing to accept his presence. He still savored their closeness and the soft pressure of her body leaning against his back as they shot down the water slide.

Gloomily he anticipated that a night of his enforced presence would ruin everything and send Megan screaming right out of his life again. Of course, he couldn't imagine anything he'd rather do than spend the night in that big pine bed with Megan in his arms.

Megan began to shake. She placed her hands over her mouth. Fearing the worst, Doug held out his arms, then hesitated to touch her. She suddenly collapsed against him, her slender shoulders shaking. She was laughing! Gingerly he placed his arms loosely around her back. Perspiration beaded his forehead as he debated the best way to deal with this new crisis. He searched his mind for everything he knew about hysteria. Perhaps he should call Brad. No. Megan would hate the humiliation of the others seeing her fall apart. He patted her back and whispered her name. He strained to make sense of the garbled sounds coming from her mouth.

"How does she do it?" Megan sputtered.

"You mean Cathy?"

"Yes, Cathy. She's even smaller than me, but all three of you big lugs tiptoe around her. You do everything she tells you to do, as though you were scared to death of her."

"I do not," Doug tried to defend himself. He felt almost light-headed with relief. Megan wasn't hysterical.

"Oh, yes you do. I don't believe it was your idea, anymore than it was mine, for us to share this room tonight. And it isn't just you. How did she get Jason to sleep in the same room with five girls? Why does A.J. have a six-pack of beer stashed in the creek, instead of in the refrigerator? Look at me! I played baseball today in the dirt, went 'bum sliding' in the creek, and now I'm sharing a bedroom with a man! Even Brad's defiance only went as far as dumping a bag of chocolate chips in her granola!"

"I think you underestimate Brad, but I guess the rest of us are a bunch of sniveling cowards."

"I just don't get it." Megan's laughter continued. "None of you are afraid of her. She never threatens, and I wouldn't call her bossy or manipulating. In fact, I really like her in spite of—"

"We all like her. She has a tremendous talent for organizing and managing, whether it's Brad's office, a Junior League Flea Market, or a little girl's birthday party." Doug struggled to act as though there was nothing unusual about Megan standing in the circle of his arms laughing. How could he explain Cathy? "She really cares about people. She believes in us to the point that we would feel like jerks if we ever disappointed her. Then again, maybe we're all just basically lazy, and have just gotten in the habit of letting her organize us."

Looking up at Doug's lopsided grin, Megan's laughter began to fade as she became aware of the broad chest brushing her cheek. Trying to appear nonchalant, she stepped away and experienced both a sense of relief and loss, as his muscular arms let her go.

She collected her robe and a nightshirt, changed her mind and reached for a soft fleece jogging suit. She turned to see Doug standing by the bed, an uncertain expression on his face.

"Uh . . ."

"Doug, I realize you can't spend the night on a rag rug in a mountain cabin, and I don't expect you to sit up all night in a wooden rocking chair either. Like it or not, we're going to have to share that bed."

"You surprise me. I thought you'd be rigid with shock at the thought of sharing a bed with me." He smiled to soften the words.

"Just because we sleep in the same bed doesn't mean we'll do anything but sleep!" Megan snapped back, heat reddening her cheeks.

"I saw an old movie once where a couple drew a line down the middle of the bed with pillows or a rolled up quilt or something."

"I don't think that will be necessary. It's a big bed."

"Do you really trust me that much?" Doug asked softly. "Make no mistake about it, Megan, I really do want to do a whole lot more than just sleep with you."

Blushing furiously Megan turned away. "I don't trust you in some things, but in this I do. Besides," she added with an impish smirk, "with your best friends, and a whole troop of little kids in the house, I don't think your masculine ego will risk my screaming the roof off!"

While Megan showered and got ready for bed, Doug sat in the rocker. There was no way he was going to lie in bed listening to Megan shower, knowing she would soon be next to him, but not in his arms. He'd go nuts. He thought of using looking for his bag as an excuse to leave the room, but Cathy had already moved all of his things into the bedroom for him.

Shaking his head over Cathy's well-meaning maneuvering, he doubted he'd get any sleep that night. He wouldn't dare close his eyes for fear he might accidentally touch Megan and set off another screaming bout. Ruefully he admitted Megan was right about that; he certainly wouldn't want to try to explain to the entire household why his wife was yelling for help in the middle of the night. Briefly he considered retreating to his truck, but he didn't want to explain that either.

When Megan returned to the bedroom she was wrapped in a thick velour robe with her damp hair hidden in a towel. "Your turn," she remarked brightly.

As he passed her on his way out of the room, Doug couldn't help wondering if she planned to go to bed so thoroughly wrapped up. It might make the night a whole lot easier. In fact it might be a good idea if he wore sweat pants too.

Megan shook the towel free and turned on the hair blower before she admitted to herself she was more than a little nervous. It would be difficult to continue pretending to be calm and unconcerned. How was she ever going to make it through the night? One minute she hoped she could fall asleep before Doug came back to the room, the next she knew she would be too scared to fall asleep at all. A traitorous corner of her mind filled her with longing to experience again the never-forgotten night in Doug's arms. She clamped down on that thought. She never allowed herself to think about that.

She finished her hair, removed her robe, and placed it near the side of the bed. She turned out the light. It would be less embarrassing if they didn't have to see each other. Quickly she climbed into bed, pulled the quilt up to her chin, and lay facing the wall. *Go to sleep* she willed herself, but she was still awake when Doug entered the room. Lying still in the dark, she followed the sound of his bare feet on the pine floor, heard the rustle of fabric falling to the floor on his side of the bed, then felt the mattress dip as he first sat down, then spread his length along the bed. Her spine stiffened and she could feel her heart pounding.

"Good night, honey."

"Good night." She managed to not stammer. She could hear him breathe. He sounded so close. *Is he wearing pajamas?* The question suddenly popped into her head. She hadn't previously considered any other possibilities. Memories of their one night together, all those years ago, reminded her that he wore pajama pants that night, but his chest had been bare. For just a moment she wished she were wearing the pink satin and chiffon gown she had worn that night with its feminine ribbons and lace, instead of the practical cotton jogging suit she now wore.

No! Don't think about it!

She carefully shifted to her back. She was uncomfortable. Belatedly she remembered she always slept on her right side and by choosing the side away from the door to avoid having Doug climb across her to get into bed she had to either sleep facing him or struggle to sleep on her "wrong" side. Valiantly she turned toward the wall again until her muscles began to ache from the effort of forcing her body to lie still in the unfamiliar position. She listened to faint sounds coming from outside. A breeze scraped a branch against the window. Doug's breath sounded smooth and even.

Fatigue from the physically demanding day eventually made her eyelids heavy and her thought processes slow. Taking advantage of her drifting mental condition, her body slowly relaxed and turned to its accustomed position.

Megan awoke. Something was tickling her nose, and there was something she needed to remember, but she was warm and comfortable, and it wasn't light out yet. She couldn't pinpoint the moment that she became aware she was snuggled against a male chest. One large arm extended beneath her neck and crooked to hold her close. Her own bent knee brushed Doug's thigh. At least he was wearing sweat pants like her own.

Expecting fear to tighten her stomach and choke off her ability to move, she was surprised to feel only a comfortable, enticing warmth. Experimentally, she wiggled closer to the warmth, then stifled a gasp as Doug's arm drew her closer and his hand slid down to her hip. She could hear his deep breathing and hoped that was an indication he was still asleep. Afraid any movement might awaken him, she lay still. How could she extricate herself from her predicament?

As the minutes ticked by she gradually relaxed. A sense of elation crept into her mind as she realized her body was reacting to this man beside her as she knew a healthy female should react to an attractive male, to her husband. He wasn't really her husband, she chided herself. *But he is,* a voice in her head argued. *He wants our marriage to be real,* the thought intruded. *That means sex. It's easy to imagine making love with a sleeping man,* a saner voice warned, *but if you wake him up, you'll be sorry.* Assuring herself he was still sleeping, she slowly began moving away. First she withdrew her leg, next she began turning toward the wall.

Not quite sure how it happened, she found herself with her back firmly anchored against Doug's chest, while his arms crisscrossed her body. Torn between an aching need to escape and a traitorous desire to stay where she was, she didn't dare move. Afraid almost to breathe, Megan tried forcing herself to think of something else, but that wasn't easy to do. She fought against the increasing temptation to relax against the warm body holding her. He felt solid and safe. Strange to think of Doug as safe. Eventually exhaustion wilted her resolve. Sleep once more claimed her for its own. Her body softened, relaxed into the bliss surrounding it, and she knew no more until the sun peeped its way through the curtains.

She awoke alone in the big bed. Relief clashed with disappointment for just a moment; relief won out. It would have been terribly embarrassing to face him in bed this morning. For a few seconds she considered she might have just imagined their pleasant contact during the night. It might have been a dream, but she knew it wasn't. She had an uneasy suspicion Doug hadn't really been asleep, but when he greeted her casually when she entered the kitchen, she was relieved to see no telling glint in his eyes.

Cathy must have noticed her quick survey of the room, because she answered her unvoiced question. "Jason and Bobbi have gone fishing with Allen. He promised to bring them back in time for lunch. I hope you don't mind."

"No, it's all right." She glanced uncertainly at Doug.

"He'll be fine," Doug assured her.

"Actually it was my idea to keep those two occupied this morning." Brad spoke up as he placed a fresh platter of pancakes before her. Turning back to the stove to lift sunny fried eggs onto another plate, he added, "Doug and I plan to cut firewood this morning, and if Jason's help is anything like Bobbi's, they're better off fishing. They can both help stack wood this afternoon, but I prefer to keep Bobbi as far away as possible while we're running the saw!"

Megan shuddered, knowing if Jason were anywhere near a power saw, his curiosity would outweigh caution. She was glad Brad had the foresight to provide a distraction. She longed for a little distraction herself. Every time she lifted her attention from her plate she encountered Doug watching her.

When Cathy began gathering up their plates and silverware, Megan hurriedly rose to her feet to help her.

"I'll get the saw." Brad rose to his feet. "Allen put a can of gas in his jeep. If you want to get that, we can be on our way."

"Okay. How about walking out to the Jeep with me?" Doug turned to Megan.

She wanted to go with him. Yet, what if he said something about the way she'd cuddled up to him last night?

"Go ahead," Cathy prompted.

Reluctantly she moved toward the door with Doug right behind her. Nervously, she looked toward the trees. Misinterpreting her motive, Doug assured her, "He really will be all right."

"I know, it's just that we've never been apart except when I'm at work." Relieved that he thought she was thinking of Jason, she made a clumsy attempt to find any topic other than the previous night to discuss.

"Speaking of Jason, I heard him tell Allen this morning that he would be in Sister Theresa's class this fall. Is he enrolled in a parochial school?"

"Yes, it's a very good school. Why? Don't you like private schools?"

"I don't know. I just assumed he attended a public school. I didn't know you were Catholic."

"I'm not." Megan was silent for several minutes. She wasn't accustomed to talking about herself or Jason, but suddenly she wanted to tell Doug about Jason. "I've never belonged to any church, but I always thought I owed the Catholic sisters a lot. So I sent Jason to a Catholic day-care center and nursery school while I finished school. He was well cared for and happy there, so it just seemed natural to send him to a parochial school when he started kindergarten."

"Why do you feel you owe them something?"

She lowered her voice. "When I left here, I had no idea I was pregnant. I didn't even know why I was sick and gaining weight until a girl in a cafe casually mentioned my condition. I was scared and angry. I looked up a clinic in the phone book the next day and made an appointment to have an abortion,"

Doug felt the color drain from his face. The gas can banged against the side of the Jeep as he momentarily lost his grip on it. He turned toward Megan, but she continued without prompting.

"As I was walking along the street to keep my appointment, I passed a large fenced yard with wrought-iron gates. Behind the fence I could see twenty or thirty children running about. An older sister wearing a long black habit was kicking a ball to a group of little boys. Her robes were flying, and she was laughing. The boys were giggling and having a marvelous time. I stood there watching for a long time. They reminded me of my little brother. After a while, the sister came over to the fence and asked me if I needed help. I started to cry, and then I remembered something my grandfather told me when he came to get me from a foster home where I was terribly unhappy: if I was ever in really bad trouble and didn't know what to do, I should go to a church and the sisters would help me."

Doug swallowed a lump in his throat as Megan added, "She did help me, and I had Jason. He was so beautiful with thick dark hair and a stubborn chin right from the beginning. He weighed almost eight pounds and slept through the night. I was so thankful to have him."

Doug sat the gas can down and placed his hand on Megan's to give it a gentle squeeze. They were both silent for several minutes. Megan had just told him more than he had ever known about her before. The back of his eyes burned, and he hoped the past few minutes were the beginning of real communication between them.

Brad came out of the shed with the heavy saw. Megan blinked rapidly and fled back to the cabin to help Cathy wash the dishes and straighten up.

Later, with Kelly contentedly sucking on her bottle, Megan settled in one corner of the porch swing with the baby in her lap. Cathy held Heidi in the other corner. The little girl was pleased to have a long cuddle with her mother while someone else held the baby. The comforting motion and soft voices of the two young women soon put both children to sleep. Michelle and Ashley came outside with a box of tiny cars and animals. Soon they were engrossed in building roads and farms in the soft dirt beneath a stunted pine tree.

"Will you and Doug be living in Salt Lake in his mother's home now, or would you rather have a newer house?" Cathy asked, then continued without pausing for an answer. "If you buy a house, I hope you'll look out our way. The new houses along Sandy's east bench are really nice. Of course since Mrs. Beckwith bought a condo in St. George, her big house is empty all winter. It's such a lovely house, and it just seems to cry out for hordes of children. Every time we go there I imagine little boys sliding down the banister of that beautiful staircase and lovely young girls dressed in elegant prom gowns floating down the stairs."

"But Doug and I aren't . . ." Megan hesitated, uncertain how to explain their situation.

"I'm sorry. You probably haven't had a chance yet to discuss anything so mundane as where you're going to live. I'm just excited because now that Doug is going to be teaching at the university instead of traveling all over the world, it will give us a chance to get to know each other and become really good friends, just like our husbands are."

"Teaching?"

Megan must have sounded surprised because Cathy burst out, "Oh, you didn't know, did you? Doug will be really upset with me now. He probably wanted to surprise you, and I've ruined it! Brad tells me I talk too much, and he's right. I really do."

"Oh, Cathy, it's all right. He probably just forgot to mention it." She found herself trying to comfort her new friend and change the subject. "I can't hear the saw anymore. Do you think they've finished?" She looked toward the trail and saw Brad emerge from the trees.

"Whew! It's hot today," he commented as he approached the porch. His shirttail was hanging out and damp half-moons darkened the sides of his shirt.

Carefully putting Heidi down in the playpen to continue her nap, Cathy followed her husband into the house. From her end of the porch swing, Megan had a perfect view of the interior of the cabin. She saw Cathy reach for the ice tray Brad had just placed on the counter top. Instead of helping him fix a drink, she dropped a chunk of ice down the back of his pants as he leaned over to get something from the refrigerator. He retaliated by holding her against the side of the cupboard with both of her hands clasped in one of his. With the other hand he slowly, methodically began dropping ice cubes down the front of her shirt. Megan could hear Cathy squeal as she squirmed to get away.

An uneasy feeling swamped Megan. She tried to look away, but concern for Cathy kept her eyes glued to the struggle inside the cabin. To her surprise she saw Brad place both hands around Cathy's waist and lift her to a sitting position on the cabinet. Her arms immediately wrapped around his neck and her legs encircled his waist. As his mouth came down on hers, Megan looked away embarrassed, but not before she recognized that Cathy was thoroughly enjoying her husband's attention. In fact, she'd instigated it. Megan recognized that what was going on between Brad and Cathy—while she'd never had any experience with it—must be a part of a really healthy marriage. They obviously had one.

Megan kept her attention directed toward the sleeping infant in her arms as the pair stepped out through the doorway a few minutes later. She heard the unmistakable sound of a quick kiss and a satisfied giggle before Brad took his leave. From the corner of her eye, she watched Brad swing several cans of soft drinks by their plastic holder as he jauntily moved up the trail, whistling off-key.

"Aren't your arms getting tired?" Cathy asked. "You've been holding Kelly half the morning. Let's put her down by Heidi." Minutes later, with tall glasses of cold fruit juice in their hands, they leaned back comfortably against the swing cushions.

"You like being married, don't you?" Megan surprised herself when the question just popped out of her mouth.

"Of course, don't you?"

"I don't like someone else running my life or thinking he owns me!"

"Doug wouldn't do that!" Cathy countered. "He and Brad think alike about a lot of things, and I've heard them talk about marriage. I've lived with Brad for ten years, so I know he practices what he says. He doesn't run my life. I'm responsible for who I am and what I do, not him. Of course, since we love each other, I'm always trying to do what I think is best for him, and he does what he thinks is best for me, and sometimes we don't agree on what is best, but somehow it all works out because we just want to make each other happy."

Megan blinked, unsure she quite followed Cathy's reasoning. Cathy continued. "Even last year when the legislature was considering a bill that would make it legal for a wife to charge her husband with rape, Brad and Doug agreed it was a good bill because marriage doesn't give a husband ownership of his wife's body. I heard Doug say he didn't believe anyone has the right to use force to make someone else behave a certain way or do something that person really doesn't want to do. He says force might sometimes be necessary to protect liberty or life itself, but it isn't warranted otherwise."

Megan wasn't sure Doug quite lived up to Cathy's lofty opinion of him—after all, wasn't he keeping her a kind of prisoner here against her will?

"Doug isn't really like Brad," Megan tried tentatively to speak her thoughts aloud. Cathy might be her ally if she knew the facts, but trusting another person with her inner self was something she had never done before. When she hesitated, Cathy forged ahead.

"No, not in looks, or personality, or career choice. They're different, of course, in all those things, but inside they share the same values and beliefs. They both care deeply about people and are committed to making this a better world. Responsibility and honor aren't old-fashioned words to either of them. They're both deeply religious men."

"Religious?" Megan felt confused. "Is Doug a Mormon, too?"

"You don't know?" It was Cathy's turn to show her surprise. "Haven't you and Doug ever talked about religion?"

"Not really. We talked a little bit to Jason about God a few days ago, but Doug and I really don't know each other very well."

Cathy's questioning look invited Megan to go on, but she didn't know what to say. Hesitating only seconds, Cathy rushed to explain.

"Doug's mother is a member of the Church, but has never been very active. His father never saw a need for formal religion. Doug grew up going to Mormon meetings and was a scout with Brad. He doesn't smoke or drink and pretty much maintains what we call LDS standards, but he has never been baptized. I asked Brad once how his friend could be a Mormon in every way except the most important one. He said for some people all the pieces may be in place—there may even be an unrecognized testimony—but until some spark is lit inside, igniting an awareness of their need to know God, they will continue to drift along, living a good life, but never developing their full spiritual potential."

"Religion is important to both you and your husband, isn't it?" Megan's question didn't belittle what she sensed mattered a great deal to her new friend.

"Yes, it's the cornerstone of our lives." Cathy was still, what for her was a long time, then she spoke with a fervor Megan hadn't expected. "Oh, Megan, I think you're experiencing some uncertainty about reconciling with Doug. I wish I could make you understand how wonderful it is to be married to a good man, and believe me, Doug is a good man and he loves you so very much. Brad told me you left Doug ten years ago, but he never stopped loving you or looking for you. Like Brad and me, You'll have arguments and disagreements, but as long as you love each other and let Heavenly Father be your best friend, you can make your marriage work. You'll be happy. There's nothing more important than a happy home."

Happy home? She and Jason were happy in their little house, but to have a marriage like Cathy's. . . . Megan felt a twinge of envy, thinking of Cathy and Brad's shared faith and recalling the way Brad played with the girls and pitched in to help with household tasks. And then there was that passionate embrace in the kitchen. . . . For a moment she felt the same pangs of envy she had felt as a child watching a neighboring family exuberantly haul chairs and tables and food into their backyard for an impromptu picnic. She had stood with her nose pressed to a crack in the fence, tears streaming down her face, while they laughed and hugged, teased and chased one another.

Pushing away the memory, she asked Cathy if Brad would object if she decided she wanted a career.

"He wouldn't try to stop me if I really wanted to go back to work." Cathy's eyes moved to her sleeping babies. "But I know he likes me being home with the girls, and it's comforting to him that he can respond to a medical emergency anytime, night or day, and know I'm with the children. I used to have a job. Actually I couldn't wait to quit. It was really hard when Brad was in medical school, and I was working every day and had to leave Bobbi with my mother or a sitter. Michelle was born during Brad's last year of residency, so he wasn't much help then either. I was tired and cranky all of the time. My job seemed stupid and boring compared to what I was missing out on at home. I was even jealous of the baby-sitter because she got to potty-train Bobbi!"

"Now that's really bad!" Megan laughed.

"I know that some women, with exciting careers like yours, must think I'm a dull stick-in-the-mud, but I really just want to be a wife and mother. I'm lucky too," she added proudly. "With the world's economic problems, there really aren't many women who have the luxury of choosing whether they want to work or not."

Megan felt confused. She'd always worked. It was the only way to survive and take care of Jason, but Cathy's words were painting a picture of family life she found appealing.

Glancing down at her watch, Megan asked if perhaps they should start fixing lunch. Deciding on salads and sandwiches which could be eaten anytime the log cutters or fishermen wandered in, the two women were nearly finished with the preparations when both little girls woke up and demanded the attention only Mommy could supply.

Seeing Cathy was fully occupied and didn't need her help, Megan decided to go for a short walk. She wandered down the trail toward the creek, where she decided to follow one of the paths that cut away from the main trail. Breathing deeply she enjoyed the clear pine-scented air. It no longer held the threat she had long associated with the smell of earth and pine.

Occasionally she stopped to take a closer look at a flower or pick up a pine cone. She laughed aloud remembering a few weeks ago she couldn't imagine actually finding a mountain environment to her liking.

Never far from her thoughts all morning, her mind returned to the events of the previous night, first the strange emotions she'd experienced as they knelt to pray, then her night with Doug filled with such mixed emotions. Kneeling with Doug and Jason had felt right. For those few minutes they were a family. More and more she recognized a need within herself to be a part of a family. If she were honest, she would admit she was attracted to Doug in some way she didn't fully understand.

Ten years ago she had awakened to see his face and known she was safe. Last night, in spite of all its awkwardness, she had never doubted her safety. Men usually made her uncomfortable, but she could handle that, unless they tried to touch her. That always renewed the revulsion she felt to Lee's touch all those years ago. She associated Doug with Lee less all the time. Last night she hadn't thought of Lee once.

Last night had accomplished one thing. Her doubts about her ability to respond physically to a man in a positive way had dimmed. Perhaps she could be a wife. Such thoughts were new to her. For years she hadn't had any desire to have a man in her life.

She had always felt that wanting a man was a trap. She could never let a man, even a good man, take away her ability to control her own life the way her mother had. She shuddered, remembering how her mother had surrendered everything, even her children, to the demands of her lovers.

With a little sigh her thoughts drifted to Brad and Cathy again. Cathy wasn't like her mother. She'd stand up for her children. Of course, Brad was nothing like Lee either. She had never been close to a marriage like theirs before, and had about decided they existed only in books. She wondered if she were to stay with Doug, would he look at her the way Brad looked at Cathy? What did Doug really want from her? Was she just the means for securing Jason? Or could this silent thread holding them together turn into something like Brad and Cathy shared? She wished she knew.

It would be wonderful to have someone to laugh and talk with, to keep her from feeling lonely and afraid. She fantasized about living with Doug, just the three of them—having another adult to talk with and having someone to share her worries about Jason's activities, his grades, and his bumps and scrapes. She twirled a curl around her finger. Would Doug give her time to adjust to a physical relationship? Was she anywhere near ready to take the risk?

She came to an abrupt stop. A frown wrinkled her face, bringing her rosy fantasy to a halt. The past two weeks had brought the past forcibly to mind with all of its terrors. Like a child with a scab who persists in scratching until the wound bleeds again, she had picked at the past, making it bleed again. She felt ashamed of the way she had treated Doug, and guilty for depriving Jason of his father. Sure she wanted marriage with a husband who adored her and made her world feel safe, but what did she have to offer him? Doug deserved someone who didn't flinch when he touched her, who wouldn't scream the house down because she felt sticky and trapped. Most of all, she thought sadly, he deserves someone sweet and innocent. She would be as out of place in his life as she had once felt in his beautiful house. *I would embarrass and shame him,* she thought.

Megan walked on, paying little attention to where the trail led until she heard voices up ahead. Old fears urged caution. She moved ahead quietly. Pressing herself against a tree, she peered into a small clearing. She recognized Doug and Brad sitting side by side on a deadfall log they had been cutting. Her gaze lingered on Doug's broad shoulders, then centered on the handsome face she loved.

Love! She clapped her hands over her mouth to prevent a cry from escaping. It was true; she loved him. No, she couldn't love him, she told herself. She didn't know anything about love. She stared in panicky fascination at the object of her jumbled thoughts. It couldn't be love; she was still childishly seeking a storybook hero. And storybook heroes and happily ever-afters don't really exist. She, of all people, knew that.

Words began to intrude on her stunned mind.

"She won't let him out of her sight." She heard Doug tell Brad. "I can't go through another night like last night, so it has to be today.

Besides, she's finally beginning to open up, and I feel the time is right."

Megan's ears burned at the reference to last night. Doug had only pretended to be asleep.

"All right, we'll take Jason with us." She heard Brad agree to Doug's plan. "But I'm not sure this is a good idea. Separating her from her child, when she's already feeling pressured and frightened, may be more trauma than she can handle. Can't you take some time to really think and pray about this? A few words to Cathy could relieve some of the pressure you feel."

Bristling with anger and embarrassment, Megan backed away. She waited until she was safely out of earshot of the two men before she even let herself consider the implication of their words.

They're going to kidnap Jason! She had just listened to Doug and Brad make cold-blooded plans to steal her child.

What a fool I am! I was actually beginning to believe he was planning a life for the three of us together. I thought he was dependable, that I had been wrong about him. I was beginning to admire him and believe he wasn't like Grandfather and Lee. He wants Jason, but not me.

Gradually her own feelings were submerged. She had to protect Jason. *I won't give him up!* Grimly she acknowledged she had run out of time. She would have to act quickly.

Ten

MOM! LOOK AT MY FISH!"

Megan had run until she was out of breath then sank down on a rock to calm herself and think what to do. Her number one priority must be to get Jason away before Doug and Brad could act. For just a moment, the thought crossed her mind that Jason might be happier with Doug than with her. No, she needed Jason. Brushing the thought aside, she proceeded to review everything she knew about the area. If they could get to the city, they'd have a chance, but how could they get away from here? At the sound of Jason's voice, she quickly stood up to find herself face to face with A.J. and an idea. He owed her. He got her into this mess.

After dutifully admiring Jason's catch she turned to the man whose eyes had never left her face since they came upon each other on the narrow trail.

"Everything okay?" he asked.

Silently she shrugged her shoulders, sensing it wouldn't be wise to appear forgiving too soon.

"Megan, I didn't mean to hurt you by telling Doug where you were." He spoke too softly for the children to hear his words. They were too busy arguing over which one had caught the biggest fish to pay any attention to the adults.

"Didn't you consider that I've always known where Doug was? If I had wanted to see him again, I could have contacted him anytime."

"Actually I did consider that. I waited three years before doing anything."

Startled by his revelation, she turned to meet his serious countenance. "Then why . . . ?"

A.J. swallowed. "For a long time I hated Doug because I thought he had ruined a young girl's life. I quit my job and followed you to Montana. I had some kind of quixotic idea that I could make everything right by marrying you and raising Doug's son."

"Marry me?" Megan squeaked the words.

"Yeah," A.J. squirmed. "I soon got the impression you weren't interested." A self-deprecating smile twisted his lips. "The night I heard you talking to Jason about his father, I realized I'd been wrong again. I was sorry to lose you, but glad to learn I was wrong about Doug. Doug was always more than a friend to me. He was a kind of hero. He saved me from bullies when we were kids, and he always had time for me when my family didn't. I thought I owed it to Doug to give him a chance to meet you again and discover his son."

"Oh, A.J. I don't know what to say. I feel so sad for all you've gone through on my account." Impulsively she reached out to touch his arm. Her fingers collided with the ever-present camera dangling from a wide strap across his shoulder. She wished she didn't need to use A.J. to effect her escape. Wiping a tear away, she continued, "I really have appreciated your friendship both for me and for Jason. You've been there for us so many times, and I've never even thanked you, which makes me feel guilty to ask a favor from you."

"Megan, I'll do anything I can. I really do care about you and want to help you. I'm not religious like Brad, but sometimes I get strong impressions about people. I believed with everything in me, that you and Doug should be together. I'm sorry I hurt you. I'd do almost anything to see you happy."

"Get us out of here. Please."

Seeing the turmoil in his eyes, she wasn't surprised when he asked, "How can I take Doug's son away from him? I can't do that. But I owe you too, and if you're as miserable with Doug as you appear to be, I can't make you stay with him. I've really made a mess of things, haven't I?"

Taking pity on him, Megan softened her request. "Just take us away for the afternoon. I'm going crazy here. There's no television or newspapers. I've finished every book I brought. I'd just like to see people wearing business suits and doing things that don't involve getting dirty or wet." She knew she wasn't being completely honest in disparaging the mountains and claiming a greater affinity for city life than was really the case, but these were arguments A.J. could accept.

"All right, Megan. I can do that. It never occurred to me that a city girl would soon get tired of all this fresh air and solitude. I certainly never meant for you to feel like a prisoner here. You decide where you want to go, and we'll leave right after lunch."

"Thank you. I'd love to just spend a few hours at the library in Salt Lake. That's the only thing I really missed after I left. I spent a lot of time there when I was a young girl, and I really would like to see it again." She reached up to touch her lips to his cheek. His hand gripped her shoulder in a quick embrace.

"Jason is happy. I wish you were, too." A.J.'s sad smile twisted Megan's heart.

"A.J.," she promised solemnly, "no matter what happens between Doug and me, don't feel guilty. I know you want all three of us to be happy, but we're not your responsibility. It touches me deeper than you'll ever know to realize I have a friend who cares so much about my well-being." She paused, "I promise I won't cut Doug off from his son. Jason needs his father as much as Doug needs him." As she said the words she realized they were true. She would have to find a way to keep her promise.

As Doug came down the trail he congratulated himself on the plan he had worked out with Brad. A couple of relaxing days without other people around, or the constant pressure of parenting, would give him a chance to really court his beautiful wife. By sending Jason back to the city with Brad and his family, he and Megan would have a few days of privacy. They would be able to really talk and ease the tension between them.

He had never wanted another woman the way he wanted Megan, but he wanted more than a superficial relationship. He was gambling for much higher stakes. Deep inside he knew she wasn't ready for the intimacy of a sexual relationship, and that moving too fast would mean forfeiting all of his dreams of a lasting commitment to each other. Trust and friendship had to come first. He broke out in a cold sweat remembering the pain of waking the night before to find Megan in his arms, and how when she had snuggled closer, he had nearly lost control. He couldn't risk that happening. She needed time, which he doubted he could give her if he had to endure the forced intimacy of the previous night again. He wasn't going to repeat the mistake of ten years ago.

His eyes roamed ahead looking for Megan. He noticed Jason and Bobbi noisily cleaning their catch. Thinking Megan might have met up with them, he hurried forward. He stopped still when he spotted Megan and A.J. standing close together. Stunned he saw Megan reach up to brush her lips against his friend's cheek, and she didn't pull away when his arm circled her shoulders. *Not Megan and Allen!* Jealousy bit deeply. Why hadn't it occurred to him before that there might be more than friendship between them? Clenching his hands he longed to smash a fist into Allen's face. It took a supreme effort to turn around and return to the cabin by himself.

Lunch was an uncomfortable meal. Doug appeared quiet and preoccupied, while Allen exhibited signs of nervous tension by talking too much. Megan jumped at each unexpected sound. Bobbi and Jason continued arguing over who caught the biggest fish until Cathy informed them it was their turn to do dishes. Then Bobbi objected loudly while Jason sulked. Even the little girls seemed to pick up on the tension and were soon fussing and whining.

Pushing his chair back from the table, Brad plucked the baby from her high chair and washed her face before plopping her in Megan's lap. Cathy firmly separated Michelle and Ashley and marched them upstairs for naps. Brad picked up a sobbing Heidi who was clutching a little blanket Ashley had "borrowed" for her doll.

"Come on, Megan." Brad motioned toward the door with his head. "Let's take these two for a walk. They'll probably take a nap too once Michelle and Ashley have settled down."

Megan lifted the whimpering baby to her shoulder and followed Brad out the door. He turned in the doorway to remind Bobbi and Jason to get started on the dishes.

"And you two," he turned to the two men still sitting at the table. "I would suggest you find a quiet corner and work out whatever is bugging you!"

Megan followed Brad into the trees. For a long time neither spoke. The girls stopped fussing almost immediately. Heidi was all smiles and laughter to have her daddy's undivided attention, and Kelly was soon lulled to sleep by the rocking cadence of Megan's steps. She was a plump baby, but her weight felt good against Megan's shoulder. Softly she kissed the downy nape of the baby's neck and was assailed with a heartbreaking litany of "what ifs."

"She must be getting pretty heavy." Brad indicated the sleeping child. "Let's rest here in the shade." He settled his large frame on a tree stump in a shady glen. Carefully Megan eased onto a smooth boulder. Brad spread Heidi's blanket on the grass before setting the little girl in the middle of it. Megan watched entranced as he turned pine cones and flowers into a doll for his daughter. She listened to Heidi's happy chatter as she played with her daddy until she grew sleepy and drifted into trusting slumber.

"There's enough room here for Kelly, too." Brad reached for the baby. Megan's eyes never left his face as he knelt beside his two small daughters, a tender expression revealing emotions she had never before seen on a man's face.

A blue jay landed in the tree beside the rock where Megan sat, the bright blue of its feathers contrasting with the deep greens and gray of the pine. Overhead a thin wisp of white provided a break in the otherwise clear blue of the sky. The buzz of insects and the distant murmur of running water were the only sounds to break the stillness of an August summer day. In the distance Megan watched as a puff of air sent the trembling leaves of the quaking aspens, flashing gray-green, then silver.

"Megan," Brad's voice came to her. "It's obvious to me you're upset and hurting. I wish I could help you. If you'd like to talk, I'm a good listener."

It was tempting to pour out her anger and fear to this gentle man. Perhaps it was the doctor in him that made her want to confide in him, but she stilled the impulse by reminding herself that he had agreed to help Doug steal her son.

When he received no response to his invitation, Brad continued. "Doug is worried about you. Please don't think he has betrayed any confidence belonging just to the two of you, but he talked to me about the guilt he has carried all these years. He married you to protect you from the abuse he suspected you were suffering at the time. He feels he betrayed your trust, leaving you with no option but to run away. He spent months looking for you. In fact, he never really gave up hunting for you all these years. Now he has finally found you, he wants to make up to you for all the hurt and loneliness you've had to endure."

"I don't want anyone taking care of me or feeling guilty because of me."

"I can understand that. I also respect the fact that what you have gone through in your life has left you with an even greater need than most to be independent."

"Why can't he leave me alone? Why can't he see I don't need someone telling me what to do or worrying about me."

"He loves you—and he loves Jason."

"He doesn't even know me."

"Why don't you give him a chance to get to know you?"

"I can't." Megan bit her lip to keep from crying.

"You don't trust anyone, do you?" There was sadness in his voice. Megan shook her head.

Brad clasped his hands together between his knees and bent forward. "I know I'm risking your anger and possibly embarrassment, but I'm going to take that chance. Doug believes you were abused as a child by the very people who should have loved and protected you. If that is true you need to come to terms with it. Until you can admit it happened, and put the blame on those who hurt you, you can't live life fully or learn to trust. Trust is an important part of life and essential to loving." He paused, and when Megan remained silent, he continued. "You need to talk to someone. There are counselors and psychologists trained to help adults heal from childhood abuse. If you're not comfortable talking to me, would you let me give you the names of several colleagues who have had experience helping adults who suffered trauma as children?"

"I'm not crazy. I don't need a doctor. I just want to be left alone to live my life without interference."

"No, you're not crazy, but you are suffering from unresolved pain. I suspect the past few weeks have put an intolerable strain on you by making you remember things you would prefer to forget. A trained counselor could help you heal that pain."

"I don't want to talk about it."

"All right. I won't badger you, but I think you should give some thought to what Jason and Doug need. They love you, both of them, whether you believe it or not, and they want you to be happy." Brad hesitated before continuing, the words coming straight from his heart.

"There's someone else who loves you too, Megan. You have a Father in Heaven who cares what happens to you, who wants you to be happy."

"I'm not sure I believe that."

"When you think of all the hurt in your life, I'll admit it's hard to have faith in God, but if you take a closer look you'll have to admit you've been blessed and watched over too. God allows people to make their own choices, and the people entrusted with your care certainly made some wrong ones, but I don't think it was any accident that Doug was there on the mountain the day a frightened, injured girl needed him."

"What do you mean?" Megan held her breath, unsure whether she wanted Brad to continue.

"We had planned to come here to the cabin that day. At the last minute Doug decided he wanted to climb the back of Timpanogos or go on one of the Sundance trails. I think a higher power knew you needed him that day."

Megan remained quiet as Brad continued. "I don't know where you were or what you've done during the past ten years, but over the past two days I've discovered what kind of person you are. You're gentle and caring, you love your son and you're a good mother. You're intelligent and well educated. Your son is healthy, polite, and well-dressed. That doesn't sound like what one might expect from an abused, pregnant teenager suddenly finding herself alone in the world. Someone has been watching over you."

"What makes you think God has been the one to help me?" Megan wasn't certain what made her ask the question with its subtle negative implication. "God wouldn't help me. I don't even know how to pray."

Brad smiled. "I believe God hears the prayer in your heart, not just the one you voice aloud. He knows how hard you've worked to provide a good home for your child and live your life as a responsible, contributing member of society. Megan, he'll help you more if you'll let him. He wants you to be happy. Has it occurred to you he might have brought you and Doug back together because he knows you're strong enough now to put the past behind you?"

"I wish I could believe that," Megan sighed.

They sat on in strangely companionable silence, both deep in thought for a long time.

Finally Brad stood, stretched, and asked, "Should we take the girls back? I doubt they'll wake up when we pick them up."

Back at the cabin they discovered Doug and Allen were still stiff with each other. Allen was being adamant about taking Megan and Jason to the library. To Megan's dismay Doug announced he was going with them. She didn't dare arouse his suspicion by objecting. Allen didn't argue when Doug insisted on taking the Bronco instead of his Jeep. Bobbi objected to being left behind. Megan felt a twinge of sadness that her friendship with Cathy was destined to be so brief. Neither she nor Jason could say good-bye to their new friends.

Jason and A.J. settled in the back, leaving the front seat for Megan and Doug. Doug boosted Megan into the passenger seat, then stepped back to talk privately to Brad. Megan worried when she noticed that they seemed to be arguing. When Brad appeared to reluctantly nod his head, Doug turned to climb into the truck. Megan's eyes stayed on Brad as he stepped to her window. Placing both hands on the open window frame, his eyes never left her face.

"None of it was your fault," Brad told her softly and emphatically. "When you're ready, come back." The words were almost a whisper.

"He knows!" Megan realized with a start of panic. Is that what they were arguing about? Does Doug know too? Her throat felt dry, and she struggled to keep her hands still. Glancing covertly at the man beside her, she saw the way his jaw clamped tightly and his hands gripped the wheel with enough pressure to turn his knuckles white.

Determined to appear unaware of Doug's displeasure and avoid suspicion, she turned as far as her seat belt would allow, to talk to Jason and A.J. Soon a lively discussion of the earlier summer Little League baseball season was underway.

"Dad, did you play Little League?" Jason called to him.

"Sure did," Doug answered showing his pleasure at being included in the conversation. "Allen, Brad, and I were all on the same team.

One year we were region champions and got to go to Kansas City for the playoffs. It wasn't until high school that we settled on different sports."

"You played basketball, didn't you?"

"Yes, I still join a league at Deseret Gym every winter. It's great exercise."

"Karl Malone plays basketball for the Utah Jazz in Salt Lake. A.J. gave me a great big poster of him for the wall behind my bed. Have you ever seen him play?"

"You bet. He's a great player, but I think my favorite is John Stockton. I've been thinking of seeing if there are any tickets left for this season. Do you think your mom might let you go with me to a few games?"

"Wow! The Mailman! You'll let me go won't you, Mom?"

Doug winced at the dark look Megan sent his way. "Hey, not so fast," he cautioned Jason. "I don't have the tickets yet, and it's not fair to your mom to put her on the spot. Let's wait and see what happens. Okay?"

"Okay, but I'll be hoping."

He was glad when Allen tactfully changed the subject by asking Megan a question about a recent fraud case she had exposed. As they discussed the story, Doug listened avidly. He knew so little about Megan's life. He had a hard time equating the woman he had seen for the past week and a half with the brilliant, fearless woman he now saw emerging from their discussion. Could they really be the same person? He was surprised to discover himself looking forward to getting to know the woman Allen was drawing out. He had fallen in love with a girl; sharing a life with the woman he now glimpsed was an exciting prospect. He felt a moment of sadness when he remembered the vulnerable girl he had come to love and whose image had never faded from his heart.

"Do you have to go back to the TV station soon, Mom? Summer isn't over yet."

"No, summer isn't over yet. We still have a few weeks."

"Monica isn't going to believe what I did this summer."

"And who is this Monica, Jason is always talking about?" Doug whispered to Megan.

Overhearing the question Allen began to laugh. "Monica," he chuckled, "is a fiery-haired nine-year-old dynamo who is an expert on everything. If you don't believe me, ask her. She's been Jason's best friend and worst enemy since first grade, and I predict she's going to grow up to be as gorgeous as her mother and just as lethal."

Turning around, Megan began to laugh. "Why, A.J. You sound like you've been burned, and I didn't even know you knew Valerie."

Allen looked sheepish. "I think I'd better plead Fifth Amendment here."

Their light hearted teasing cheered Doug immensely. The kiss he'd seen her bestow on his friend had disturbed him, and several times he'd noticed Allen giving her casual touches which she didn't seem to mind. He didn't want to jump to conclusions, but Jason's casual references indicated Allen was a frequent, welcome visitor in Megan's house. At first he hadn't even considered the possibility there might be another man in her life. Since seeing them together, he hadn't been able to get the thought out of his head. That she might be involved with one of his best friends caused a double pain. Listening carefully, he was relieved to hear no jealousy in her voice as she continued to tease Allen about Valerie and some femme fatale at the television station where they both worked.

Suddenly the day regained its brightness. They emerged from Parley's Canyon and saw the city spread out before them. Doug smiled as he contemplated getting Allen alone for a few minutes so he could gain his cooperation. If Allen would take Jason back to the cabin, leaving Doug and Megan to enjoy a quiet dinner together, perhaps they could finally talk and start making some plans for the future. They could stay at the house tonight. He was glad Cathy had mentioned his mother was returning to St. George this week.

Doug didn't drive straight to the library. Instead he took a short detour first to show Jason the Delta Center, home of the Utah Jazz. Casting a defensive glance at his mother, Jason announced he would really like to see the Jazz play the Seattle Super Sonics there.

"I didn't think finding a parking spot near the library would be this hard," Doug commented as he made a second swing around the block. "I usually go to a smaller county branch library closer to home or use the University library." Spotting a parking space, he swerved into it before someone else could take it.

Megan was glad he wasn't too familiar with the main city library. It would complicate her plans if Doug and A.J. knew the building as well as she did.

As they entered the south doors, she took a moment to look around, assuring herself no extensive remodeling had taken place since the time she had spent most of her waking hours between school and dark sheltering there. She quickly noticed that reference desks and departments were a little different, but no real structural changes seemed to have been made.

She pointed out, ostensibly for Jason's benefit, the stairway and elevator, a few steps from the door. Rounding the corner of the elevator wall she indicated the escalator to the two upper floors and the north doors opening onto a large courtyard.

"Actually this floor is the middle of the library," she told Jason. "There are two more floors below this one that can only be reached by stairs or the elevator and two above which can be reached by escalator."

Leading the way, she crossed the wide expanse of floor, stopping twenty feet from a huge two-story-high painting. Slowly allowing her gaze to drift upward, she was assailed with all the feelings of hope that painting had instilled in her bleak childhood.

"What's it supposed to be?" Jason whispered.

"It looks like a bird flying over a cyclone to me," A. J. whispered also.

"No, you have to start at the bottom. A librarian explained it to me once. It shows the history of the people who first settled this valley. They were chased out of their homes back east because they were different. You can see the dark times of trouble they went through, then better times when they were more hopeful. Do you see the bones and broken wagon wheels that hint of the terrible struggle they went through crossing the plains? Even then, there were more bad times ahead, and some good ones. The bird at the top represents a seagull because the birds rescued the pioneer's crops when a black swarm of crickets would have eaten everything, leaving the people with a long, cold winter and no food."

"It reminds me of the legendary Phoenix rising out of the ashes of the past," Doug added.

"I always thought it showed that if someone keeps trying, even when everything looks black and hopeless, better things will happen, and if you keep trying long enough, you can escape into the sunshine and be free like that bird." Megan finished on a wistful note. Her mind flashed Brad's final words to her, "Come back."

Watching her expressive face, Doug found himself wanting with all his heart to give her the happiness and security he sensed she had missed all of her life.

"Hey, look at this!" A.J. drew everyone's attention to a display of books about the national parks of the United States and Canada. "Remember that backpack trip we took across Yellowstone?"

"The lady's room is on the second floor." Megan interrupted. "I'm going there for a minute. I'll introduce Jason to the children's library on the way." Without waiting for a response Megan took Jason's hand and walked away.

Doug's eyes followed them as they stepped onto the escalator. He admired the way her short flowered skirt swayed as she walked, and the matching cropped jacket clung to her figure. He grinned in appreciation as she took a large step onto the moving stairs, revealing her skirt wasn't really a skirt, but a clever pair of dressy short pants. Turning back to Allen he grasped the opportunity to acquaint his friend with his plans.

Before reaching the top, Megan informed Jason she wouldn't be going into the children's library with him, but she wanted him to go to the far end of the large room to wait for her. She didn't want anyone to remember seeing them together. Leaving him at the door, she hurried around the open area linking the three above-ground floors.

Below she could see Doug and A.J. with their heads still bent over one of the display books. Casually she walked past the fiction desk and entered the restroom area. In a stall she quickly reversed her shorts to a solid black and removed her jacket to reveal a plain white blouse. She stuffed the jacket in her handbag.

After a glance around, she stepped through a recessed door. A few swift steps carried her across a small amphitheater to another door. Cautiously she opened the door. She breathed a sigh of relief. Jason stood a few feet away. A bookcase obstructed the children's librarian's view of that corner. Drawing Jason behind her she retraced her steps. A quick glance revealed the fiction librarian was busy and had her back to them. They slipped behind the paperback racks into a recessed alcove.

Seconds later, she and Jason entered a staff elevator she had discovered by accident a long time ago. It carried them to the basement and an underground staff parking lot with an exit a block away.

Entranced with his mother's mysterious game, Jason never hesitated to follow her lead. They ran hand in hand for the distant opening onto the street.

Eleven

DOUG GLANCED AT HIS WATCH. "WASN'T MEGAN coming right back down?"

"They probably found some interesting books and lost track of time. Do you want to go upstairs and look for them?"

"I'm not sure." Doug glanced both directions. From where they stood, he could see both doors clearly. A nagging uneasiness was creeping into his mind.

"You don't think . . . ?" Allen looked stricken.

"No, I've had both doors in sight the whole time they've been gone. I wish we'd gone upstairs with them though. Come on, let's go take a look."

"I think one of us better stay right here. She may be waiting for us to go looking for her. That would give her a chance to leave while we're upstairs. You know she resents being kept at the cabin. If she wants to leave, she'll find a way."

"You stay," Doug agreed grimly. Taking the escalator stairs at a run, he stopped at the top to check the children's library. He scanned the room as rapidly as possible. He saw a six-foot stuffed kangaroo and a number of snug little nooks where a child could curl up with a good book, but no familiar faces. A sick feeling started low in his stomach. Back in the hall he hurried to the fiction area and began circling the open area to check the stacks. Again without luck. He questioned the librarian. She told him she hadn't seen a blonde woman with a young boy. She took pity on his increasing agitation and volunteered to check the rest room for his missing wife. No Megan.

He rushed back to the escalators and rode to the third floor. They had to be there! They weren't. On the way back down he checked with the librarians at both the fiction and children's desks again. No one remembered seeing a pretty blond woman in a pink and black suit with a dark-haired boy. Where could they be? The sick feeling grew stronger.

Back on the first floor the two men consulted together before they rushed to the doors at opposite sides of the building.

A quick scan of the streets and courtyard again brought negative results. Where could they be? They couldn't just disappear. Together Doug and Allen began a meticulous search of the building, finally recruiting the help of the security staff. Then they learned of the underground exit. It was nearly an hour later that Doug admitted defeat by calling the police to report his wife and child missing. He made another call to Judge Williams before the police would initiate a search, since they saw the missing mother and son as a domestic dispute, rather than as a possible crime.

Allen drove and Doug stared out the window all the way to the police station. Megan wouldn't run away again, would she? How could she do that to him? What if someone took them? Jason wouldn't leave without a fuss—they're so protective of each other. If one thought the other were being threatened. . . . He was too scared to complete a thought.

It didn't take long to fill out all of the papers and answer the detective's questions, but Doug was antsy. They should be doing something. When he and Allen were finally allowed to leave, they raced to the airport. If Megan had run away she would probably return to Missoula as quickly as possible.

Doug dropped Allen at the terminal entrance before heading for the parking terrace. He left the Bronco in the first open space he could find, slammed the door behind him and sprinted toward the terminal building. He took the skywalk, then the moving sidewalk at a run. He stopped in front of the departure screens to hastily jot down information concerning any flight headed north, particularly to Idaho or Montana. His heart pounded. He prayed they weren't too late.

Dusk had fallen, leaving only a few red streaks behind the western Oquirrh Mountains, by the time they finished checking every concourse and questioning every ticket agent. Wearily they returned to the Bronco. Doug grimly gripped the steering wheel in silence as he negotiated the airport exit and entered the freeway. Thirty minutes later they pulled into the driveway of Doug's east bench home. Doug went straight to the phone to check in with the police.

"Nothing?" Allen asked seeing Doug's shoulders sag before he hung up.

Doug shook his head and sank onto a deep leather sofa. He cradled his head between his hands. Over and over, one word was screaming in his head. *Why?*

Allen picked up the telephone. First he called a friend in Park City who agreed to drive up to the cabin to alert Brad to return to the city and to let him know they wouldn't be going back to the cabin that night. He placed another call to his boss in Missoula. After five rings the Prescot's answering machine asked him to leave a message.

"This is A.J.," Allen said, leaving Doug's area code and phone number. "This is an emergency. Get back to me fast!"

The night passed slowly. Around midnight Allen went to the kitchen to fix sandwiches. He returned to the study to nibble morosely while Doug mostly ignored his. Alternately they paced the floor and sat silently staring at the telephone. Eventually Allen made his way upstairs and sprawled across a bed; Doug yielded to a fitful doze on the short sofa in his study just as the first light of morning was painting a pink and gold glow above the rugged Wasatch Mountain peaks.

The shrill ring of the telephone instantly brought Doug to his feet.

"Douglas Beckwith, here." Tension stiffened his shoulders as he waited for the caller to speak.

"Hello," Allen echoed from the upstairs extension.

"A.J.?" A brusque voice demanded. "What's going on? If you're planning to quit too, forget it. I expect to see you back here September first, and if you've got anything to do with Megan Nordfelt running out on me, you're fired! You bring her back with you and there will be a b—"

"You've talked to Megan? Where is she?"

"With you, I thought. She called me late yesterday, said she had some personal problems. First she asked for a six-months leave of absence, and when I refused to give it to her, she quit."

"Do you have any idea where she was calling from?"

"No. Noisy place, lot of racket in the background."

"Look," Doug interrupted. "I'm Megan's husband, Douglas Beckwith. It's vitally important that I find her and our son. If there's anything you can tell us, I'd really appreciate your help."

"Husband! A.J., you'd better start explaining. I won't stand for any ex putting pressure on my best reporter. Besides I thought you and she . . . uh . . ."

"Megan is married to a friend of mine. They've been vacationing together, and yesterday they had a little tiff. Megan took off, and we can't find her. We're worried about her; that's all. If you hear from her again or have any idea where she might be, if anyone contacts you for a job reference, anything like that, please get in touch with us. Okay?"

"Okay. Oh, Megan did say to let you know her house key is taped to the bottom of the middle drawer of her desk here at the station, if you want it."

After assuring Prescot he would be back on the first, Allen hung up the phone. Back in the study he faced Doug. "I can't believe it. She's given up her job and obviously has no intention of returning to her house. What about her car, her clothes? How can she just walk away from everything?"

"I've got to find them," Doug groaned. "Anything could happen to them out there. Where is she? I don't even know what I did to make her run again!"

"It's my fault." Allen took the blame. "I had no business meddling in her life."

"Don't blame yourself. I'll always be grateful you gave me a second chance. I'm the one who somehow frightened her into running away again."

Both men showered, shaved, and forced down cold cereal before setting out to check the bus station, taxi cabs, motels, and car rental agencies. Periodically they checked with the police. A little after noon, Doug was told to go back home and wait for the police to contact him. There had been several reports of possible sightings of the runaway pair, but the most promising was from the Nevada Highway Patrol. An officer reported seeing a biker headed west with a blonde woman and a kid on the back of his bike. The woman had caught the trooper's eye because, unlike her companion who was attired in the usual denim pants and black leather jacket, she was dressed in a bright pink and black suit like she was going to work in an office or something. He didn't get a good look at the kid.

Doug paced the floor, jubilant one minute and angry the next. "Wait 'til I get my hands on her," he growled. "She should have better sense than to go off with some stranger on a motorcycle. Doesn't she know how dangerous those things are?"

"You can't be sure it's her," A.J. cautioned. "Somehow I can't imagine the woman who hates riding in a convertible with the top down ever climbing on a motorbike."

"How do you know she doesn't like sports cars?"

"Convertibles. She hates convertibles. Every time she rides in mine, she complains about the wind messing up her hair."

Doug didn't like the picture that came to his mind of Megan and Allen riding around in a convertible together.

"She might not have had a choice," Doug scowled. "If the guy threatened Jason, she'd do anything to protect him."

The doorbell rang, and Doug charged to the door. He flung it open to find Brad and Cathy standing on the doorstep.

"Any news yet?" Cathy asked as they stepped into the hall.

"Come on in." Briefly he explained the possible sighting. Doug paced the room as he talked. His fingers scraped through his hair.

"If it is her, what are you going to do?" Brad asked, his eyes full of concern.

"Go get her. I've already called the airport to arrange for a private plane. It will be ready to take me anywhere I need to go as soon as I get word."

"Doug, sit down," Brad advised. "Have you considered that she might not want to come back with you? She ran away, and unless you plan to keep her a prisoner, she'll run away again the first chance she gets."

Doug sank into a chair. Despair slumped his shoulders and he could feel a slight tremor in his voice as he whispered hoarsely, "I can't just let them go. I love her. I've loved her since the day I found her all broken and bleeding up there in the mountains. And I've only just discovered Jason. I can't lose him now."

"I don't want to upset you, Doug. Just tell me to butt out if I'm prying where I shouldn't, but what happened to make her take off like that?"

"I don't know. I've asked myself that same question a million times. We got off to a rocky start. She was so scared she passed out when I barged into the cabin in the middle of the storm that first night. I hadn't even shaved yet; I must have looked like a wild man. I was so excited about seeing her again, I never considered she wouldn't be glad to see me." It was difficult to speak around the lump in his throat. "When I found out Jason is my son, I lost my temper and made a lot of crazy threats to take him away from her."

Doug lunged to his feet. He paced a relentless path to the window and back. He could feel his friends' eyes following him. He didn't want to look too closely to see if they held censor or pity.

"We were just starting to get to know each other when I found out she's been worrying I might send her to jail for taking the money I tried to give her father."

"What money? Why would you give her father money?" Allen was clearly puzzled.

"Lee Fergus threatened to make trouble so I gave him money to go away. I thought it would protect Megan. Just then my mother collapsed from her heart attack, and Lee ran."

"Did they ever catch him?" Cathy wanted to know.

"Everything went wrong. Lee must have dropped the money while he was jumping out a window, and Megan took the money."

"Wait a minute." Allen went back to an earlier point. "You think it was her father who attacked her?"

Doug nodded.

"When we were at the cabin, Megan began to talk about what happened ten years ago when the bunch of you showed up. I thought that might make matters worse, but actually it seemed to help. The first day we were all together she seemed happy, and for the first time I began to really hope."

He paced the length of the room again, pausing with his back to his friends, before continuing.

"The night we spent together after your arrival was a rough night. I thought Megan would have hysterics when she found herself alone with me. She's terrified of being touched."

Allen seemed about to interrupt, but Doug didn't give him a chance.

"I know, it's not touching; it's being restrained she can't handle. Actually she handled spending the night with me quite well. I was the one who found sharing a bed with someone I love but can't touch too difficult. That's why I asked Brad to help me have some time alone with her. I thought if Jason wasn't around and we didn't have the pressure of sharing a bedroom, we might be able to really talk to each other."

"She sounded pretty desperate when I met her in the woods," Allen put in. "She asked me to help her get away. When I told her I couldn't do it; she begged me to just take her away for a few hours, and stupid me, I didn't even suspect what she had in mind. As protective as she is of that kid, if you threatened to take him away, no wonder she ran." The look he gave Doug revealed more than Doug wanted to acknowledge.

Cathy turned angrily on Doug and Allen. "How could you do that to her? After being treated badly by her parents and having a baby alone when she was a teenager, she probably doesn't have much reason to trust anybody. You didn't help matters by tricking her into a situation where she had no control. No wonder she thinks you're trying to run her life, Doug."

"I'm not trying to run her life," Doug tried to defend himself.

"Yes, you are. And you," she turned on Brad, "could have told me the truth. Didn't it occur to you I might have helped her if I had known what was going on, instead of placing her in a position too uncomfortable to tolerate." She glared at them.

The ringing of the telephone cut through the discussion. Doug picked it up. They learned little as Doug listened carefully and then hung up. He swallowed twice and cleared his throat before turning to face his friends.

"That was the highway patrol. The Nevada troopers caught up to the couple on the motorcycle. It wasn't her. She obviously set it up though. The woman claims some high class lady approached her at a restaurant near the bus station in Ogden and offered her fifty bucks to trade clothes. She agreed because she and her boyfriend needed the money to buy gas to get to California. The kid wearing a helmet turned out to be a dog."

A bitter little laugh escaped Allen. "Now that sounds like the Megan Nordfelt I know."

"The Ogden police checked with the bus station. No one remembers seeing anyone fitting the descriptions of Megan and Jason. The only child's ticket they sold yesterday was to a child traveling with both parents to Denver. They aren't even sure whether the child was a boy or a girl. They're checking on the possibility she may have attached herself to some guy traveling alone in order to disguise their departure."

"It looks like she anticipated being followed and is taking steps to cover her trail." Brad picked up a pen. He appeared deep in thought as he twirled it between his fingers. "Perhaps we ought to be trying to discover where she's going and how much money she has at her disposal. Did you find out where she went when she disappeared ten years ago?"

"No. All I know is she had the baby in a Catholic hospital, but I have no idea which state she was in. Allen found her in San Antonio, and she's been in Missoula, Montana, ever since. She sent me a cashier's check from a bank in Chicago three years ago to pay back the money she took. I hired a detective agency to trace every Fergus in the country, poured over records at the genealogy library, and nothing. The police notified me when Megan's parents were killed in a car accident in Oklahoma. When I checked with the authorities there, I found that Lee had served ninety days in a county jail for some kind of petty theft right after they left here. They left the same time Megan did, but the detective I hired said she was never with them. I flew to Oklahoma and paid for burying them in hopes Megan might show up."

"Why Fergus?" Allen asked clearly puzzled.

"That was the only name I had. Her father was Lee Fergus and the name on our marriage certificate is Margaret Karel Fergus."

"You really don't know anything about her, do you?"

Doug bristled. He glared resentfully at his friend.

Allen was silent a moment, then spoke with difficulty. "I'm sorry, Doug. Megan's last name was Karel. Lee never legally adopted her. Her own father is unknown. She lived with her grandfather, Walter Karel, on a little farm not far from San Antonio when she was a child. She was placed in foster homes a couple of times because of neglect and abuse. She left Texas with her mother, Lee, and a little brother in 1977."

"Did she tell you all this?" Doug asked, incredulity and jealousy mingling in his voice.

"No, not Megan. She never told me anything. When I found her in San Antonio, I followed her to an attorney's office where I got friendly with her attorney's legal assistant. What she didn't tell me, I found out from the old man's neighbor, a gossipy old terror who didn't mind telling me everything she knew about the scandalous Karel family."

Allen walked across the room to the grand piano. He gave the metronome a little shove, then turned to face the group again.

"Megan's grandfather was an alcoholic with a mean temper, but when he was sober, he took care of Megan pretty well. She and the little brother were inseparable. It was Megan, not her mother, who took care of the boy. The neighbor said she suspected Lee beat the girl, and even the boy was often bruised. Before the old man died, he sold his patch of ground for a lot of money to a big corporation who built luxury condominiums there. Megan was in San Antonio to settle his estate when I happened to see her. He left everything to her except a small trust fund for her brother. The legal assistant told me Megan stayed in touch with her grandfather by phone."

"Where is her brother?" Cathy asked eagerly. "Maybe she's with him."

"No one seems to know."

"Megan mentioned a little brother once," Doug said, "but the detective I hired didn't turn up any information about a brother, and he certainly wasn't with the Ferguses when they left here or when they died in Oklahoma." Doug felt nauseated. He'd seen what Lee had done to Megan. What kind of fate had the other child suffered?

"Could you get any information by tracing her grandfather's money or her checking account in Missoula?" Brad wondered.

"I'd be willing to bet the answer is no," Allen answered before Doug could respond. "By now she's probably gotten her hands on a computer and wiped out every trace of that money."

"Do you know where she got the Nordfelt name?" Doug hoped there might be a hint to her whereabouts in the name.

"I haven't a clue."

Doug felt he was floating in space without an anchor to cling to. Allen's remark was too true. There wasn't a clue.

"If you'll excuse me," Doug said quietly. "I'm going to call a detective friend of mine. I don't think the police are going to find her." He stepped into his study and closed the door behind him.

An hour later Brad tapped on the door. "May I come in?" He hoped he could offer his friend some comfort.

"Yes." Doug sat behind his desk with both elbows resting on its smooth expanse, his hands cradling his head as though it ached fiercely.

Brad settled in a chair and looked at Doug for several minutes before speaking. "When you first decided to marry Megan, I understood you never intended it to be a real marriage but simply a way to protect her. You obviously changed your mind. I can see you love Megan and Jason and how much you want to stay together. In your place I would want to maintain the marriage too, no matter what. However, have you really looked at her point of view? What does she want?"

"That's the whole point isn't it? I've never looked at her point of view. In my arrogance, I thought because I love her, she had to love me, too."

"There's another unpleasant factor you have to face. It's obvious she was severely abused as a child. She may not be capable of participating in the kind of loving, trusting relationship you want."

Doug raked his hair back with one hand. "I thought she would get over that in time. Now I don't know if she ever will, and I'm afraid I hurt her worse than Lee did. If I hadn't been married to her, what I did would have been considered statutory rape because of her age, though I swear, there was no force involved."

"Doug, don't be too hard on yourself. I know you didn't mean to hurt her then, anymore than you want to cause her pain now. Abuse is seldom a one-time occurrence. Years of pain and fear leave deep scars. I doubt that day in the mountains was the only time her stepfather attacked her."

Doug raised stricken eyes to his friend's face. "She's been through so much pain and grief. At the cabin I really tried to reassure her. I wanted to comfort her and relieve her of some of the responsibility she has shouldered alone for so many years. She accused me of sexually harassing her. I thought it would help if she became accustomed to me touching her. Obviously I only succeeded in reminding her of that filthy scum."

"Doug, I'd like you to talk to a friend of mine who counsels abuse victims and their families. If you ever find her again, you need to be prepared to cope with her unique problem. You have to understand that all the years of pain and helplessness she survived left deep scars."

Brad was right. He definitely needed help. He needed to find out why Megan was afraid of him and why she'd run away again. Most of all he had to find her. "I won't give up. I believe with everything in me that behind all her fear, she loves me, and we belong together. It's a good thing her stepfather is already dead, or I'd probably kill him."

"Try to let the hate and anger go," Brad cautioned. "When you find Megan, you mustn't muddy your relationship with any lingering thoughts of revenge or regret. Remember, she needs help in learning to let go of the past."

A silent tear slipped down Doug's cheek as he turned beseeching eyes to his friend. "There has to be something I can do. When she disappeared ten years ago, I nearly lost my mind. She was just a kid with a broken arm. I had nightmares of her being attacked, turning to prostitution to feed herself, of having nowhere to sleep, or taking up with criminals. Then I became angry. I told myself I didn't care. She deserved whatever happened to her because she turned her back on my generosity. Next I became angry at God. It wasn't fair to give me a miracle then take her away. Why did I experience that burning certainty that she was meant to share my life, if she wasn't? This time I not only feel as though half of me is missing, my son is missing, too."

"You can't blame God."

"No, I stopped doing that a long time ago. If anyone is to blame, it's me."

Brad clasped his shoulder in an understanding embrace.

"Actually I find myself turning to God more every day. He's the only one who can help me now. More importantly, I've got to believe he's helping Megan and Jason too."

They sat together quietly as the shadows began to lengthen. A long, long day was drawing to a close. Once more the telephone rang. Without much hope, Doug lifted the receiver.

"Hello, Douglas Beckwith speaking."

"Daddy!"

"Jason!" Doug nearly shouted. "Are you all right? Where are you?"

"We're just fine. Mom said I could call you, so you wouldn't worry about me."

"Is she all right? Is she there with you?"

"Yes. We're both kind of tired."

"Son, where are you?"

"I don't know the name of the town, but we're at an airport."

"Put your mother on the phone. Tell her I want to talk to her."

There was a pause. Sweat trickled down Doug's face and the telephone receiver became damp in his hand.

"She said no, but she said to tell you not to worry. We'll be fine, and she'll let me call again when we get to where we're going."

"Where are you going?"

"I don't know. Mom won't tell me. Dad, I didn't know we were going away without saying good-bye. Will you tell A.J. and Bobbi good-bye for me?"

"Sure, son."

"And Dad, I have to go now, but Mom said we'll see each other again. I wish we could be together all of the time."

"I do, too."

"Bye, Dad."

"Don't hang up yet."

"I have to."

"All right. Call me again soon. I love you. Tell your mother, I love her, too."

Hearing the click at the end of the line, he still continued to hold the receiver until Brad took it from him and gently placed it back in place.

Twelve

SUMMER TURNED TO FALL AND DOUG FOUGHT despair. Megan and Jason had disappeared into thin air. The detective he'd hired provided him with a report verifying everything Allen had told him of Megan's childhood. It made him sick and angry. Social services' records were sketchy, but they painted a picture of a little girl who frequently went hungry, lacked adequate clothing, and was alone too much. This little girl clung desperately to her elderly, alcoholic grandfather.

There were periods when she lived with her mother. Those periods always ended with emergency treatment in a hospital and a stint in a foster home. Case workers labeled her quiet, uncooperative, shy, sullen, stubborn. The last notation indicated her mother had married.

Doug had a pretty good idea of what kind of life Megan lived after that. So he was even more astounded at her work and all she had accomplished during her three years in Montana. He felt admiration for her strength and determination. The detective discovered she had gone to Channel Two highly recommended from a station in Chicago. In Chicago the trail disappeared. She had only been there a few months and evidently made no friends. Personnel couldn't produce her application, and all trace of her background was missing from their computer files.

He returned often to the mountains where, alone, he could think. One day he found himself in the clearing where he had picnicked with Megan and Jason, the day Jason first called him Dad. He lay on his back staring at the sky. Bare branches were silhouetted against gray. The spruces looked dark and forbidding. Snow would come soon.

Where was Jason? he asked himself. Would his son grow up without a father? Slowly he sank to his knees. *A boy shouldn't grow up without a father when he has one who wants to be there for him as badly as I do. Please let me be more than a voice on the telephone to him.*

Jason had called twice since that first call. The calls were brief and unsatisfactory. Even so, Doug knew Jason was angry over their separation. He feared the boy would give Megan a hard time. He didn't want that. After a couple of long sessions with Brad's therapist friend, he had a better idea of what his threat to take Jason had done to Megan. He suspected that whatever sent her running from him was somehow linked to that threat. *Keep Megan safe and help her learn to trust me. Give me a chance to assure her I'll never take our child from her.*

A wave of helplessness swept over him. He'd never felt so out of control. All his life he'd known that if he worked hard he could get good grades; a job well done brought praise and better pay. Kindness to his neighbors resulted in their consideration for his mother while he was gone for long stretches. He enjoyed the benefits of friendship by being a friend. Now he wanted something with all his heart, something good, not evil, and there was nothing he could do to obtain it. He dealt with formulas every day, but for this problem there was no formula.

That's it! He jack-knifed to a sitting position, then scrambled to his feet. This is what Megan feels. This utter lack of control. He paced the clearing. He could see the helplessness of a child who couldn't count on a meal or an uninterrupted night's sleep—a child who never knew if a simple word or action would bring pain and misery. Suddenly he thought of Allen's description of her house, of the neat precise way she dressed, the way she had cut off the links to her past. Megan created stability in her life by inventing a safe island she could control. She made the rules, set the boundaries, and only allowed Jason inside. Only with Jason could she be herself. Jason was the one person she trusted, and he had threatened to take Jason away. Would she ever feel safe enough to let him in too? Doug spent weeks pondering that question.

By Thanksgiving the snow was deep, but he wasn't interested in skiing or snowmobiling. Doug found an old set of scriptures his mother bought him the year he'd taken seminary with Brad. He found the books comforting when he sat before the fireplace alone each night. He never wanted to be far from his telephone. He instructed his secretary to accept all calls and put any call from his wife or son through immediately. Only on Sundays did he allow Brad to drag him away to attend church. After one of Jason's hurried calls he indulged in a flurry of Christmas shopping.

Christmas came and went with only a telephone call, a little longer this time. Gradually he faced what he had to do. On a Sunday in January he sat across the kitchen table from Brad and Cathy. "Next time Jason calls I have to get a message through to Megan. I have to let her know I won't interfere in her life anymore, and I won't take Jason from her."

"Oh, Doug." Cathy covered his hand with her own. "Will she believe you? And can you really do that?"

"I don't know. It's all I can think of. I've been reading a lot lately about free agency. The message I'm getting is that even when I know she needs love and security, I can't force my version of that onto her."

"It would be better if you could talk directly to her. If you suddenly stop searching, Jason might think you don't love him."

"I know that. But how can I talk to her when I can't find her."

"I've been thinking about that," Cathy mused. "You've done everything to trace Megan, but perhaps you should be tracing Jason. There was a little girl he talked about last summer. . . ."

Rain slashed across the bus windows with renewed ferocity as the clumsy vehicle slowed to a stop. Megan pulled her coat tighter and checked to make certain her scarf was knotted securely. Picking up her bag and umbrella she prepared to exit. She shivered in the cold when the driver threw open the door to the blustery, wet afternoon. Puddles were everywhere.

She stepped from the bus and splashed her way to the curb, carefully keeping her face turned away from the stinging force of the icy rain. Dodging puddles she hurried across the street and through wide iron gates. She pulled open the door and entered the welcoming warmth of the grand old mansion. The scuffle of feet and the sounds of children's laughter filled the air.

"Meggie!"

She found herself facing her old friend and benefactor. The sister's face shone with an inner light, causing her rather plain face with its colorless eyebrows, once freckled nose, and thin mouth to appear beautiful.

"You're soaked to the skin, child. You'll be catchin' your death of cold if you're not careful. Tsk! Look at you. Seattle in the winter is no place for a Texas miss, I'm sure. Here, come into my office for a hot cup of tea."

Megan pulled her wet scarf from her head, sending a spray of moisture flying as she stepped into the cozy room. She was soon settled in a roomy wing chair with a hot cup between her hands, warming her fingers. She turned her face expectantly toward Sister Mary Katherine, who sat frowning as though concentrating on a weighty topic. Her fingers tapped against the side of the china cup which sat untouched on her desk.

"Megan, dear," she began. "I've been thinking long and hard about you and your little lad. He's not happy here, you know."

Megan nodded her head as Sister Mary Katherine continued, "He's a young man meant for wider spaces and greater activities than we can offer here. And he's missin' his father." She paused. "You're for missin' the man, too, aren't you now?"

Unable to say the words aloud, Megan admitted with a nod of her head that she too missed Jason's father.

"You could take the boy and go on home," the sister suggested. "The semester ends soon. It would be a good time for him to transfer to another school."

"It's not that simple," Megan objected. "I've thought about it for weeks now, and I know Jason needs to be in a school with older children. I suspect it was mostly for his sake you extended your program to include the fourth grade this year. He misses playing ball, and yes, he misses his father, but I can't go back, and I can't give him up." Anguished tears welled in her eyes.

"I wasn't meanin' you should give up the boy," the sister hastened to assure Megan. "He's needin' his father, but that doesn't make him need you any less. I was thinkin' you should all be together. And it's plain to me you're longin' for the man. Do you think maybe he isn't missin' you and the boy?"

"Oh, he's definitely missing Jason. Jason called him on Christmas, and there's no mistaking how much he wants his son to be with him. I'm not sure how he feels about me, though. He says he wants me, but I'm not certain that's enough. Even if it is enough, I couldn't go back now."

"Do you trust this husband of yours?"

"I'm not sure. Sometimes I think I do, then I remember he tried to take Jason from me."

"Have you talked to him about that?"

"No." Megan took a slow sip from her cup, slowly savoring its warmth. "Jason talks to him, but I haven't spoken to him since we left Salt Lake."

"You should, you know, but to do that you'd have to trust a wee bit. Your trust has been betrayed, so it's natural for you to expect hurt and betrayal. 'Tis a vicious cycle, child. That's for sure. You have to trust before you can love, but you'll have to love a whole lot before you'll dare to trust." She reached inside her desk and handed a slip of paper to Megan. "Call this number," she urged.

Megan looked at a woman's name and a telephone number. "Who is she?"

"Years ago when Emily Baker was going through a bad time we became friends. Later she became a doctor who specializes in helping children and adolescents deal with trauma. Among her patients are a number of adults who were physically and emotionally injured as children. I'm sure she'll see you. Perhaps if you better understand your own childhood, you'll feel more confident about meeting Jason's needs."

"Last summer someone else told me I should see a counselor or therapist, but I wasn't ready to listen." She folded the paper and tucked it in her bag. "Perhaps now is the time."

Later that evening Megan sat across from Jason in the living room of the small apartment she was renting. Though clean and neat, the simple furnishings left the room lifeless. Perhaps it was the lack of personal touches that lent a bleak air to the rooms. She could buy nicer furnishings; she still had a little of grandfather's money left, and she'd earned a good salary at Channel Two. She stared resentfully around her. They'd been happy in Missoula. She missed their house and her work. If only A.J. had minded his own business! No, she didn't really blame him. He'd only wanted to help. Each day the conviction grew that she did need help. First thing in the morning, she'd call Emily Baker.

While Jason watched television, Megan tried to read. Her mind strayed not to the house in Missoula, but to the cabin. Over and over she relived the days spent there. A faint smile turned up one corner of her mouth as she remembered Doug's laughter over her big fish.

"Mom, Missoula got eight inches of snow, and Park City got fourteen." Jason looked disgruntled as he added, "All Seattle got is rain and more rain."

Megan sympathized with her son's disappointment. He was restless and unhappy.

"Can we go home pretty soon? I'm missing winter. Last year A.J. took Monica and me sleigh riding, and he was going to teach us to ice skate this year. Remember the fort we made in the backyard and all the snowman Indians we built to attack the fort?"

"It was fun, wasn't it?"

"Dad said he bought me a snowmobile suit for Christmas. He said he got some other neat stuff for me too and some stuff for you. He's going to leave them all wrapped up so they'll be surprises when we go to his house. He said he hasn't gone snowmobiling or to a Jazz game yet. He says they wouldn't be much fun without me. When are we going to Dad's house?"

Megan found it increasingly difficult to deal with Jason's desire to see his dad, and he was still unforgiving of their quick departure from Salt Lake and the promise she had extracted from him to not tell his father where they were now living. It wouldn't be long before he rebelled against that promise. She had been only a couple of years older when she'd found a way to sneak calls to Grandfather without Lee's knowledge. Grandfather had accepted her collect calls, sympathized, but done nothing. Doug wouldn't just do nothing. If Jason asked, Doug would be on the first plane to Seattle.

She was beginning to feel she hadn't been fair to Doug either. She shuddered thinking how it would be if their roles were reversed—if Doug had Jason and she didn't know where they were.

A trip to the library while she waited for her first appointment with the doctor yielded a large number of books, some written by therapists or victims. Some she rejected, some made her cry, and some opened her eyes so that she saw her past in a different light and held out hope that she could plan a future instead of running from her past.

She dressed with care for her appointment. When she was ushered into the doctor's office she was surprised to see a thin woman in her mid-thirties lounging on a sofa in tight black pants and an over-sized poncho. Emily Baker's wispy short hair emphasized her huge eyes and too generous mouth. Megan liked her at once, although still she felt uncomfortable talking about the things that had happened to her as a young girl.

"You need to talk about it," Emily told her one day. "Unlike some abuse victims, you've always known what happened to you, but until you end the secrecy, you won't be able to stop the isolation and begin to connect with other people in a positive way."

It became easier with each session to talk about Jason and eventually Doug, but the years with Lee were too painful to verbalize. Each time she tried to say the words out loud, fear swamped her, and she stammered like a frightened child.

Night after night she lay in bed, and no matter how hard she tried to block him out, her thoughts always turned to Doug. She questioned whether she might have misunderstood the conversation she overheard between him and Brad. Had she acted too hastily? Brad's words the afternoon they took a walk with the little girls kept returning to haunt her. Could it be true Doug really cared about her? Whenever she let Jason call his father, Doug never failed to tell Jason to tell Megan he loved her.

For months after they reached Seattle, she found her sleep interrupted by tormenting dreams of being in Doug's arms. He would touch her face with the tips of his fingers, then lean forward to kiss her mouth. Before his lips touched hers, Lee would thrust them apart. She could hear Doug calling her over and over while Lee stood over her and laughed. Then she would be all alone again, and so cold she felt like she was carved out of ice. But lately she didn't think of Lee at all, asleep or awake. Instead she found herself growing increasingly frustrated to awake from dreaming of Doug and realize he wasn't there beside her.

Sometimes she regretted taking such drastic measures to cover her flight. She had anticipated Doug might find a way to trace her credit card purchases or the transfer of bank funds, so she had deliberately searched for a job in the banking industry where she would have computer access and could cover her trail.

It was a Thursday morning a few weeks later when a watery sun peered through the clouds as Megan dropped Jason off at school. He'd dawdled around getting ready, spilled his milk, and cried because she wouldn't let him stay home. He complained his stomach ached until they missed the bus and she had to call a cab. Her high heels clicked rapidly on the sidewalk as she returned to her cab waiting in the thinning mist. Suddenly her feet flew out from under her as one heel slid on a small patch of ice. Before she crashed to the pavement, strong arms gripped her tightly, helped her gain her footing, then slowly, as though with reluctance, let her go.

Megan gasped for breath, then raised her eyes to thank her rescuer. Her eyes widened, and her mouth formed a little round O.

"Doug?" she whispered.

"Hello, Megan." His eyes never left hers. They looked flat and bleak, making Megan shiver.

"I . . . How did . . . ?" What could she say? She looked longingly at her cab. Could she reach it before Doug could stop her? As though reading her mind, Doug stepped to the curb, handed the driver a bill, then waved him on his way.

"No!" She stepped toward the curb. "I'll be late for work!" She turned accusing eyes toward the big man who appeared even bigger in his heavy fleece-lined jacket.

"My car is right over there. I'll take you wherever you need to go." He didn't touch her as he ushered her toward a dark Buick. Seconds later she was seated beside him in the close confines of the car. For just a moment he sat hunched over the wheel staring straight ahead.

Time and light seemed to telescope while she waited for him to turn on her. She noted the way the dark hairs on the backs of his hands curled slightly. She was aware of small rivulets of water forming drops where his wet hair was too long and tended to curl. The drops, one by one, found their way to the white fleece of his collar. Faint sprinkles of moisture soaked into the navy blue of his coat, losing their sparkle to become simply darker spots on the denim. The denim of his jeans stretched tightly across his thighs and down his legs to disappear into familiar saddle tan boots. Raising her eyes, she found deep blue eyes devouring her from head to toe.

"Where to?" he asked grimly.

They rode in silence for several blocks. Megan looked everywhere but at the man beside her. Nervously she clenched her fists inside her coat pockets.

"Relax, Megan." His voice sounded more tired than vengeful. "I didn't come for a pound of flesh. I only came because I need to know if you're all right. I can't face another ten years of wondering if you have enough to eat and a safe place to sleep."

He stopped the car in front of the building where Megan worked. "What time do you get off work?"

"I don't work a full day." She hesitated before adding. "I leave at three each day to pick up Jason."

"I'll pick you up right here at three, then."

Megan reached for the door handle. She paused, seeing the fatigue in his face and every move of his body.

"What will you do until then?"

"Don't worry. I won't go after Jason." The words were laced with strangely gentle sarcasm.

"I didn't mean that; you look tired. I just wondered if you have a place where you can rest for awhile."

"I'll get a hotel room and sack out for a few hours."

"Here." Megan withdrew her apartment key from her bag. Quickly giving him the address, she added, "If you oversleep, don't worry. We'll be there by four." Turning she hurried through double glass doors.

Doug sat staring at the key in his hand until honking horns behind him reminded him he was double parked. Could he trust her to be waiting at three? He could go to Jason's school and wait to see if she went to get him. No, if he wanted her to trust him, he had to trust her, too. She said she would see him by four.

Once she reached her desk, she made a quick telephone call to Sister Mary Katherine. She asked the sister to keep an eye on Jason and make certain he didn't leave the school with anyone else, especially his father, before she arrived to pick him up.

After hanging up, Megan sat for long minutes staring blankly at the computer screen before her. Her knuckles turned white as she clutched the edge of her desk. Slowly one hand formed a fist and she brought it to her mouth. Not even the pain of her own teeth sinking into the tense flesh of her hand lessened her anguish. She could no longer hide from Doug. It wasn't fair to Jason. If only she were stronger. They could go with Doug, live in his house. But he would expect her to be a wife in every way. Could she do that? Even for Jason?

Gradually she became aware of a hand shaking her shoulder. Her eyes slowly drifted upward to the face of a concerned co-worker.

"Are you all right?" The woman—Megan thought her name was Marsha or Cindy—appeared concerned.

"Yes, uh yes, I'm fine," Megan stammered.

The woman looked at her uncertainly. "You don't look well. Why don't you go to the ladies' lounge and lie down for a while? If you don't feel better in an hour or so, perhaps you should go home."

Megan studied the worried face of a woman who appeared to be a few years older than herself. It suddenly occurred to her that she had been far more alone during the past ten years than she had needed to be. How many Marshas or Cindys or even Cathys had offered her friendship, but she had been too absorbed in her fears to see? Something was happening to her. Where was the calm shield that kept her from caring, from feeling?

"Thank you, I think I will," Megan responded softly. On shaking legs she made her way to the quiet lounge. There she leaned weakly against a cool marble wall trying to gather her thoughts. Suddenly barely audible words poured from her heart. *Dear God, help me be strong enough to do what is best for Jason.*

Rain was falling again by the time Megan left the shelter of the bank building that afternoon. She immediately spotted the Buick parked at the curb. The sight of the driver hunched over the steering wheel watching her through the rain sent a shaft of summer light flashing to a deeply hidden recess in her heart. Doug leaned over to swing the passenger door open as she approached. She slid onto the seat and quickly brushed water droplets from her sleeves. She placed her closed umbrella on the floor. They exchanged tentative smiles before Doug pulled into traffic.

Driving took all of Doug's attention at first. Once out of the heavier traffic, he glanced over at the young woman sitting quietly beside him.

"Before we pick up Jason, I think you should know he didn't tell me where to find you. Monica did."

"Monica! But how did she know? Jason hasn't been in touch with her."

"He didn't have to. She's awfully good at putting two and two together. Cathy suggested I ask her, since, according to Jason, she's the expert on almost everything. She said he might have gone to see his grandmother. She said you usually spend Thanksgiving with her. Since I happen to know his only living grandmother is my mother, I doubted that. But then, she added that his grandmother is a nun who teaches school in Seattle. I remembered what you said about a nun helping you when Jason was born, his interest in the Super Sonics, and that Jason said it was raining on Christmas. I caught the first flight leaving Missoula for Seattle. The telephone directory told me the rest."

"I see. You probably won't believe me now, but I was going to call you this weekend to ask you something. I would have given you our address."

"What did you want to ask me?" Doug suspected he knew what she wanted, and despite his resolve, he cringed waiting for her to say she wanted a divorce.

"Maybe we could talk about it later."

"Okay." Doug was willing to put off the discussion. "May I take you both to dinner tonight?"

"I'm not dressed to go out." Megan attempted to discourage him, but was secretly pleased when he brushed off her excuse.

"Neither am I. We'll just go some place casual like a pizza parlor or a fast food place. Okay?"

"Jason will love that. You won't believe it when you see the amount of pizza that boy can put away!"

When they arrived at the school, Doug helped Megan from the car. She almost had to run to keep up with his long steps as he hurried to meet Jason.

"Dad!" Jason let out a wild whoop and tore down the hall to be caught up in his father's arms. Doug swung him around in an ecstatic bear hug. Megan found herself wiping away a tear as she watched their enthusiastic greeting. Feeling a slight movement beside her, she turned to meet Sister Mary Katherine's beaming face.

"Jason, go get your coat," Megan broke in softly. "Hurry, your dad is taking us to dinner."

Doug placed Jason back on the floor. Immediately he began to dash down the hall. Midway he stopped, rushed back to give his dad one more hug, then ran back to his classroom. Doug watched until the boy disappeared through the door. Swallowing hard he turned back to Megan.

His eyes widened slightly as he beheld the tall nun, attired in a stately black robe. Something white and starchy surrounded her face and a long chain held a flat, gold cross to her bosom. His experience with nuns was very limited. As a young boy he had visited the Cathedral of the Madeline in Salt Lake City with a group of friends, but the sisters he saw there weren't dressed like this one. Once his company sent him to South America where he remembered a couple of nuns jaunting around in a jeep to all the small villages. They were dressed in blue street-length dresses and wore little scarves that seemed to flutter from the tops of their heads. He'd probably seen sisters dressed in white at several Catholic hospitals he had visited over the years. This one reminded him of his mother's favorite Julie Andrews movie. He half expected her to begin singing. Awkwardly he extended his right hand.

Her eyes twinkled as she firmly shook the offered hand. He only half heard as Megan introduced the nun as Sister Mary Katherine. He felt like a fish out of water. Nothing in his experience had prepared him to know what to say to such a person until his eyes met hers. Something in their depths put him at ease. Somehow he knew she had witnessed many things in many years and had become adept at understanding. He felt overwhelmed with gratitude for this woman who had rescued Megan and Jason ten years ago and had provided them with a point of stability ever since. A spark of rapport seemed to pass between them, and Doug found himself chatting easily with her until Jason came charging back down the hall.

Jason's coat hung from one arm and his boots flapped on the wrong feet. Megan took a moment to straighten him out before they waved good-bye to Sister Mary Katherine. Jason gripped one hand of each of his parents as they dashed through the rain to the car.

They ordered pizza with everything but anchovies on it. Jason picked off the green peppers. "Peppers are okay when they're cut in little pieces, but I don't like them in big round circles." They laughed and joked their way through dinner. It seemed to Doug that a magic circle had been cut in the rainy night, creating a private haven of warmth just big enough for the three of them. He longed with all his heart to keep the magic circle, but he knew it couldn't be. He'd traveled a hard road to reach this point. He knew what he had to do.

Later at the apartment Doug removed his boots to avoid making wet marks on the carpet. Jason followed suit. Together they popped popcorn and talked until Jason began to yawn and rub his eyes. Megan was surprised to see how late it was and hastily sent him to get ready for bed. At first he resisted, demanding to know whether his father would still be there when he got up in the morning. When Doug said he would get a hotel room nearby, but be there in time to give him a ride to school, Jason wasn't satisfied.

"There are two beds in my room. You can sleep with me," the boy pleaded. "Please." Hurrying to his mother's side he continued his plea. "Tell Dad to stay, please Mom."

"If you want to stay, Doug, it really is all right. It is kind of late to start looking for a hotel."

Jason hugged her tight. Doug's eyes met hers over the top of their son's head. Doug sent the boy on to bed, assuring him he would join him later.

The apartment was small and seemed smaller with Doug's presence. He seemed to fill every corner. Megan sat at one end of the sofa, and Doug at the other, making her conscious of how short it was. Only inches seemed to separate them. Several times she tried to start a conversation, but the words always died in her throat before she could push them past her lips. Doug shifted restlessly as though he might have the same problem.

Absently she reached for the popcorn bowl on the coffee table in front of her. Her hand closed around Doug's. Instead of quickly releasing the hand, she found herself examining it as though she had never seen a man's hand before. She ran her fingers across the fascinating hairs across the back. One finger traced the thickness of his thumb nail. Her thumb brushed lightly across the smoothness of his palm to calluses at the base of his fingers.

Doug sat still, afraid to move, before slowly raising his other hand to her face. Gently he smoothed back her hair, then let his fingers trace the outline of her face. They lingered at her mouth.

Hesitantly she transferred her hand to his face. Slowly she explored his features like a blind person committing every detail to memory. As her fingers traced the outline of his lips, his arms encircled her, drawing her closer in a careful embrace. His eyes seemed to hold her mesmerized. Somehow her fingers slipped from his mouth and her arm slid around his neck. Doug's mouth descended gently onto hers. She wasn't afraid.

She wasn't afraid! For a crazy moment she thought, *I can do it. I can go with Doug. Jason can have both a father and a mother.*

"Look at me. Open your eyes and look at me." Doug's voice came as though from far away. Opening her eyes she looked directly into his.

"I won't let what happened ten years ago happen again." Doug's voice was hoarse.

She stared uncomprehending into his eyes. Didn't he want her? Was it really only Jason he wanted? No, she wasn't a naive girl, she knew he wanted her. Slowly she leaned forward until her lips barely grazed his.

"Love me, Doug. Please, love me," she whispered.

"Megan, I do love you, and I want to love you every way a man can love a woman, but when I wake up in the morning I want you there beside me, and every morning after for the rest of our lives."

"Doug, I can't promise you that." Tears quivered on the tips of her eyelashes. Forever was too much to ask.

"I know, honey." A big hand cradled the back of her neck, drawing her face against his chest. Her shoulders trembled, leaving him aching to comfort her.

"I don't understand." She raised solemn damp eyes to his. He could see the pain and uncertainty there. It made no sense to her that after all his efforts to make her accept his physical advances, now he was refusing hers. He wasn't sure why she was offering herself to him, but instinct told him she felt no real desire to consummate her love for him.

He knew without being told, that all her life she had felt rejected and unwanted and right now she was feeling he was rejecting her, too. Slowly his hands framed her face, one fingertip brushed away a single crystalline tear. Deep within his soul he prayed for a way to make Megan understand the depth of his love for her and that she didn't have to do anything she didn't really want to do.

"Megan, remember that night when Judge Williams talked to you in the study? Without meaning to, he hurt and frightened you. You ran to your room to cry yourself to sleep. I was angry with him and wanted to go to you. He insisted you needed some privacy, some time to think about what you wanted to do with your life. He said the attraction between us was all mixed up with my exaggerated desire to be a hero, and your desperate need for a parent to love and care for you. He said we had poor reasons for marrying. He warned me that by marrying you so hastily, I had carelessly tossed aside the social taboos that otherwise would give you the time you needed to grow up. Our relationship needed an opportunity to develop the trust which should exist between two people who love each other. I was irritated with his moralizing."

Never taking his eyes from hers he continued. "Over and over I've told myself that when I went to you later that night I only meant to offer you comfort, but the truth is, just as I used protecting you from your stepfather as an excuse to marry you, I used your need for comfort as an excuse to make love to you. I wanted you to be mine, but I was going away, and I was afraid I would lose you while I was away. My lack of faith in our relationship caused us both years of needless pain. Can you ever forgive me for all I've done to you?"

"Doug, I needed you that night."

"You needed a friend, not a lover."

"I don't regret having Jason."

"No, darling. Neither of us will ever regret Jason, but my actions then were selfish and irresponsible. Jason should have come to us when we were both ready to be parents. I didn't really consider your needs then, anymore than I did when a miracle occurred, bringing you back into my life last summer. Neither time could I accept that your needs might not be the same as mine."

"I still don't understand why you. . . . I'm not a child now."

"No, you're definitely not a child now, but I want more than a lover, I want a wife."

"But no matter what happens in the future, right now we are married, and it wouldn't be against my will, so how can it be wrong? I could try to be what you want me to be."

"Oh, Megan, you're making this difficult." Lightly he touched his lips to her temple. "I don't want you to change yourself into some image you think I want. I want you to just be you. I want you to trust me and love me. I want you to come to me for no other reason than because you desire me."

Megan squirmed uncomfortably in his arms. He let her go.

"Just now you told me you aren't sure you want to share your life with me. I see marriage as a total commitment, not a legal technicality. For right now, I'm only asking you to think about giving us a chance to know each other better. I swear I won't pressure you for sex, because to me a physical relationship means commitment. I'm ready to make that commitment, but you're not. Until you're ready, I can wait."

"I'm not afraid."

"That means a lot to me, but it's just the beginning. All my life I've been taught that the physical relationship between husband and wife is a beautiful and desirable part of marriage, a sacred gift from God to be cherished and enjoyed by both partners. Lately I've come to recognize that those standards mean more to me than I ever understood before. If we skip the preliminaries again, there's no way I will be able to give you the time you need to discover whether you want to spend the rest of your life . . . and maybe beyond, with me. Megan could you allow me that one thing, just for us to get to know each other?"

She leaned her head against his chest. The room was silent and neither one spoke for a long time. Against her ear Megan could hear the steady beat of Doug's heart. It comforted and soothed. She was tired and wasn't sure she understood all he had said. Could she let Doug get to know her better? There were things in her past it would be better to keep secret. Some undefinable light in Doug's eyes would be lost if he knew. Little by little she lost the battle with fatigue.

Tenderly Doug lifted the sleeping woman in his arms. He didn't interrupt her slumber as he carried her to her bed and gently removed her shoes. His hands lingered as he pulled a comforter over her. When her small fingers grasped his wrist he glanced uneasily toward her face. Wide, lake-blue eyes gazed back at him.

"Stay with me tonight," she whispered. "Please just hold me until morning."

A silent groan rose in his throat but never passed his lips as he stepped out of his shoes and lifted the quilt to slide in beside her. Was it a good idea? He couldn't deny Megan's first acknowledgment that she needed human warmth.

They lay still for long minutes, then Doug lifted one arm to cradle her against his side. He lay motionless, staring at the ceiling he could barely see in the darkened room, listening to Megan's breathing return once more to the gentle pulse of slumber.

Father, please help me, the words thundered in his head. *I can't forget for a moment this woman is my wife. We are married, and I want this marriage. Help me to understand her needs and know what to do to make our marriage last. If she would be happier without me, give me the strength to let her go. I'm so afraid of hurting her again.*

Thirteen

MOM!"

Megan struggled to open her eyes.

"Mom! Dad's gone. He didn't sleep in my room." She heard the frantic note in her son's voice just before the door to her bedroom crashed open.

"Mom! Dad isn't . . ." His voice trailed off as he spied his father's tousled head emerging from beneath the comforter on his mother's bed.

"Dad!" Tears streamed from the boy's eyes. He hurtled across the room to throw himself into his father's arms. "I thought you were gone," he sobbed.

"I'm right here." Doug's arms closed around the child.

Megan felt a lump in her throat as she watched Jason and Doug, their curly, dark hair blending together as Jason leaned his face against Doug's crumpled shirt.

"I wanted you to sleep in my room." He turned his face up to speak. Doug placed his hands on either side of the boy's face.

"I know you did. You wanted it to be like when we were at the cabin. That was a special time for both of us."

Jason looked at his mother, then back at Doug. Color began creeping up his neck, turning his ears red. Looking at the floor he mumbled, "Monica says . . ."

"Never mind what Monica said," Doug cut him off with a chuckle. "We can talk about what Monica said some other time. Right now it's time for you to get ready for school. I'll fix your breakfast this morning. Let's give Mom a chance to sleep in, okay?"

"Isn't Mom going to work?"

"Not today," she murmured. "I arranged to take the day off."

"Good," Doug whispered as he planted a quick kiss on her upturned mouth.

"I'm not going either, then," Jason announced.

"Yes, you are," Megan informed him in no uncertain terms. "This is the last day of the term. Your dad will still be here after school. Scoot now!"

Brushing one finger against the tip of Megan's nose, Doug grinned before stepping out of bed. He pulled the comforter up to her chin and admonished her to go back to sleep. She lay in bed listening to Doug's deep voice coming from the kitchen, then Jason's higher-pitched tones. Laughter reached her ears. She hadn't heard Jason laugh like that for months, not since she took him away from Utah. As soon as they left for Jason's school, Megan dialed Emily Baker's number.

When Doug returned to the apartment after dropping Jason off at his school, he found Megan fully dressed in navy blue slacks with a feminine silky white and navy polka-dot blouse. Her eyes wouldn't quite meet his as she stepped back to allow him entrance. Though his arms ached to gather her to him, a voice of caution warned him to go slowly. Methodically he removed his coat and boots. He waited for Megan to speak. When she nervously straightened a stack of papers on a small table without saying anything, Doug sighed. A cold fear began to take hold of his insides.

"Come sit down." He indicated a place beside him on the sofa. Seeing her hesitation, he continued, "I just want to know what you're thinking."

Gingerly she sank into a wing chair near the end of the sofa where he sat. Doug watched her clasp her hands tightly.

"Megan." A deep sadness filled him. Reaching out he placed one hand on the arm of her chair. "I didn't come here to frighten you again or to make you do anything you don't want to do. Last night was . . ." He swallowed. "I never expected to hold you. It was a fantasy, a miracle come true. When you left last summer, I thought it was because you couldn't bear my touch. It both helps and hurts to learn I'm not completely repugnant to you."

"I left because I heard you making plans with Brad to take Jason away from me." Nervously she chewed the side of her thumb, afraid to meet Doug's eyes.

Doug's weary sigh was the only sound in the room. He flexed his fingers, then clasped his hands together. "Obviously you didn't hear my whole plan. It was never my intention to take Jason from you. I only wanted some time alone with you." He stared at his clenched hands. He sucked in a long, shattering breath and continued, "Actually I came to Seattle to set you free. I can't bear the thought of you running and hiding, afraid to use your own name, always looking over your shoulder to see if I am coming to tear Jason away from you. He's yours. You can go anywhere you want, do what you want. I won't interfere. I only ask that you'll let me see him occasionally."

Megan ran her tongue across dry lips. She couldn't look at Doug.

"Are you saying you want a divorce?" There was a noticeable tremor in her voice.

"No!" Doug exploded to his feet. From the corner of his eye he saw the way she flinched away from him. He made an effort to control his voice and avoid any threatening gestures. "I don't want a divorce, but I'll give you one if that's what you want. Last night I let myself hope, but if you can't . . ."

"Doug, sit back down." She reached for his hand. Her eyes wouldn't quite meet his as she struggled to find the words she needed to say. "I didn't grow up the way you did." Her voice was so soft he had to strain to hear her words. "My childhood was full of fear and insecurity. Sometimes there wasn't enough to eat, several times I was placed in foster homes with strangers, and I was . . ."

"I know, honey."

Megan looked startled at first, but continued with more confidence. "My grandfather cared more about me than my mother did, but he was an alcoholic who was never strong enough to place my needs over his need to drink. I don't know who my father was. My mother was a weak woman who followed one lover after another until she met Lee. She would do anything to hold him." Megan's hands formed fists, and she swallowed hard before continuing. "She let him give my little brother away—actually, he probably sold him. I was so helpless. I couldn't protect Buddy."

"Don't tear yourself apart remembering old pains, Megan." Doug ached to take her in his arms and soothe away all of the hurt. Instinctively he knew he couldn't do so, even as he sensed the terrible toll the past had taken from her.

"No, I have to tell you."

He quietly stroked her hand as she continued, "I tried to stay out of Lee's way, but he always found ways to make me feel trapped and afraid. He locked me in closets, he held me down and tickled me until something would snap and I couldn't feel anymore. He held me by my hair and forced me to kiss him before he would let me go. My hair seemed to hold some fascination for him, which is why I keep it short now. I was scared to go near him for fear he would reach out and grab an arm or a leg. He beat me with his fists when I didn't do what he wanted me to do quickly enough. My little brother and I slept under my bed at night so he couldn't get us while we were asleep."

Painfully she gripped Doug's hands as she relived the nightmare. Her voice lowered to a raspy whisper. "I didn't grow up as fast as most girls do, and I was nearly sixteen when my body suddenly changed. Lee noticed and I found myself constantly dodging his hands. I would wake up in the night and he would be in my room. He held me down and . . . and . . . When I complained to my mother she got angry and accused me of trying to take him away from her. I hated her for not protecting me. That day . . . that day . . . he . . . the day you found me he . . . he hurt me . . . he . . . ."

"I know what he did to you." Doug knew better than to tell her it didn't matter; that it was all in the past. To his sorrow he knew it still mattered very much to Megan. He ached for her pain, and though he had struggled for months to overcome his own anger toward the man who had so badly abused her, he felt rage sweep through him again at the injustice of an adult so misusing his power over a child.

"To this day I don't know whether my mother finally tried to protect me by letting me marry you or whether she thought she was getting rid of competition." Her voice rose as she left her chair to pace with short, jerky strides across the room. She paused to look back at him, her face contorted with the magnitude of her emotions. "I hated her. Does that shock you, that I hated my mother? I'm glad she's dead. She was weak and stupid. Lee beat her, but she stayed with him. She knew what he was doing to me and did nothing to help me." She swiped a fist across the tears streaming down her cheeks.

Doug walked toward her. His big hand pulled her face against his shoulder. He held her gently while she sobbed. Perhaps voicing her pain would help to free her. He had expected hate and rage directed toward Lee, but he hadn't understood how deeply her mother had hurt her, too. He understood something of the hopeless despair that kept battered wives from leaving their abusive husbands, but he suspected Megan wasn't ready to hear anything that might exonerate her mother even a little.

The memories were painful, but Emily had been right. The words had to be said. She felt compelled to make Doug understand. "I hated them both so much that before Jason was born, I decided I couldn't bear for my baby to have any of their names, and I didn't feel I had a right to use yours, so I changed my name. I didn't know what name to use until Sister Mary Katherine said her papa's name was Nordfelt. He always felt badly because he didn't have a son to carry on his name, and since nobody was using it, she thought it would be all right if I borrowed it."

Tears were falling, muffling her voice, as Doug sat down and lifted her to his lap. He tried to soothe her as though she were still the hurt, lonely child of which she spoke.

"No one is ever going to hurt you again like that. Shh, you're safe now. I'll take care of you."

"Doug, I don't want you to take care of me." Seeing the hurt in his eyes, she continued, "Don't you see? I have to be strong within myself. I have to be able to take care of me."

"I don't understand what you're saying, unless you're telling me you don't want to give us a chance, that you don't trust me. Last night taught me one thing. Even though you have my word I'll never try to coerce you to be my wife, in my heart and in my head, I can't get past knowing you are. I have strong feelings about providing for and protecting my family. You are my family—you and Jason. I love you, Megan. I want you with me. If you want a career, fine, but I want the right to take care of you."

Megan tried again. "I'm not explaining this well. I have hurt inside for so long. I've been afraid to let anyone close to me for fear they would hurt me. I've felt guilty because I couldn't make grandpa love me enough to stop drinking, guilty because my own mother preferred a cruel sadist to me. I've wallowed in guilt because I couldn't save Buddy. It was my fault Lee tried to blackmail you and the judge thought you hurt me. I took your money and the whole horrible mess caused your mother to have a heart attack. I was wrong to keep you and Jason from knowing each other. I feel so much guilt and anger. I'm not ready to be a wife, especially yours."

"Why especially mine?"

"You're good and honorable. You deserve a wife with a background like yours, someone who is trusting and unafraid, who doesn't know the things I know, someone who isn't dirty."

"You have a right to feel anger, Megan, but the last thing you are is dirty because of someone else's rotten choices. None of that was your fault—not the tiniest bit. Don't let the anger destroy you. Express it and forget it," Doug urged. "Nothing your parents or grandfather did was any fault of yours. You were a child, there was nothing you could have done to protect yourself or your brother. My mother is fine— you don't need to feel guilty about her, and there is still time for Jason and me. All we need is to be together with you. Please be my wife."

"I can't! Find someone who . . ."

"I only want you." Taking her face between his hands he enunciated clearly as he looked deeply into her tear-reddened eyes, "Megan, believe me, you have nothing to feel guilty about. You were a child. The people who were responsible for you are the guilty ones. They betrayed you. You have nothing to feel guilty about, and don't you dare ever again think of yourself as dirty."

"I can't help it, I know I'm not good enough for you."

"Don't say that; don't even think it. I'm not perfect, but I do know you're perfect for me. If you won't share my life, there won't be anyone else. I discovered a long time ago, I'm strictly a one-woman man, and you're the one woman for me. I love you, Megan, and I think you love me."

Megan shook her head painfully. She couldn't accept his words. She couldn't deny them either. From the first time she'd opened her eyes to see his worried face she'd felt something pulling her toward him.

"Lee said I was born a tramp, mama accused me of being a tease, and I've seen the same look in other men's eyes that I saw in Lee's.

Doug, you said some beautiful things last night, but I wasn't raised that way. I never really knew anything about sex except dirty jokes. I just knew I didn't like Lee to touch me. He hurt and frightened me."

"Did I hurt you, Megan?"

"No, but after I saw you give money to Lee and I thought you were buying me, I felt ashamed, cheap, dirty. I never wanted anything to do with sex again."

"Then what was last night all about?" He brushed her temple with his lips.

"That was selfishness," Megan choked. "I needed . . ."

"You needed to be held and I needed to hold you. That's part of love. It can lead to sexual fulfillment, but it doesn't have to. When it does happen for us it will be right and beautiful. There's nothing dirty about sex with the right person at the right time."

Megan was silent for a long time. She bowed her head against Doug's chest as she pondered his words. She wasn't being completely honest. The words were difficult to say.

"It was more than that. Jason needs you, he's unhappy here with me. I thought if I could sleep with you, maybe I could go with you and Jason would have both of us."

"You don't have to sleep with me to come with me. You can have your own room if you want. We have the rest of our lives to get to know each other, and when you're ready for an intimate relationship, it will happen."

The rough texture of Doug's sweater felt good against her cheek. She felt surrounded by his warmth, his scent, and his love. If the time ever came when she could join her life with any man, it would be with this one. She wished she could walk into the bedroom, pack a bag, take his hand, and go wherever he led. Why couldn't she? An icy shiver shook her shoulders, a faint line of perspiration glistened on her face. No, she couldn't do it. She'd told him the truth when she said she wasn't ready to be a wife. Worse she wasn't ready to be a mother. She'd closed her eyes too long to what she was doing to Jason. She hated her parents for what they'd done to her. She loved Jason, he was her world, and she would never hit him or deny him food, but emotionally she was hurting him. Someday he would hate her for denying him a normal childhood.

Straightening so she could see Doug's face, she reminded him, "Remember when you first arrived I told you I planned to ask you something?"

He nodded his head.

She took a deep breath. "When you go, will you take Jason with you?"

Doug sighed in defeat. "Oh, honey, I'm not taking Jason from you. I was wrong to have threatened to take him. As much as I love him and want to be there for him as he grows up, I only threatened because I was trying to hold on to you. I knew you'd never leave him, and as long as you thought I wouldn't let him go, you'd have to stay too."

"No, Doug. That isn't what I mean. I want you to take him. You were right about Jason; he really does feel too much responsibility for me. Besides, he's unhappy here. I have to do what is best for him. Right now it looks like staying with you is what is best for him."

"But you'll come too, won't you?"

"I can't. I'm not giving him up. I won't ever do that, but there's something I have to do here first. Last summer Brad told me I should seek help to deal with my past and Sister Mary Katherine gave me the name of a doctor here in Seattle who helps her patients deal with the aftermath of childhood trauma and abuse. I've only been seeing Dr. Baker for a few weeks, but I feel strongly that I should go on seeing her."

Doug gently squeezed her fingers. She could see understanding and acceptance in his eyes.

"There's something else I have to do too, and I can do it best if I start here where I know the library and university research materials best. Later I may have to go back to Texas. I have to find my brother. I've wanted to search for him for years, but I've been afraid."

"Afraid of what?"

"Afraid of what I might find, afraid I wouldn't find anything, afraid of the memories."

"And what if you don't find him?"

"I don't know exactly, I just know I have to try. I'll call every week so Jason won't forget me, and if I'm ever able . . ."

"Not if, *when*. When you're ready to come to us, I'll go anywhere to get you, meet any flight. And every day I'll pray that one day you'll come to stay."

"Your feelings might change."

Doug smiled gently. "No, if you can't believe anything else, please believe my feelings for you will never change. I love you. I've loved you for ten years, and I'll love you forever."

His commitment touched her. Deep inside she understood that it took a man of special strength to love so unconditionally.

When Doug realized he couldn't change her mind, they spent the remainder of the day talking quietly while Megan packed Jason's belongings. When she wished aloud that Jason could collect his things from the house in Missoula, Doug told her he already had the key; Allen had given it to him. He promised they would stop to pick up anything Jason wanted, and he offered to send her whatever she needed for herself. Eventually they decided he should sell her house and arrange to have her car shipped to her.

Megan made arrangements to transfer her son's school records from both Seattle and Missoula to whatever school Doug chose. She gave him a small card from her wallet outlining Jason's immunization record.

"Oh, and don't let him have a dog."

"Why not? Don't you think a boy should have a dog?"

"He'll beg for one, but don't give in. He's allergic to dog hair."

Looking sheepish Doug admitted, "I am, too. My mother wouldn't let me have one either, though I used to sneak in a few good romps with Brad's old collie."

"And probably spent the night scratching and sniffling."

With a guilty smile, Doug admitted he had.

Together they decided that making the break as quickly as possible would be best for Jason. Doug called the airport and made reservations for an early morning flight the next day.

When they told Jason he was returning to Salt Lake City with his father he was ecstatic until he realized they would be leaving his mother behind. Then he rebelled, refusing to go until both parents managed to assure him he would see his mother again, and he could talk to her on the telephone as often as he liked.

"It's not the same thing." He tried unsuccessfully to hold back his tears. He threw his arms around Megan's neck. "Why can't we all live together like we did at the cabin?"

How could Megan explain to him that she still had too much anger and fear to work through to adapt to the kind of life both of the "men" in her life wanted for her. She needed a period of mourning for the little girl who was never allowed to be. And just as important, she had to find Buddy. Jason wasn't mature enough to understand that another little boy's face still haunted her dreams at night nor to understand her abhorrence of losing her independence. She couldn't explain to herself why she viewed marriage as being swallowed alive by someone stronger and more powerful than herself. Perhaps it was linked to all the years she had felt like a thing rather than a person. And there was no way to explain that being away from her for a time would be best for his own emotional development.

"Mom, let's go back to our house in Missoula. Dad could come, too. I don't want to go to another strange school where I don't have any friends."

"Jason," Megan glanced self-consciously toward Doug before continuing. "When we were at the cabin last summer, Bobbi's Mom and Dad told me about a friend I didn't even know I had. He's your friend too, and he'll be wherever you are. Sometimes I talk to him when I'm scared or lonely, and he helps me feel better."

"Who is he?" Jason was clearly puzzled. "Do you mean A.J.?"

"A.J. is our friend, yes, a far better friend than I ever suspected, but I meant your Heavenly Father."

"She's right," Doug echoed softly. "I've learned to talk to him, too."

"You mean praying? Mom, I'm getting kind of big for that!"

"I thought I was too, but lately I've found out I was wrong. When you get to Salt Lake, talk to Bobbi's daddy. I taught you lovely verses about God, and the sisters at school taught you one way to pray, but Bobbi's daddy can teach you how to really talk with God."

"Why can't Dad teach me?"

Megan caught her breath. There was an unmistakable challenge in Jason's voice, and she knew Doug hadn't missed it.

"I can, if you want me to." She hadn't expected Doug's calm response.

"Well, all right, I guess." Jason didn't sound enthused.

"I'll take you back to your mother if you don't like living with me," Doug promised. "And you can call her every week, every day, as often as you like."

Hugging him tightly Megan assured Jason that she would always love him and that she wasn't abandoning him. They would be together again soon.

"Jason, you don't have to be cut off from me or your Dad ever again. You're too grown up for that. You know names and telephone numbers now, and I promise I'll never ask you to keep secrets from your father again."

When Jason asked if his dad would sleep in his room that night, Doug glanced at Megan. She glanced away.

"Your mother and I need to talk for awhile, son." Doug bent over to give the boy's quilt a tug. "We'll be in the living room if you need us." In truth, he didn't know how he was going to make it through the night.

He hadn't expected Megan to make it easy for him, so he was caught unaware when with a wry smile, she dumped an armful of pillows on the floor.

"I don't think either one of us is brave enough to set foot in the bedroom tonight." Her honest bluntness caught him unprepared. "You said we were going to talk, so talk." She sank gracefully onto a fat, square cushion.

Doug grinned at the woman sitting cross-legged in a pink track suit on her pillow who looked as innocent and young as a child. Lowering himself to a reclining position, he propped the arm supporting his head on another pillow and began to talk.

He told her about his childhood, his father, and his work. She coaxed him to keep talking. He spoke of his beliefs and values, and still she urged him to continue. Little by little, he began to realize one lifetime wouldn't be long enough to share all his hopes and dreams with Megan.

He wanted her to open up too, but he hesitated to ask questions about her painful past. Earlier he had witnessed her hurt and rage, but when she began to speak, it was of the little brother she wanted to find. She shared Jason's early years and her own stumbling effort to be a good mother, and her drive to complete her education and become self-supporting. They talked of their questions about life, shared their doubts and concerns, and spoke about the newly awakened hunger they both were experiencing to become acquainted with spiritual power. They laughed together until Megan's laughter turned to tears.

Doug wiped her eyes and held her hand until long after she fell asleep. For long hours he lay on his back with the fingers of one hand entwined with hers. His own tears ran across his cheeks and down the sides of his face before disappearing into the pillow beneath his head. With all his heart he wanted to take her back to Salt Lake with him. He would have to draw on every reserve of strength he had to be patient and wait for her. He knew she wasn't offering him any promise that she would ever live with him, but giving him Jason, even temporarily, had to mean there was some hope.

Sometime after midnight he heard Jason leave his bed in the room next door, pause in the bathroom, then silently enter the room where Doug lay, wide awake, unable to sacrifice to sleep one precious moment of being with Megan. The child trailed the comforter from his bed behind him as he walked. He felt Jason curl up on the other side of his mother. Doug was glad the boy had come. They needed to be together. He reached across the woman sleeping between them to draw the comforter around the child's shoulders and tug it across Megan to enclose the three of them in its warmth.

When morning came, no one could swallow any breakfast. By silent agreement they determined not to shed any more tears. Megan had dressed in a soft gray wool skirt and a pale pink angora sweater and checked her hair and makeup carefully. It was important to her that Doug carry away with him the best image she could manage.

She decided not to go with them to the airport. It would be too hard to keep her composure if she saw them actually board the plane.

Doug didn't argue with her decision. He had his own nightmare vision of leaving her standing alone in a bare, impersonal air terminal and of her finding her lonely way back to an empty apartment. He feared that in the trauma of the moment, he might grab her and force her to go with them, ensuring her hatred forever.

Doug carried their bags down to his car, leaving Megan and Jason alone for the last time. Struggling to keep back the tears, they hugged each other tightly.

"Call me tonight." She ran her fingers through his curls.

"I will, Mom. If you get lonesome, I'll come right back."

"I'll be fine, though I'll miss you very, very much."

"Come with us, please, Mom."

"Oh, honey, I wish I could, but there are things I have to do first."

"Someday you'll come, won't you, Mom?"

"Yes, someday."

"Is that a promise?" Doug's voice caught as his arms came around Megan, too. He wasn't sure he had the strength to walk away.

"I think it is." Her voice held a touch of wonder. Her eyes raised from where her face pressed against the rough denim of his coat to the firm jaw, lingered on his full lips for a breathless moment, then met the deep blue of his gaze. She marveled at his dark, thick lashes so like those of their son.

Bending his head his lips brushed hers lightly, then settled firmly in a kiss so deep and giving she felt as though he were lending her his height, his weight, and all his strength. In exchange she gave him a promise of hope. Only the hope that she would some day come to him made it possible for him to walk out the door.

Leaning her forehead against the glass window of her tiny breakfast nook, she could see the street below. It did no good to tell herself it would be better not to watch, she couldn't help herself. As the black Buick, carrying Doug and Jason, left the parking area and pulled onto the street, her tears began. In just seconds the car disappeared from sight. For a long time she continued to stare at the street where it had disappeared.

Rivulets of rain streamed down the glass marring the view, but she didn't seem to notice; the storm in her heart sent lashing rain streaming down her cheeks in greater torrents than the one wetting her window.

Fourteen

ARCHING HER BACK, MEGAN SHIFTED uncomfortably in her chair. Her eyes felt gritty, and her stomach rumbled noisily. She glanced across the room, slowly blinking several times before her tired eyes focused on the face of a round wall clock mounted high on the wall. The library would be closing in thirty minutes; she couldn't take a break now with half a roll of microfiche still to be viewed. With a sigh she lowered her head once more to the viewing screen.

She slowly turned the knob that fed the film through the viewer. For the past two months the Seattle Public Library had been methodically acquiring the Houston area newspapers for her, beginning with the year she last saw Buddy and slowly working forward. She had long suspected that Lee had sold the baby through some black market scheme. Her only hope was that at some point Lee's contact may have been arrested for a similar crime.

When Doug and Jason had returned to Utah, Megan had quit her job in order to devote herself full time to locating Buddy and getting the professional help she needed to come to terms with her past. She could live on her savings and the money from the sale of her house for one year. She continued her visits with the therapist who had become her friend, and through the support groups Dr. Baker had recommended, she had shared her grief with others who had experienced similar losses. In this way, Megan learned how to grieve for the child who had not received the love and security every child deserves.

Doug had insisted on hiring a private investigator to help her in her search for Buddy, and though she resisted the offer at first, she finally agreed when he pointed out how much time might be saved and assured her the detective would answer to her rather than him.

Being separated from Jason was incredibly painful. She knew sending him away would be difficult, but the reality was so much worse than she had anticipated. She lay awake until the early hours night after night, then awoke before dawn. Early one morning, unable to sleep, she pulled on a fleecy sweat suit and a waterproof jacket. She left the apartment building at a run. Two miles later she staggered to a stop, turned and slowly walked back. After that she ran every morning. It helped. She slept better and felt more alive.

She devoted most of her time to the search for Buddy, which was somehow as therapeutic as the reading her therapist gave her. Megan had wondered for so long that now, just doing something about Buddy made her feel more in control of her life. She contacted adoption agencies, wrote to child welfare and law enforcement agencies, and met with Chad Harris, the detective who specialized in missing person cases. Chad was a nondescript brown-haired man who might be anywhere between thirty and forty, the kind of man no one seemed to notice. But his office was equipped with a sophisticated computer system that offered an expertise designed to accomplish a thorough search of all available records. But so far, nothing.

Twice she flew to Houston chasing leads that only led to disappointment. She wondered if she should move to Houston, but her own healing was progressing so well here with Dr. Baker's help. Besides, some instinct told her Buddy wasn't in Texas. He had probably been moved somewhere else long ago.

The lights flickered, warning patrons the library would close in ten minutes. Wearily Megan began rewinding the film. Her back and shoulders were stiff from the long hours she had spent fruitlessly poring over newsprint on the small screen.

Tiredly she shrugged her waterproof jacket over her shoulders.

"Would you like to use the phone?" the librarian asked as Megan returned the film to the desk. Sometimes Megan called a cab to take her back to her apartment, but most nights she waited for a bus which stopped just outside the library. Her car had arrived from Missoula, but she didn't like driving in Seattle's heavy traffic.

"The fog is really thick tonight. I wouldn't want to be walking from a bus stop."

"No, I'll take the bus." She shook her head wearily. "It should be coming any minute, and I don't want to wait for a cab." She had learned not to depend on taxis for transportation when the fog was thick or the heavy rain slowed their arrival time and increased the demand for their services.

Fifteen minutes later she raised her hand close to her face to peer at her watch. The bus was late, and she was anxious to get back to her apartment and a long, hot shower. There might even be a letter from Cathy, Brad's wife. Warm and chatty like Cathy herself, her letters had begun just after Jason had gone to live with his father. Cathy managed to fill Megan in on the details about "her men" that Doug and Jason never thought to mention in their frequent telephone calls. The letters always included a thought or observation which left Megan feeling a little happier, a little more hopeful.

She could barely make out the shape of several other would-be passengers standing several yards away, most of whom had left the library at closing time also.

There was something about fog that always made Megan uneasy. When she first came to Seattle, before Jason was born, she tried to convince herself the fog was her friend; it hid her from those who might be looking for her. But she hadn't been able to convince herself. As the whiteness billowed and puffed around her, so thick she couldn't see her next step, then thinning to offer a brief glimpse of a wall, a car, or a figure coming toward her, her imagination warred between a sense of disorientation and panic. Was she about to step off into unknown space? Or might the precarious fog suddenly swirl away leaving her exposed to an enemy?

She shifted her weight from one foot to the other. It was hard to see anything. She wished the bus would hurry. Voices drifted to her and she could see vague shapes a short distance away. There was an occasional cough and the shuffle of feet against the damp pavement. The sounds seemed muffled by the fog, lending them an eerie quality. Nervously she edged further away.

Megan caught the sound of a heavy diesel engine. She breathed a sigh of relief. Lights glimmered faintly for a second before she caught the whoosh of the opening door and felt the concerted surge of bodies moving determinedly toward the vehicle. Just as Megan stepped from the curb, she felt a tug on her arm. She jerked violently away and lunged for the open door. Fingers slid down her arm toward her brief case. She swung the bag abruptly forward, then jerked it backward. The bag made contact with a jarring impact. She heard a grunt of pain, then she was through the door and scrambling up the steps.

She fell trembling into the first empty seat. Nervously she watched as three huskily built teenagers boarded. A shudder passed through her as her eyes dwelt on a trickle of blood oozing from the arm of one of the denim and leather clad trio. Moments later she watched a man who appeared to be in his mid-thirties make his way slowly down the aisle. He walked hunched over as though protecting a sensitive midsection. He looked angry and hurting.

Megan shifted uneasily. She felt a pain in her chest where her heart was pounding crazily. *Take deep breaths*, she reminded herself. Feeling a prickling sensation in the back of her neck, she fought slipping into the yawning blackness she knew awaited her if she allowed panic to win.

I will not freeze or lose consciousness. I can take care of myself.

Slowly, determination began to win. As a child she could not protect herself from adults who misused their power over her, but she was an adult now. As an adult, she could protect herself most of the time, if she remained aware and used her head.

Megan gazed out the window at a shadowy, white world. Had she been attacked or had someone tried to steal her brief case? She wasn't certain. Was the person on the bus? Would she be followed when she got off? Her head spun as she tried to formulate a plan for reaching her apartment safely.

If only she had someone strong to walk with her. She thought longingly of Doug for just a moment. The advice she'd given Jason came into her head. When he was afraid, she'd told him, he had a friend who would help him. She could turn to that same friend. "Father, please help me know what to do," she whispered.

Gradually she became aware that the bus was slowing down. She tried to appear nonchalant as she gazed through the window in an effort to get her bearings. She was surprised to see the fog had lifted considerably and the bus was pulling into a well-lighted shopping mall. People began making their way to the center aisle. Quickly she stood up. Her heart pounded as she stepped into the aisle. She didn't like crowds and she was wedged between people pressing toward the door. A wet fur collar tickled her nose. An elbow jammed her ribs. She steeled herself to stay calm. Then she was through the door gulping in the clean wet air.

She looked around for a telephone to call for a taxi. Her glance lit on a cab unloading passengers in front of the theater entrance a few feet away. Her feet flew as she ran to it.

It was with a deep sense of relief that she closed her apartment door behind her half an hour later and flipped on the light switch. Her legs felt weak, and she nearly staggered as she made her way to a chair. Slowly sinking into its soft depth, she closed her eyes, and leaned back against the cushion. She was so tired and so alone.

She didn't have to be alone. Jason could be with her. She smiled thinking of how he would mix a cup of hot chocolate heaped with marshmallows for her. His grin would be a little lopsided, and his hair would fall across his forehead.

Stop tormenting yourself, she reminded herself sternly. *Jason is perfectly happy with Doug. It wouldn't be right to keep him caged here.*

"But, oh, how I miss him," she spoke out loud as she struggled to keep tears from falling.

In a burst of honesty she admitted she missed Doug too. If he were with her now, she wouldn't be cold and lonely. For just a moment she luxuriated in the imagined feel of Doug's strong arms holding her.

"This is madness!" Megan jumped to her feet only to stop with her eyes fastened on the telephone. "All it would take is one telephone call." She stared hungrily at the instrument which had taken on fascinating proportions.

"I'm all right. I felt fear, but I didn't panic or freeze. I found a safe way out of a potentially dangerous situation. I can take care of myself."

A wry smile trembled on her lips. She valued her independence, but more and more she caught herself looking for excuses to drop her search and hurry to Doug and Jason. She wanted to be with them, but something held her back. She no longer felt an aversion to being touched by Doug. He'd promised her he wouldn't press for a deeper physical relationship until she was ready, and she believed him. The aloofness and poise she had carefully nurtured had been a child's frightened attempt to protect herself from hurt and betrayal. She knew that now, so why couldn't she go to them?

A small red light was blinking on her answering machine. The significance of that light penetrated her mind slowly. How long had she stared at the telephone without really seeing it? A surge of adrenaline sent her rushing toward the play button.

When Doug's voice reached her ears her first thought was fear that something had happened to Jason. Her worries were quickly put to rest as Doug's message continued. He and Jason were on their way to dinner and a basketball game, but he had learned something earlier today he thought she should know. He had joined Brad and his father for lunch, and they asked about her. When he mentioned her search for her brother, the judge had offered to check a few sources. Later he called Doug to tell him he might have a lead.

"Call me later tonight for details." Doug's voice came to the end of the message space.

With trembling fingers Megan dialed the now familiar Salt Lake City number. There was no answer. She sat the phone down and drummed her fingers impatiently on the table top. Picking it up again she redialed. She counted the rings. After fifteen rings she knew Doug and Jason had not returned to the house yet.

Between hanging up her coat, fixing herself a sandwich, and taking a shower, she tried to call Doug. It was almost eleven o'clock when the telephone rang just as she was reaching for it. She didn't know whether to laugh or cry at the welcome sound of Doug's voice.

"I'm sorry," he apologized. "I didn't plan to keep Jason out so late. He's been looking forward to this game for some time, and I agreed to take him before I learned tip-off time would be later than usual. He fell asleep in the car on the way home, so I undressed him and put him to bed before calling."

Talking to each other on the telephone had been awkward and stilted the first few times she spoke with him, but after two months their conversations had become long and comfortable. Now it seemed natural to discuss their son, Megan's frustrated search for her brother, and Doug's adjustment to teaching. They never discussed their marriage or hopes for the future.

"Megan," Doug finally brought up the judge's information. "Judge Williams remembered a black market ring based in Albuquerque, New Mexico, that was broken up about twelve years ago. The babies involved were acquired mostly from Mexico, but some were traced to Texas. They were sold to couples all across the United States who didn't meet the usual adoption standards or who were too impatient to wait and had available cash."

"San Antonio is a long way from Albuquerque. How could Lee have been involved with anyone there?" Megan's voice sounded a bit skeptical.

"When you left me last summer, Megan, I hired a detective to help me find you. He didn't find a trace of you, but he did find out a great deal about Lee. It seems your late stepfather dabbled in a lot of illegal activities, including smuggling drugs and illegal aliens across the border. He has been arrested in every state bordering Mexico for some infraction of the law. I think he might have had the same contacts as the Albuquerque group."

When Megan hung up the phone some time later, she had the name of a retired F.B.I. agent and a New Mexico deputy who had worked on the case. Judge Williams had also made arrangements to send her copies of the court records. She was so excited she could hardly sleep.

Early the following morning she contacted Chad Harris to give him the information Doug had given her. Harris was both careful and thorough. Megan appreciated his methodical checking and cross-checking, but she wanted to scream at the time it consumed. She was grateful for her own expertise with computer searching, and when she returned to the library, it didn't take long to locate several newspaper articles concerning the Albuquerque case. The more pieces of the case came together, the more convinced she became that Lee had sold Buddy to the black market group, but how would she ever know for sure?

Over and over she found herself on her knees asking for help. If all Cathy had told her about families being important to God were true, surely he would help her to be reunited with her brother.

"Look at this!" Chad threw a handful of papers down on the desk in front of her. They were in his office, and he was peeling pages off the fax machine. "They actually kept records of the children they sold. There's no record of where the babies came from, but they kept a thorough dossier on the people who bought them. Do you suppose they had a little blackmail in mind for the future?"

"Might have. Judge Williams said most of the babies came from Texas or South America."

"Right! These records show each child's racial background, sex, and age, so let's start looking for Caucasian two-year-old males."

"Chad," Megan lifted her head an hour later. "Have you noticed most of these babies were infants less than six months old, and they were adopted in batches? I've only found three males listed over a year old."

"I have five. That's eight. You go on home now. I'll give you a call as soon as I check these out."

"I want to stay."

"Megan, it could take days, maybe weeks to check out these names. I'll call you every day whether I find anything out or not. Okay?"

"Okay." Megan smiled weakly. She gathered up her coat and started for the door. With her hand on the doorknob she stopped. "Chad, what happened to the babies the F.B.I. traced twelve years ago?"

"Most were allowed to stay in the homes they were in, a few went back to Mexico, and the rest were turned over to legitimate adoption agencies for placement in more suitable homes."

"Why didn't they trace all of the babies, if they had the records we just went over?"

"There could be a lot of reasons. Some of the children may have passed hands several times, the adoptive parents may have changed names, divorced and remarried, or even lied about their names and addresses in the first place."

"Do you think some of the babies died?"

"Probably. Some weren't healthy. Some may have died of the usual accidents and illnesses that strike children. But don't borrow trouble. As far as we know Buddy was healthy."

A week passed before the call came. The phone was ringing as she fit the key into her lock after her morning run. She left a trail of mud on the carpet all the way from the door to the telephone.

"Hello," she said, gasping for breath.

"I think this is it!" Chad's voice rang with excitement. "I just got back from Leyeton, California. A couple there adopted a two-year-old boy in 1978, four days after Buddy disappeared. They were in their forties at the time. The boy is a senior at the local high school and doing very well."

"Have you seen him? How soon can I meet him?"

"There's a problem. The father is deceased and the mother adamantly refuses to talk to me. Her brother is the chief of police, and he made some nasty threats about my future well-being if I decide to contact her or approach the boy."

"I'm not giving up."

"I didn't think you would. Look, I can meet you at my office in two hours. There's something I want to show you." He hung up the phone.

Megan's hands shook as she replaced the telephone. She laughed and cried as she rushed through showering and dressing. She pushed to the back of her mind the possibility that she wouldn't be able to break down the woman's resistance to her meeting the boy.

In Chad's office he confirmed her conviction that he wasn't one to give up easily. He told her how he had nosed around looking for corroborating evidence of the boy's identity. He concentrated on ingratiating himself with neighbors who had known the Wadoups family at the time they adopted the boy they named David. He hit it lucky when he befriended the divorced mother of one of David's classmates, a proud mother who was delighted to show off the family photo album. Chad left the woman's home that night with two purloined photographs, one of a tiny girl surrounded by her little friends blowing out three candles on a birthday cake and one of two weary toddlers sleeping on a blanket beneath a big tree.

Megan cried when she saw the photos. The brown-eyed toddler was Buddy. She knew it.

Three weeks later she flew with Chad to the small town in northern California. Together they walked to the courthouse.

Random snowflakes fluttered from a steel gray sky. Winter hadn't quite released its hold. She wasn't surprised to see two familiar figures standing on the steps, a faint dusting of white on their dark coats let her know they had been waiting for some time. Doug and Judge Williams had taken an active part in arranging for an informal hearing before a judge in the little town.

Doug gripped her hands in his as his eyes searched her own. She found it strangely comforting to have him there.

Judge Williams stepped forward. "Hello, Megan."

"Judge Williams." Megan felt like a tongue-tied teenager again as the judge extended his hand toward her. Doug released her, and she shyly extended her right hand. It trembled slightly as their hands met. The judge brought up his other hand to gently enclose her small hand.

"Megan, I never meant to frighten or worry you all those years ago." A warm smile replaced his serious demeanor.

Hesitantly Megan returned the smile. "Thank you for helping me look for Buddy. I feel so certain David Wadoups is Buddy, but even if he isn't, I am grateful for your help."

Megan's hand gripped Doug's tightly as they proceeded into the room. She didn't remember when Doug had taken her hand or if she had been the one to reach out. She only knew her hand felt right in his.

Immediately her eyes scanned the small group of people already gathered there. Her heart leaped as she caught sight of a slender young man seated a short distance from the long table that dominated the room. His hands were clasped and his dark head bowed. Something about his posture looked vaguely familiar.

A woman with gray hair piled on top of her head sat beside him. She was wearing a plain black dress and dabbed at her eyes frequently with a bit of white lace. The youth didn't look up as they entered the room, but the woman couldn't conceal her emotion. Anger, fear, and possessiveness were all there.

Megan had come prepared to dislike the woman who had fought her every way she knew how to prevent this meeting, but as she looked into the face of the woman who had mothered her brother for most of his life, her heart softened. For just a moment she remembered her own reaction to the threat Doug represented when he had so implacably appeared in her life.

Doug helped her to a seat directly across the table from David. Silently she willed him to look up, to speak to her, but the boy continued to look down. An obscuring lock of hair fell across his eyes.

She was aware of the men in the room shaking hands and taking seats at the table, but her concentration was centered on the boy, really a young man, seated across from her.

Everyone stood when the judge entered the room. He promptly told them to be seated. "As you are aware," he began. "This is not a formal court proceeding. David Wadoups is legally a minor, therefore this matter falls under the jurisdiction of juvenile court. As a juvenile court judge I agreed to this informal discussion as the least painful way of determining whether the court should pursue the possibility that Buddy Fergus and David Wadoups are one and the same, and whether charges should be brought against any party, or a petition for change of custody should be entertained."

He turned first to Mrs. Wadoups. Tearfully she told how she and her husband had been turned down by the state and by numerous adoption agencies because of their age. A friend had told them of an attorney who could help them with a private adoption. She told how they had used all of their savings and mortgaged their home to pay the attorney's fee. Quietly she added, "It was worth it because David is the child of my heart."

Megan observed the tender way the young man reached for the older woman's hand, giving it a gentle squeeze. A picture flashed through her mind of Brad making pine cone dolls for his small daughter, Heidi.

Mrs. Wadoups' attorney handed the judge documents verifying David's blood type, photographs taken of him shortly after his adoption, and a statement from the Wadoups family doctor stating that in his opinion the child had been seriously abused and neglected before being placed in the Wadoups home. Megan closed her eyes, remembering.

Judge Williams presented the California judge with a copy of Buddy's birth certificate, documents verifying that Lee and Marla Fergus' blood types both matched that of David Wadoups, and pointed out that the Wadoups received David four days after Buddy was left behind in Houston. He also produced a statement from a recently paroled courier for the Albuquerque group, stating that her boss owned a house in Houston and that she had transported babies from there to Albuquerque several times. She distinctly remembered picking up a little boy, approximately two years old and delivering him to an attorney's office in Sacramento.

Turning to Megan, he asked her to tell of Buddy's early years and of their separation. When she finished she was crying, and so was the elderly lady seated beside David. Megan watched as the boy patted his adopted mother's hands and gave them another quick squeeze, then he lifted his face to look directly at her. Fury and loathing were in his voice as he spoke for the first time.

"You are not my sister. Those horrible people are not my parents. This is my mother. My father was a wonderful man who d-died two years ago." He put his arm around the sobbing woman. "I won't leave my mother, no matter what you say."

"Buddy . . ."

He glared at her, his eyebrows bunched together, and he lifted one hand.

Suddenly Megan's tears stopped. She stared at David in astonishment. Surprise gave way to joy. She clutched Doug's hand tighter as she beamed at the belligerent young man facing her. God had answered her prayer.

"Bud—, er, David, you definitely are my brother. Right now you look exactly like our grandfather." She hastened to tell him of the fierce, old man who had cared for them the best he could in spite of his alcohol addiction. "David, he loved us; he wanted to take care of us. For years I could not forgive him. Only recently have I come to understand that he was sick, but in spite of his illness he did all he could for us. When he died he left a trust fund for you, enough to see you through college."

When the boy continued to scowl, Megan swallowed her disappointment. Her eyes turned beseechingly to Doug for help. His eyes told her what she had to do. Once more she turned to the boy, her little Buddy, who was now nearly a man.

"Yes, I can see that Mrs. Wadoups is your mother. I wish I could make you both understand what it means to me to know at last that she has been here all these years to love you and take care of you. I don't want to take you away from each other. I want you to be happy and loved. I'll stay out of your life if that's what you want, and I'll make arrangements for you to receive your trust fund."

When the boy said nothing, Megan continued softly, "Try to understand that I needed to know if you were alive and being cared for." In her emotional state she echoed the words Doug once spoke to her.

Silence filled the room. The judge cleared his throat. "If there is no further evidence I'll study the testimony and evidence given today. I expect to have a report ready for you to act on by the end of the week."

"Your honor," Megan spoke up. "I don't wish to proceed any further. I have no intention of interfering in the adoption of my brother by Mrs. Wadoups. He will soon be of age and will do as he wishes anyway. I am satisfied he is in good hands."

Mrs. Wadoups smiled tentatively at her. David refused to meet her eyes.

When the judge dismissed them, Megan hurried to reach David's side as he left the room. She stopped in front of him and reached out to touch his arm.

"David?" She wanted to touch him, to establish contact before he disappeared. He looked pointedly at her hand, reached for his mother's arm, and brushed past Megan. Megan watched them make their way down the courthouse steps. Buddy didn't look back once.

Doug was suddenly beside her, his arm around her shoulder. She hurt too much to cry.

"Come back to Salt Lake with me."

She shook her head.

"It might help to be with Jason," Doug tried to persuade her.

She walked stiffly toward the exit. Her eyes remained dry all the way to the airport.

"Megan, what will you do now?" Concern was evident in Doug's voice as he walked her to the small plane waiting to carry her and Chad back to Seattle.

Megan shook her head as she blinked back the tears that were finally beginning to fall. She couldn't answer.

"Honey, please reconsider. Don't rush away like this. Couldn't we go somewhere quiet for dinner and just talk?"

"No, Doug, I can't," she choked on the words. Buddy was so disgusted by her, he wanted nothing to do with her. She felt like a leper who contaminated everyone close to her. Someday Doug, and yes Jason too, would want nothing to do with her.

Doug reached out with a clean white handkerchief from his pocket to wipe away her tears. His arm settled around her shaking shoulders, and she didn't resist as he pulled her against his shoulder.

"It's been an emotional seesaw of a day for you. Please let me buy you dinner. Jason sent you a dozen messages, and I have something important I want to discuss with you."

"Doug, it isn't going to work!" She pulled angrily away from him. "Your rosy dream of turning us into a family isn't going to work any more than my dreams of getting my brother back are ever going to happen. It's too late!"

Doug reached out to help her as she stumbled in her hurry to board the plane. His hands fell short, leaving him watching helplessly as the door closed and the little plane began its slow taxi away from the gate.

Fifteen

ONE, TWO, THREE," MEGAN COUNTED ALOUD. SHE straightened, then stretched the other leg. "One, two, three." She left the stairs at a fast walk. Midblock she broke into a run. Two blocks into her run, her muscles moved easily and her mind floated free. Sharp, clean air pumped through her lungs. A hint of spring lingered in the air, and for once, it wasn't raining. Some mornings, her thoughts were as mechanical as her body, other mornings her mind and body stretched and explored. This morning she only wanted to escape.

How many times did she have to run away? No, she couldn't run anymore. To run, she had to stop feeling again, and she couldn't do that. She had changed. She couldn't freeze out the pain.

They all betrayed her. First Lee, then Doug. No she couldn't compare Doug to Lee. *Doug didn't betray me, not really. I only thought he did.* She had finally found the faith to pray, and God had let her down. *No, I only asked God to help me find Buddy.* A.J. tricked her. *But he wanted to help me.* Jason turned to Doug. In some way she couldn't fathom, she felt she had lost Jason as surely as she'd lost Buddy. He too was happier in his new home than with her. *But he didn't turn from me. He calls every week. He sends long letters and wants me to come live with him.* What about Buddy? *Buddy hates me!*

Buddy! Buddy, the only bright spot in my childhood. Why did you turn on me?

Megan suddenly stopped. Another early morning jogger swerved to miss running her down. He scowled in her direction, picked up his pace, and disappeared around a corner.

Buddy did to me just what I did to Doug. I know Buddy is my brother, but he doesn't know it. I didn't want to remember the past, Buddy wants no part of that past either. He's clinging to what makes him feel safe, just as I did. It made sense. She wouldn't give up, not any more than Doug ever gave up on her. She hadn't understood before why Doug clung so tenaciously to their marriage. She began to tremble. She knew how deep her tie to Buddy ran. If Doug's feelings for her ran that deep, what should she do? She wasn't certain she wanted him to care that much.

Slowly she turned around. She wasn't running. Her steps were slow, but she didn't feel the cold. She felt warmer inside with each block she traveled.

As soon as she got back to her apartment she wrote to Buddy. Days went by and she received no answer. She wrote several long letters to Jason, but she didn't call. She treasured the long childish scrawls he posted to her twice a week. The days drifted slowly by. She knew she had to make some decisions about her future, but she felt unable to think clearly. She let the answering machine take Doug's calls, she wasn't ready to talk to him. She spent hours reading a Book of Mormon that Cathy sent to her. It comforted her even though she didn't always understand it. Vaguely she wondered if she might be using her study of the book as an excuse to put off making plans.

She didn't want to go back to work at the bank. She toyed with the idea of returning to Channel Two, but something kept her from picking up the telephone and calling Mr. Prescot. She had enjoyed investigative reporting, and she felt confident he would give her back her old job. Still she delayed. She felt suspended, unable to make a decision. Running became her one escape.

Muddy water splashed her ankles. She ran on. It didn't matter anymore whether the fine mist coated her eyelashes and flattened her hair against her scalp. Physically she felt good. Never before had she thought of her body as a source of pleasure. Now she reveled in the strength of well-toned muscles, the music of coordinated movement, the freedom of knowing her own capacity for endurance. She cut across the grass of a small park that reminded her spring would soon come to Missoula and the grass would turn green around the house she bought for herself and Jason nearly four years ago. That house had been sold, but she could buy another one.

If she returned to Montana she could have Jason with her again. But would he want to return to their old life? What about Doug? It would be unbearably cruel to both Doug and Jason to separate them. She splashed through another puddle. *I don't want to separate them; I want to join them.* There! She finally admitted it. At last she could acknowledge her desire, but could she find the courage to act on it? And if she went to them, could she stay? Would the first threat to her independence send her running? Was she really through looking backward and ready to concentrate on the future? Emily Baker seemed to think she was ready to move forward. Each day the future loomed larger in her thoughts than the past.

Megan slowed to a cooling walk. Dark clouds portended more rain. The temperature was dropping rapidly too. Her apartment building was in sight. A new excitement filled her with an unfamiliar euphoria that carried her through the front door. She stripped off her clothes on the way to the shower. A tingling sense of anticipation sustained her actions until she sank onto the worn sofa to nibble on toast and drink her orange juice. Knowing what she wanted didn't settle her doubts and fears. She thought about calling Emily, but it wasn't the doctor she wanted to talk to.

When she reached for her glass on the table beside the sofa, her hand brushed a stack of letters and sent them spilling across the floor. Scrambling to her knees she picked them up one by one. They were Cathy's letters. She thought of the vibrant redhead. Cathy wouldn't hesitate, she'd know what to do.

She picked up an envelope, drew out the pages and began to read. Megan remembered one paragraph in particular that had stood out when she first read it. She reread it slowly.

I've been really worried about my father. He's going to have to have a pacemaker. Friday I went to the temple. When something's on my mind and I just need to think and talk it over with my Heavenly Father, I like to go to there. I always seem to think more clearly and feel more at peace in the temple.

Could that work for her? Megan scrambled to her feet. She ran to the closet for her jacket. There was a temple in Seattle. She couldn't go in it; Doug had told her only Mormons could go in their temples, but she could walk through the gardens, watch the fountain, maybe find a bench where she could sit for a while.

The temple was only a few miles away. The freeway ran right past it. A light sprinkle of rain dotted her windshield as she exited the freeway. A few blocks further and she turned her car into the temple parking lot. The parked cars looked forlorn in the gathering gloom. They sat like abandoned toys waiting for children who had gone away. She tightened the drawstring of her rain hood, picked up her umbrella, and stepped outside just as the wind blew a gust of cold rain in her face.

She was disappointed to see that after a week of balmy spring weather, the bitter, winter rain had returned. Her hands dug deeply into the pockets of her jacket as she walked briskly across the wet lawn. She wanted to get as close to the stone walls as possible. Her shoes were soon soaked, and she dismissed the possibility of finding a quiet garden bench. Tulips and pansies bowed their heads against the slashing rain. In a few minutes she returned to her car to sit and stare at a single spire pointing its way upward through the icy torrent. She had noticed the building before from the freeway and admired its graceful beauty. Now she was struck by its strength and majesty. It didn't just defy the storm, it rose above it.

There was a message here if she only knew how to find it. She wondered what it would be like if she could walk inside to sit in calm silence. She imagined shutting out the storm and the noise of the world. She tried to focus her mind and pray from the depths of her soul. A quiet peace permeated her heart. She sat until her teeth began to chatter from the cold.

Then she started the car engine and turned up the heater. She blew on her fingers to warm them before backing out of her parking space. In a few minutes she was back on the freeway. Whether she had accomplished what she set out to do or not she wasn't sure, but she did feel calmer. The answer would come.

Megan was relieved to find traffic wasn't as heavy now as it had been earlier. The storm decreased visibility rapidly. She slowed her speed. The windshield wipers slapped with a fury to match the storm. A fine line of ice formed where their downward sweep ended. Thoughts of reaching her apartment and a warm shower were uppermost in her mind now. She caught a glimpse of a green highway sign. She should take the next exit. It would be just over this small hill. She peered through the torrent.

Suddenly there were cars! Cars everywhere, turned every direction in a massive pile-up. Flashing lights! She was headed right into them. She had to stop! She hit the brake. The car slid sideways. She skidded, careening sideways across lanes of traffic. Her car made a complete circle. Her hands froze to the wheel. A torrent of water streamed across her windows. The cement barrier rushed toward her. She would hit it! No way to stop!

"Take your foot off the brake. Ease the wheel to the right."

A man's voice spoke clearly and calmly. Without hesitation she obeyed. "Tap the brake several times, softly." The voice went on, talking her through the wild ride. She completed another half circle, stopped. The engine died, but she was off the road. She saw the man in the car closest to her, his mouth open as though holding a suspended scream.

Other cars were still coming on the scene—startled drivers having to stop unexpectedly. A van and a pickup slowed to a stop beside her. From the passenger window, a woman stared at her with wide eyes. Cars whipped by in the outside lane. She heard the squeal of brakes, but she was safe.

"Doug . . . ?" Her voice trembled as she turned to the seat beside her. It was empty. Of course, it was empty. Doug wasn't here. But the voice. . . .

With shaking hands she reached for the ignition key. The engine instantly purred to life. Oncoming traffic paused to allow her to pull into the exit lane. A highway patrolman gave her a modified salute and shook his head wonderingly when she slowly pulled past the tangled cars.

Her shoulders shook and she choked back tears as she left the freeway. She was alive! She would see and hold Jason again! She could tell Doug she loved him! She didn't know how or why she had been spared. Something happened, but she wasn't sure what. Why did she think Doug was beside her? She knew it was his voice she heard. Perhaps she had imagined it. No, definitely not. She didn't imagine anything. It isn't possible for anyone to be in two places at once, is it? It couldn't have been Doug.

But if God wanted to send me a message would I know his voice, or would he use the voice of someone I trust? Her fingers tightened on the wheel. *Someone I trust to the farthest reaches of my soul. Doug!*

She pulled into her parking space and turned off the engine. And the tears came. It didn't matter whether Doug sat beside her, whether God spoke to her, or if she just heard Doug's voice in her head. It was still a message from her Heavenly Father. She had her answer. She heard Doug's voice because her inner self knew she was safe with him. That knowledge set her free to love and be loved.

She scrambled out of the car and dashed for the door. Her hands delved in her purse. Her fingers closed around her apartment key. She had to get to the telephone.

"Hi!"

Startled by a familiar voice, she spun around. A.J. stood in the lobby, leaning nonchalantly against the elevator panel. For just a moment they stood awkwardly staring at each other before Megan reached out to take his arm and invite him inside her apartment.

"I'm so glad to see you," Megan told him, taking in the strained expression on his face. He had lost weight, she could see, and he was clearly troubled about something.

"Doug gave me your address. I'm on my way to Vancouver, next stop Alaska," he told her. "I wanted to give you a little present before I go and make certain we're still friends."

"Of course, we're still friends. Why wouldn't we be? Actually, I owe you an apology for using you to make my escape."

"No apology needed. I should apologize for meddling in your life."

"It's okay, A.J. It really was time I met Doug again and time he met his son. Jason is better off now."

"But are you?" Allen asked bluntly. "And Jason would be happier if you . . . Anyway, here!" He held out a flat parcel, then helped her remove the string wrapped around it. She tore away the paper to find herself peering at a portrait of three people. It was Jason, Doug, and herself laughing and clinging to each other as they shot down the natural water slide near the cabin. Jason's hands were high in the air, and a grin flashed from one side of his face to the other. Doug's mouth was open. His eyes sparkled with excitement, and water streamed from his hair. Megan's arms gripped him tightly, her cheek turned against his sun-warmed back which had contrasted so vividly with the shock of the stinging cold water.

She hardly recognized herself in the laughing, joy-filled young woman in the photograph. Her eyes misted over as they hungrily devoured the image of the two people she loved with all her heart. The photograph symbolized a moment, when clutching each other they soared free of all their fears and misunderstandings. A mixed wave of homesickness and hope swept over her, not for a place, but for the people she knew would always mean home to her.

She saw then the little girl huddled on the car seat with her legs tucked beneath her body and her cheek leaning against her grandfather's rough work shirt as his battered old pickup truck carried them through the heat and glare back to the farm and away from the house where they said she was naughty. She saw chubby brown fingers grip the sides of a wooden wagon as tiny white teeth gleamed, brown eyes sparkled, and children's laughter echoed against a blazing Texas sky. Looking up through a fog of pain and fear, she saw intense blue eyes and the steady features of a man she knew would love her with the steadfastness of the mountain. Her arms ached with the pleasant weight of her newborn son and a stab of joy filled her heart as her lips touched his silky head. And she heard Doug's voice guiding her to safety.

"Oh, A.J. It's priceless. How can I ever thank you?" Impulsively she stood on tiptoe to kiss his cheek, her own cheeks damp.

"You can thank me by getting back there with them where you belong," he pretended to growl.

"I intend to."

"Oh, Megan. When?"

"Now. As soon as I can call Doug and can catch a plane." She was laughing and crying.

"Stop your blubbering and call the man." A.J. grabbed her hand and rushed her across the room to the telephone.

Her fingers trembled as she dialed the number. The voice she wanted to hear came on the line, and Megan found herself unable to speak. She feared he would hang up before she managed to stammer his name.

"Megan? Megan, is that you? Is something wrong?" Across the miles she felt his love and concern.

"I—I'm fine. I just called to tell you I'm leaving tonight."

"Megan, oh honey. You're not running away again, are you?"

"No. Yes. I—I'm coming home."

"Home?" Doug held his breath.

"Yes! If you still want me to be part of your life."

"Darling, I want you beside me forever."

"Doug, all my life I've dreamed of a real home, a place where I would be safe with people I love and who love me, but I never believed I would ever have it. I want to be with you, but I'm so scared."

Her hands shook, while her voice trembled, and she was afraid she might drop the phone and bolt for the door.

"Megan, you're doing fine." A.J. encouraged her to continue before he walked into the next room and closed the door behind him.

"Something happened this afternoon." Suddenly she wasn't afraid anymore. She was safe in every way with Doug. She told him of her near accident. "It wasn't narrowly missing being killed that made me realize I love you and I'm ready to spend my life with you. It was learning that you will always be there for me. It was the sense of safety and security that enveloped me when I heard your voice.

"When I got back to my apartment A.J. was here. He showed me a picture of you and me with Jason, and I realized you are my home, my love. The past is over. The ugliness is gone. I don't have to be ashamed or alone and frightened. I want to be with you and Jason." Her voice quavered, making speech difficult. She hadn't had much experience voicing her feelings. "I want to give you all you've given me."

"You're really coming?" Megan heard a catch in his voice. "You just made me the happiest man in the world."

"I—I love you, Doug."

"And I love you."

"Tell Jason . . ."

"I will, love. Hurry home!"

Megan stood with the phone pressed against her mouth. Tears were streaming down her face. A.J. walked back in the room.

"Are you all right?"

She nodded. Her face shone with joy through her tears. Looking at her, A.J. realized the ice princess was gone forever. He felt a twinge of regret that he hadn't been the one to awaken her. She was alive and beautiful, radiant as only a woman in love can be. She gulped noisily as she tried to speak.

"I have to pack and call a cab. What about my car? Oh!" Her face fell, "I don't know if there's even a plane. I don't have a reservation."

"Leave it to me, lady," A.J. cut in. "I'll call the airport, and since I'm heading that way too, you can forget about calling a cab. If we hurry we can have everything, including your car, packed and ready to ship before you leave, so you won't have to come back here at all."

Laughing and wiping away her tears, he helped throw Megan's few possessions haphazardly into boxes. She rushed to her landlord's door to pay a generous sum in lieu of notice. She arranged for storage and later shipment of the personal items she had acquired in the months she had been in the city while A.J. made arrangements to ship her car to Salt Lake.

During the ride to the airport, A.J. talked about the job he had accepted doing a wildlife documentary in Alaska, and he filled Megan in on all of the news he could think of about their old colleagues at Channel Two.

Conversation turned serious when Megan asked him, "Are you running away like I did?"

"I honestly don't know," he admitted candidly. "Sometimes I think I am, but I don't have any idea what I'm running from. If my life and safety were threatened as yours were, I'd know what I'm trying to escape. As it is, all I know is I can't go home and there's something I have to find."

"You know A.J., you're the one person I could never freeze out or fool. I think I always knew you were a fellow runaway, because you understood me too well. You were right, it's time to stop running from the past. I had a hard time finding the faith to risk love; I hope faith won't be so difficult for you to find."

"Here we are." A.J. found a parking space.

Running down the concourse with her luggage slapping against their sides, they heard the call for Megan's flight.

They stopped abruptly at the boarding gate. A.J. let the bag he was carrying slide to the floor, freeing his hands to grasp Megan's shoulders. His mouth quirked up on one side as he looked into her face.

"Oh, what the heck!" He pulled her into his arms and kissed her soundly on the mouth. "Be happy, little one." He abruptly turned her around and pushed her toward the line of people disappearing down the ramp. He walked away before she could regain her breath or see the tear that threatened to slip from the tip of an eyelash.

Sixteen

SOMEBODY GET THE DOOR!"

The buzz of the doorbell could scarcely be heard over the uproar taking place in every room of the big old house.

"Mom, tell Heidi she's too little to play basketball with us," Bobbi pleaded from her position in the middle of a half dozen gangling, would-be athletes. The little girl wrapped her arms more securely around Jason's leg. She refused to budge without him. Jason looked up at his father with a helpless, embarrassed grin on his face. A couple of boys snickered. The doorbell sounded again.

"All right, Muffin, come with me." Doug scooped up the child as he made his way through the crowded room. Over the heads of children playing tag, fellow faculty colleagues, friends, and neighbors, his eyes made contact with his wife's. He gave her a broad wink before throwing open the front door.

Heidi shrieked when she saw the figure standing there. Ducking her head into Doug's shoulder she peeked, through her fingers at the woman attired completely in black from head to toe.

"It's a witch," the little girl whispered.

Looking from Sister Mary Katherine to the flustered child in his arms, Doug hid a smile before reaching out one arm to draw the stately older woman into a quick embrace.

"No, Heidi, you've got it all wrong. Some angels wear black."

Megan quickly detached herself from a circle of friends, to greet her old friend. Jason and his grandmother quickly followed suit. It wasn't long before Sister Mary Katherine was swallowed up in the noisy crowd.

Several hours later Megan settled herself on a step of the grand old staircase with a plate heaped high with fried chicken, rolls, relishes, and salads. As she slowly made her way through the mound of food she gazed around the room at her family's many friends. A touch of melancholy flitted through her thoughts, causing a faint shudder as she recalled how close she had come to missing it all. The adjustment hadn't all been easy, but it was certainly worth it. Glancing down she saw Doug, her beloved husband, standing at the foot of the stairs. She held out her hand, then patted the spot beside her, which he soon occupied.

Doug pointed out little Heidi sitting cross-legged on the floor as close to Jason as she could get. His chuckle sounded warm and loving in Megan's ear. Jason sat with Bobbi and almost his entire Little League team. She smiled, seeing the happy glint in her son's eyes. She watched him flip one of Heidi's curls and knew he really didn't mind his little shadow. Across the room Kelly was snuggled in Judge Williams arms, sound asleep, while the judge carried on an animated conversation with her co-host from the in-depth news show she broadcast three times a week. She overheard several neighbors compliment Doug's mother on the lovely party as they carried their loaded plates toward the patio.

Megan nudged Doug to draw his attention to Cathy and Brad, who appeared absorbed in conversation with Sister Mary Catherine. The three looked as comfortable as old friends.

"Want to bet they've got her talked into a tour of Temple Square tomorrow?" Doug drawled.

"Cathy always plays fair; they'll take in the Cathedral of the Madeline, too," Megan added with a smile, remembering the tours she had taken with Cathy. She remembered too her astonishment when she finally agreed to listen to the missionaries, only to discover that through the letters she sent her in Seattle and the tours, Cathy had already taught her most of the discussions.

"Of course, we probably should warn Sister Mary Catherine that Brad isn't just plain old Dr. Williams, that he's also Bishop Williams."

They sat quietly, each lost in thoughts of the past year. Both of "her men" had cried and hugged her as she stepped off the plane and back into their lives to stay. For weeks both Doug and Jason followed her constantly with their eyes, as though afraid if they looked away she might disappear.

Doug's mother, Elizabeth, hadn't spent as much time in St. George as Cathy had once implied she would. It was hard for her to tear herself away from her adored grandson and the "daughter she had always wanted." Megan had discovered she enjoyed having a mother to fuss over her. In fact, the party had been Elizabeth's idea. She was appalled when Megan casually mentioned once that she had never had a birthday party, not even a birthday cake as a child, and had immediately determined to throw a party for Megan's birthday.

They had a second reason to celebrate too, one that brought tears to Megan's eyes. Earlier this afternoon Doug had taken her in his arms and slowly lowered her beneath the waters of baptism. One of the surprises awaiting her when she reached Salt Lake a little more than a year ago was learning that Doug had joined the Church and that Jason was awaiting her permission to do the same.

Doug explained how much he had wanted to discuss his decision with her when they met in California for the hearing, but she had been too hurt by her brother's refusal to acknowledge their relationship and in too big a hurry to return to Seattle. He had been afraid it might upset her further, so he had said nothing.

Wisely, Doug hadn't pressured her to be baptized, too. Patiently he waited. He hadn't interfered when Jason made his own campaign; rather he'd watched quietly as Jason convinced his mother his decision was his own and not a misplaced desire to please his father and his new friends.

She had studied the Church with the same thoroughness she put into any news story she had ever investigated and found much to admire, but no sure testimony. For her the sweet recognition of truth came the day Brad was sustained bishop of his ward. Standing before the congregation, he bore his testimony with a quiet strength that touched the last frozen corner of her heart. Doug softly squeezed her fingers as Brad sat down and Megan realized her husband knew the truth of all his friend had testified, and so did she. She sat through the rest of that meeting savoring a warmth and comfort beyond anything she had ever imagined possible.

Her thoughts returned to the party, and she found herself thinking of her selfless friend and wondering where A.J. was tonight. Once she thought he owed her, now she recognized how much she owed him.

"I wish your brother could have come," Doug said, mistaking the reason for the tears she quickly brushed away.

"I didn't think he would. He isn't comfortable with me. We're still strangers and probably always will be, though his happiness will always be in my prayers. Just knowing he grew up with people who love him, goes a long way toward making me feel better about him. I'm glad he decided to accept the money Grandfather left him to go to college.

"Actually I was thinking of A.J.," she added. "I wish he had been able to come."

"His sister said he called two nights ago to tell her he wouldn't get here in time for the party. A man he met up there in Alaska had some kind of accident and Allen promised to drive the guy's truck back here for him. It will take him a couple of weeks."

Doug set down his plate so that he could wrap his arms around Megan. Even though he knew she loved him, he still sometimes felt a little twinge of jealousy whenever she spoke of Allen. To his ears her voice seemed to take on a special warmth. She had a right to care, he reminded himself, just as he had a great deal to thank Allen for. Allen had been a positive role model in Jason's life when the boy had no one else, and he had loved both Megan and Doug enough to sacrifice his own dreams for their happiness. Instead of jealousy, Doug felt a surge of gratitude for the honorable friend who touched his family's life.

"Do you think anyone would notice if we disappeared up the stairs?" Her fingers found their way behind his back to tease their way along his spine. The sparkle of laughter in her eyes held a hint of mischief, which left no room for jealousy.

"No running away before you cut your birthday cake." He grinned as his mother wheeled into sight a huge, three-tiered birthday cake loaded with icing and candles. "But hold that thought."

Deep in the night, long after friends had departed and family and guests were all settled in their beds, Megan awoke. She stretched luxuriously, then snuggled closer to her husband's side, happily reliving the day.

Running her fingers lightly across her abdomen she hugged their secret hope to herself, feeling certain this special day would be remembered forever in the form of a new life to cherish and love. Dreamily she imagined Doug in a white suit and herself in a long white gown, kneeling, facing each other. Then Jason would walk into the room wearing a suit like his father's and carrying his baby sister. The dream seemed so real she could see the flutter of lace and ribbon on the baby's dress as the children's hands joined hers and Doug's.

"I love you," she whispered as she pressed her lips to Doug's bare shoulder.

Immediately his arms pulled her closer and his earlier words surfaced briefly as his mouth closed over hers. "No running away."

"Never again," her heart answered. She was home to stay.

About the Author

Jennie Hansen was raised in Idaho and Montana as the fifth of eight children. In her teen years she often ran their dairy farm while her father was fighting fires or on lookout in the forest service. She graduated from Ricks College in Idaho and Westminster College in Salt Lake.

Jennie has been a newspaper reporter, editor, and librarian because of her love of reading and writing combined with her desire to know something about everything. National Press Women awarded her second place for best newspaper editing in the United States. She is presently a technical services specialist for the Salt Lake City Library System and has been on a number of library committees including WHICLIST.

Jennie's church service is equally varied. She has been a teacher in every organization, has been in stake and ward Primary presidencies, and served as a stake communications director and ward chorister.

She has lived in the Salt Lake area since her marriage to Boyd K. Hansen. They are the parents of four daughters and one son. Jennie is the author of five best-selling novels for the LDS market: *Macady, When Tomorrow Comes, Some Sweet Day, Run Away Home,* and its sequel, *Journey Home.*